ELIZABETH PEWSEY

Elizabeth Pewsey was born in Chile and educated in Calcutta, London and at St. Hilda's College, Oxford. She has worked as a civil servant and publisher, and now lives in Dorset with her husband and two children. *Finding Philippe* is her eighth novel following *Losing Larry*, published by Hodder & Stoughton, and the Mountjoy series: *Children of Chance*, *Divine Comedy*, *Unholy Harmonies*, *Volcanic Airs*, *Unaccustomed Spirits* and *Brotherly Love*, all published by Sceptre.

FINDING PHILIPPE

Elizabeth Pewsey

FLAME
Hodder & Stoughton

A CIP catalogue record for this title
is available from the British Library.

ISBN 0 340 71865 X

Typeset in Bembo by Hewer Text Ltd, Edinburgh
Printed and bound in Great Britain by
Mackays of Chatham plc, Chatham, Kent.

Hodder and Stoughton
A division of Hodder Headline
338 Euston Road
London NW1 3BH

For Sylvia

France, 1943

He could feel nothing.

He wasn't surprised. He'd read about soldiers receiving terrible wounds and injuries in the heat of battle, and being unaware of any pain until hours later.

True, this wasn't a battle, this war of his was a more private affair. He assumed he'd been shot in the back. He had certainly felt a thump between his shoulders. More like a kick from a horse than anything else. He remembered the time when Jupiter had lashed out with an enormous hoof and left him bruised for days. He could see the scene quite clearly, the stableyard, and the bay with his huge, round rump and thick, muscular neck. There he was, on a rope attached to a big iron ring on the brick wall. It was strange to think of that now. It was a sunny day, and his nostrils were filled with the smell of hay and horse. He could see himself, beside the horse. How old was he, sixteen? Seventeen? Had he really been that thin? He was putting up a hand to pat Jupiter, normally so mild, now with his ears laid back, sending a message that he hadn't had the sense to notice. His mother was standing by the gate, laughing at him. Odd to watch it like this, from outside, as though he were an observer and not a participant.

His mind drifted. Why had they shot him? No, that wasn't a sensible question. He was the enemy, of course they'd shoot him on sight. Strangers arriving from England in a plane that flew and landed by moonlight were always unwelcome to the Germans.

What about Raoul? Had he got away? He wasn't really called

3

Raoul, of course. That was his code name. His real name would be Archie, or Freddie, or some other absurd English name.

And why had he been left here, lying on the ground, alone? He didn't expect mercy from the Germans, but you had a right to expect efficiency. That was what they were expert at, so you were always being told. Where was the officer, with a group of men to heave him into a van or even, just possibly, an ambulance? If they wanted to preserve him for interrogation, then it would be an ambulance, and they'd stitch him up before taking him apart again.

He could always crunch on the cyanide pill. That would be sensible, but really, he couldn't be bothered. He felt all right, not frightened, not in pain, not, seemingly, suffering from shock. No, the pill might come in handy later, but for now he'd wait and see. Maybe a French local would notice him. A Frenchman riding home on his bicycle by the light of the moon, fresh from a romantic assignation. Or, more likely, from an illegal gathering, a reconnaissance trip, attending at a drop.

Jean-Luc and Marie should have been here to meet them. Where were they? Perhaps they'd gone to the other landing place. Raoul had insisted on this one, and the pilot had been too anxious to be done with the job to argue about it. Ops had got it wrong, Raoul said. He'd fixed it up with the Ludo network before he returned to England, this was where their French colleagues would be waiting. The pilot hadn't waited to find out if Raoul was right or not, he'd wheeled the plane round and was taxi-ing for take off almost before his and Raoul's feet touched the ground. You couldn't blame him. These night-time missions were so bloody dangerous that flying one gave most of the pilots the shits.

So where was Raoul? He must have gone for help. He'd be back soon. Meanwhile, he himself wasn't exactly conspicuous, and maybe the German who'd shot him and then doubtless rushed off for reinforcements wouldn't remember where he was. He should try to move in a little while. He felt he could. It might cause more damage, but if he were badly hurt it wouldn't be so painless, and his head wouldn't be so clear.

Could he summon up an image of Vicky if he tried? Why not, there wasn't much else to do to pass the time. Good thing it wasn't

4

cold or damp; that was surprising, really, considering the time of year.

There she was, shutting the doors of a garage. She'd just come off duty, she'd returned the ambulance to the depot. Now she'd walk to the corner of the street and wait for an all-night bus to take her home. She looked tired. No, exhausted was the word. Smudges of grey beneath her beautiful eyes, and a droop to her mouth. Her hair could do with a wash. With a cut and a shampoo, actually, but those were luxuries in wartime; indulgences, not weekly or monthly routines. Such a pretty colour her hair, gleaming with those red lights. He felt if he called her name, she would hear him.

'Vicky,' he whispered. She stopped in her tracks, her eyes wide open. She spun round, looked up and down the street which was shining black from the recent rain. It was deserted. She gave a depressed little shrug, turned back, and walked slowly on towards the corner.

1949

Chapter One

———— ❧ ————

'You'll be sick, Miss Vicky.'

'I won't,' said Vicky, teeth gritted.

She was.

'I told you it was a mistake to come on this nasty boat. Keep away from the sea, was what my old dad used to tell us, and he was right.'

Vicky, still green in the face, wished Mrs Shipton would topple overboard. The boat gave an even more violent lurch, and Vicky hung on to the rail. Why, oh, why did it have to be so rough on the day she was making the crossing?

'Of course, this isn't what I'd call rough,' Mrs Shipton went on. 'I remember on a voyage to India there was a terrible storm in the Bay of Biscay. Oh, awful, it was, hardly a passenger left standing. That was when I was looking after the Palmerston twins, ever such nice boys, one killed in the war, though, and the other's in prison now. Fraud. Pity, really.'

Vicky's stomach heaved.

'You stay here, I've got something in my cabin that will make you feel better.'

'I don't want anything,' she shouted into the wind as Mrs Shipton headed for the interior of the boat, her firm steps sounding on the deck planking. She could have saved her breath, her old nanny would dig up some foul remedy and force her to take it and then she'd be sicker than ever. Oh, hell. And why wasn't Nanny seasick? She and Mr Hutt, who was no doubt still sitting peacefully in the saloon reading his newspaper and smoking his foul pipe, were fine; why did she, Vicky, have to suffer so?

It had seemed a good idea at the time. It was an idea that had come to her on a particularly grim day, a grey Wednesday in March. She had gone to the East End, to make some sketches of streets and the river for the book she was illustrating. The day had started badly, the morning's work hadn't gone well, and, she felt as she waited for lunch, it seemed fated to get worse. She was sitting at a table in the British Restaurant in Candle Street, London. It was foggy outside, no doubt building up for a peasouper. The lights in the restaurant were switched on, the forty-watt light bulbs only adding to the dinginess and general disagree-ableness of the surroundings. An uninterested waitress, whose face quite clearly said bunions, handed her a scruffy, hand-written menu.

'I'll have the mutton stew, please.'

'Mutton's off,' the waitress said with a dispirited sniff. 'There's venison, but no one's been able to eat it yet.'

'Is it actually venison?' asked Vicky, fearing the worst. She was right.

'No. It's old goat. You can eat venison when it's horse, but not when it's goat. I'd have the Hamburg steak, if I were you.'

'What exactly is Hamburg steak?'

'It's leftovers, with lots of bread mixed in. Same as a hamburger, just a fancier name.'

It sounded revolting. Still, that was what she'd have to have, there was hardly much choice.

'There's Spam, of course,' the waitress offered helpfully. 'You could have that with a nice piece of beetroot.'

'No, Hamburg steak, please.'

Vicky didn't have the energy to take out the book she'd brought with her. The smell of bad food permeated the atmosphere. The other customers looked grey and unwashed and downtrodden, and hungry. Everyone in the country, she thought, from Land's End to John o'Groats, was hungry and grubby.

The waitress made her weary way back to the table and put a plate of food in front of Vicky.

She gazed down at a round, leathery-looking item with two scoops of watery mashed potatoes flanking it on one side, and a pile of soggy carrots on the other. 'It looks disgusting.'

'It does, doesn't it?' the waitress agreed. 'Tastes nasty, too.'

Vicky got up from the table, picked up her sketchbook.

'Aren't you going to eat it?' the waitress said disbelievingly. 'It mayn't be very nice, but you won't find any better anywhere else, not outside the posh restaurants, and you pay through the nose there.'

'I know, and also they are a long way from Candle Street.'

Another sniff. 'Everywhere's a long way from Candle Street. You'll have to pay for that, mind.'

'I suppose,' said Vicky, handing over half a crown, 'that it will go into the leftover pile for tomorrow's Hamburg steak.'

' 'Sright,' said the waitress, waiting to see if Vicky would leave a tip.

She slid two penny coins on to the none-too-clean tablecloth. Her shoes squeaked slightly on the linoleum floor as she walked to the double door, swung the right hand side open, and went out into the street.

She consulted her wristwatch. A quarter to one. The afternoon stretched in front of her. She looked up and down the street. There was a small, grim café round the corner, perhaps a cup of unpleasant lukewarm coffee would persuade her stomach that it didn't actually want to eat anything.

She pushed open the door of the café, and her nostrils were assailed by the scent of coffee. A rich, sense-tingling aroma, bringing memories of other times and other places, pre-war places where coffee was coffee, not ersatz grounds of God knew what. The woman behind the counter was new to her; the only previous time she'd been in here, an unsavoury man in a dirty jacket had been ladling out plates of beans on thin grey bread toasted into nothingness.

'Where's Albert?' she asked the neat, dark woman who was doing something miraculous with coffee beans. There was no one else in the café.

'Off sick,' she said. 'I'm his sister-in-law, what do you want?' She had a foreign accent, French, she thought.

'I can smell coffee. Real coffee.'

'You know real coffee when you smell it, eh? This isn't for the customers. Their coffee comes out of a bottle.' She gestured to the familiar square brown bottle standing on a shelf above a sink.

Vicky closed her eyes in an agony of desire. 'Please,' she said. 'Please.'

'Okay,' the Frenchwoman said. 'Sit down, I bring it to you. Only you don't tell other people, okay?'

'I promise I won't.'

She brought a thick china cup and saucer, filled to the brim with black coffee. 'You want milk in it?'

Vicky shook her head, sniffed the steam rising from the dark liquid, drank. Nectar couldn't have touched this, she hadn't had a cup of coffee like this for months.

'You hungry?'

She nodded.

'I make you an omelette. I got eggs, don't ask me how. It will cost you.'

'That's all right,' said Vicky. 'Made with butter?'

'Of course made with butter. It is what I make for myself, you think I eat the grease scrapings they call margarine?'

'Where do you get butter?'

'Don't ask, and you won't get told lies.'

She brought the omelette, and talked to Vicky who, in a daze of greedy delight was savouring every perfect mouthful.

Her name was Madame Lafarge, she was indeed French, a window; her husband had been killed towards the end of the war. 'By the Germans, on their way out.'

'I'm sorry,' said Vicky, unashamedly licking the last traces of butter and egg from around her mouth; too precious to be wasted on the napkin Madame Lafarge had provided.

The Frenchwoman shrugged her shoulders. 'Too bad, it happens.'

'And your brother-in-law?' asked Vicky, more out of courtesy since Madame Lafarge seemed to want to talk than out of any interest in the slob who had served her last time she had come into the café.

'He is ill, he drinks too much bad beer. My sister was married to his brother, it is not a close family tie. My sister's husband, as mine, is now dead. We are both widows.'

'I'm sorry,' Vicky said again. 'The war . . .'

'It wasn't the war, he drank too much and fell into the Thames.'

'Oh.'

'Good riddance, he was a burden to my sister, and he beat the children when he was drunk. Now she goes back to France.'

'And you?'

'I, too, go back to France. Tomorrow,' she said, smiling for the only time in their conversation. 'Tomorrow I leave the fog and the marge and the rationing and the queues and I go back to Paris.'

'Surely France is in an even worse state than England,' said Vicky. 'I mean, after the Occupation and everything, there's ferocious rationing, isn't there?'

'That's a story made up to keep you English happy and not complaining about the rationing and controls. In France there is food.' The flat statement brooked no contradiction. 'Not for everyone, maybe, but for my family, with good farms in the country, there is food. And with the black market, there is money. Also, people pour into Paris, the Americans, for example, with their dollars to spend. My brother has a restaurant in Paris. He writes to me and to my sister: Come, we need you, there is work for you here, and good money to be made. So, goodbye England!'

Lucky you, thought Vicky.

The woman gathered up Vicky's plate. 'You like your food. Most English people don't care what they eat, but if you do, then living in this country is like being in Purgatory. Take my advice, come to Paris. In Paris you will be able to eat like this every day, only much better, like a king. If you have money, that is.'

Vicky had noticed the Frenchwoman's eyes running over her coat, bought before the war, shabby, but still carrying an unmistakable message of wealth and taste.

'Twenty-five pounds is all this government allows you to take to France. Even with the exchange rate as it is, it doesn't go far.'

'A young woman like you, full of resource, you should find a way. There's always a way. Come to Paris, and when you do, come to my brother's restaurant, the Lion d'Or in Rue des Saints Pères.'

'Whereabouts is that?'

'You know Paris? It is in St-Germain-des-Prés.'

Vicky sat perched on a capstan, her cheeks pink with the cold, looking out over a dingy Thames, its dirty water mirroring the clouded sky. Her sketchbook was on her lap, but it was closed, her fingers were too cold to draw any more. It was strange, this dockland scene. She remembered it, vividly, on the night of a raid, with flaming warehouses sending jets of brilliant orange sparks into the sky, the river water dancing yellow and red with reflections of the blazing building. Firemen with hoses tried to battle with the fires; pin men against the raging furnace. It had smelt, of burning wood and of the noxious fumes given off by the contents of the warehouses: paint and chemicals and sugar; the hot smell of caramel had been sickening.

Now it was all deserted, the only sound that of the gulls as they wheeled above with their plangent, mewing calls. Derricks stood dilapidated and unused, rails rusted in the ground. Such a desolate place, but it suited her mood. She thought back to those days of the war, when she, like all the other Londoners, had been so often in danger. Yet then her life had felt worth living, she'd had times of such happiness. She'd been a different person, nothing like she was now, as she sat contemplating the dreary scene in front of her. A barge chugged up river, the sound of a school bell shrilled out from some unseen, begrimed brick building.

'Come on, Vicky. Snap out of it.'

The words jerked Vicky out of her reverie, and she sprang to her feet, shaking herself. Her notebook slid to the ground. She looked round, then across the river, even up into the tangle of metal above her. There was no one there, of course not. These were words in her head, some part of her subconscious taking on the very sound of Philippe. She bent to pick up her sketchbook, then stood up, her shoulders defeated, her face a mask of unhappiness.

Vicky looked at the slab of gelatinous white fish sitting in a lumpy sauce, flecked with unpleasant grey specks, that lay like something out of the morgue on the plate in front of her.

14

Her aunt had already eaten. 'I can't change my hours to suit you, I've a meeting to go to at seven.'

Vicky told her about the omelette she'd had for lunch.

'You're greedy, that's your trouble. You've always liked your food, ever since you were a child. When your mind should have been on your books and on God, you were thinking about what was for lunch. Just be grateful for what I put on your plate. There's many a poor soul in this world hasn't got a mouthful for their supper and will be dead of starvation by the morning, think about that. And greedy for food is greedy for other things, sinful things, that's what you should have been taught. Gambling and dancing and champagne, it's all one lustful state, leading you on the path to destruction.'

She whisked her thin, spiky grey form out of the gloomy dining-room, shutting the door behind her with a defiant click.

Vicky sprinkled some salt over the mess on her plate and banged the bottom of the pepper pot more out of hope than expectation. A few pale grains fell on to the fish, and she stirred them in with her fork. A glass of water had been placed by her plate, and by means of taking a gulp of that after each mouthful of fish, she managed to force most of it down.

'There,' said her aunt, coming in triumphantly, dressed ready for the street in a dark brown coat and a hat like a man's. 'I knew you'd enjoy it. Now, there's a nice bowl of tapioca for pudding.'

Tapioca wasn't too bad. At least, it was; it was so appalling that there was no way Vicky could manage a single spoonful of it. The advantage of tapioca was that her aunt's huge tabby cat loved it. Vicky tiptoed to the door and listened, heard the front door open and then shut. She made a chirruping noise, and Falstaff, who had a sixth sense where food was involved, appeared as if by magic and wound himself round her legs. Vicky went back into the dining-room, watched the cat polish off the tapioca as though he hadn't been fed for a week, and then put the bowl back on the table with the spoon in it. I bet that cat gets half my rations, she told herself, looking at the cat's portly profile and shining fur. She rolled up her napkin and put it in the napkin ring, a silver one in need of a polish, with an ornate V engraved on it. When she had moved into her aunt's house, her aunt had exclaimed how lucky it was that her name began with a V. Her late husband's name had been Vincent, and it had been his napkin ring.

Vicky hated it, just as she hated the heavy mahogany furniture, the thick, brown carpet on the stairs and landings, the huge and lumpy bed, the wardrobe with two oval mirrors whose door flew open in the night with a violent cracking sound, and the dark green bathroom papered with curling notices in her aunt's handwriting, laying down the law as to depth of water, frequency of use, habits of the geyser, times when weekly baths could and couldn't be taken and the drying of towels. They dated from the war, when her aunt had taken in carefully selected lodgers as her war effort, but Vicky supposed they would stay until they finally dissolved into a soggy mess to be be washed away down the plughole with the meagre allowance of hot bathwater.

She lay on her back in the cooling water and stared up at the familiar cobweb of cracks on the ceiling. It was badly in need of a coat of paint, like every other surface in London. She though about Paris, wondered how long one could last on twenty-five pounds; how much was that in francs? And how much did it cost to live in Paris?

She hadn't the vaguest idea. All her trips to France had been with family or to stay with family friends. Her single visit to Paris had been before the war, in 1938. Good God, more than ten years ago. She'd been a schoolgirl of fifteen, on the threshold of life, unaware of just what lay ahead of her, and of all of them. She and her mother had spent a few days in the capital on their way to the south of France for a holiday with her aunt, the one who had scandalised her family by marrying a Frenchman of no position or distinction. Only she'd had the last laugh, for her devoted husband had turned out to have the Midas touch, and he had left her a rich and contented widow enjoying life in her enchanting villa in the hills behind Nice.

Vicky's heart was thudding in that way it always did when she thought of France. She stirred the water with her hands. Of course she couldn't go to France. She supposed she might be able to find twenty-five pounds, if the publisher for whom she was doing the illustrations of London paid her promptly. Only as soon as those drawings were finished, she'd need to look for another commission. Either that, or be thrown back on her father's allowance. 'It's there whenever you want it, but you'll have to come and live at home. Unmarried girls should be with their families.'

Not if they've got fathers like you, they shouldn't, she thought, sliding down into the water until it was level with her mouth. She blew bubbles to distract herself. It was her birthday next week. Perhaps if Mummy gave her a cheque . . . but she wouldn't. Daddy wouldn't let her.

How expensive was France? Prices, in that different, vanished, pre-war world, had passed her by. She would need enough for a cheap hotel. Transport, once she got to Paris, would be next to nothing, she could walk, there was the metro, didn't people say what amazingly good value it was?

She stood up, dripping and shivering. These were pipe dreams. Twenty-five pounds, though, even allowing for a very favourable exchange rate, wouldn't last long. And if she had the money, could she bear to be in France, the country that would have been her home if only . . .

She took hold of the threadbare towel and did her best to dry herself. She mustn't think about that. That was in the past, this infinitely less promising present was what she had to cope with. She mustn't think about Philippe and those might-have-beens. Think about money. If she could come by some more money, could she take it out of the country illegally?

Tricky; she had heard how tough and unforgiving the Customs were to people trying to smuggle currency, and what would her father say if she were caught? Imagine the embarrassment it would cause him. She laughed at the idea, but knew she wouldn't laugh if it happened and his wrath descended on her. And Duggie would be scandalised, he had an acute respect for the proprieties in these matters.

She padded, still damp, across the landing to her room. She jumped into bed and pulled the covers up, waiting for the chill sheets to warm up and finish drying her icy body.

Her eyes fell on three envelopes propped up against the ornate mirror of the over-large mahogany dressing table. She slid out of bed and picked them up, checking to see if her aunt had steamed them open. Probably not, since the handwriting on two of them was feminine and the third looked official. Her aunt was too mean to waste gas by allowing the kettle to steam unless she could be sure of discovering some impropriety.

One had a French stamp, and for a wonderful moment her heart rose, then, with a pang of disappointment, she recognised the writing. It was from an old school friend, Martha. She tucked the envelope under the other letter, which she knew was from Mrs Shipton, her old nanny; she would open that one first. The long envelope with a typewritten address looked dull; she'd leave that one until last.

Vicky clambered back into bed and stuffed a thinly filled cushion behind her head. The light from the single central bulb was almost impossible to read by, but she was used to it. Her aunt disapproved of bedside lights for young people; beds were for sleeping in, and the only book you needed to read before going to sleep was the Bible, and that was best read when you were still on your knees from saying your prayers. The ill-fitting window let in thin wisps of evil fog that caught in Vicky's throat. She knew a peasouper meant that London would be invisible the next morning, a city without a dawn, and when you went out, you'd be wrapped in a foul-smelling blanket so dense that you literally couldn't see your hand in front of your face.

No fog in Paris, not like this, anyhow, she told herself as she opened Nanny's letter. It was full of venomous tales of the doings of wicked neighbours and the trouble Mr Hutt, Mrs Shipton's lodger and Vicky's father's one-time chauffeur, had had with his new uppers and lowers. He's been eating too much of the grey, tasteless bread that was all you could buy at the baker's these days, thought Vicky.

Nanny rebuked her for not having written. When were they going to see her again? They might go somewhere for a day out together, did Vicky fancy Margate?

Vicky did not, but a thought stirred in her head. Day trip, well, why not? Why not a day trip to somewhere more exciting than Margate. What about a day trip to France? A day trip for them, that was, but maybe, just maybe, a longer trip for her. Now, how could she arrange it? And how could she persuade them to go? Musing on this, she opened the letter from Martha. In fact, it wasn't a letter, just an address in Paris typewritten in the centre of the page and a note in green ink scrawled below. *Come and visit if you can ever escape.*

Escape. What an odd word to use. Possibly an accurate one, but how was Martha to know that?

Escape.

Escape from dull, miserable, ration-bound England. Escape from the worrying search for work, from the effort of scratching a living from her drawings and paintings. Escape from her father. Escape from Duggie. Escape sounded good.

Without any great interest, she opened the third envelope and read the brief, formally worded letter that was inside it. She shut her eyes, then opened them, blinked and read it again.

The next morning, she was up an hour before her usual time, startling her aunt as she brewed tea in the kitchen, opening the front door to let in swathes of evil fog; was it too thick to venture out in? No, it wasn't. Was it so bad that people wouldn't be able to go to work? Some people might be defeated, but she felt sure that the representatives of the firm of Glassonby, Bassenthwaite and Hawkes, as signed at the bottom of her letter, would be the sort of people who would always make it into the office.

She sat in the dining-room with her aunt, who was reading a few religious tracts she had collected the previous evening. 'Aunt Julia, did you know my Aunt Belinda?'

Aunt Julia chewed a piece of stringy toast. 'Your mother's sister? Oh, yes. A giddy woman, who married a foreigner and became a Papist. She died during the war, I remember your mother telling me, only it took a long time for the news to reach her. She was quite upset about it. Yes, I met Belinda. She'll be regretting that she ever set foot in a Catholic church by now, you can be sure of that.'

'Oh, hellfire you mean,' said Vicky after a moment's reflection. 'I don't think so. She was so lively and funny and kind. No loving God would cast her into the sulphurous pit.'

Her aunt rattled her cup in its saucer. 'If you were younger, I'd wash your mouth out with soap for such a remark. What brought your Aunt Belinda to mind?'

'Oh, nothing,' lied Vicky, not wanting to raise any suspicions.

'You nearly went the same way, with that Frenchman you were

so friendly with in the war,' her aunt went on. 'Such a good thing nothing came of that. I rarely agree with your father, but he was right about that. You were thinking of marrying him, and I told him so; you young people did such foolish things in the war. It wouldn't have done.'

Vicky stared at her. 'Which Frenchman?'

'The one who vanished in France. Dead now, just as well. I expect he had a wife and family tucked away in France while he was dallying with you over here.'

Vicky's face was white, her eyes alarmed. 'Aunt Julia, are you talking about Philippe? You never knew him, so why are you saying these horrible things about him?'

'Was that his name? I saw you two together, walking along the street. It was obvious what he was to you. To anyone with eyes. I told your father, of course I did. 'Put a stop to it,' I told him. 'Or who knows where it'll end, and then there'll be tears.' And don't go wasting time thinking about him now, Victoria. Your father wouldn't like that at all, nor would Duggie.'

'Philippe's dead,' said Vicky. Out of reach of tongues like yours, she thought, but oh, what wouldn't she give to have him back, to discover that it had all been a mistake, that he hadn't been killed, that he was alive. Only, of course, he couldn't be. If he were alive, he would have come back to England to find her. Wouldn't he?

Her aunt sniffed, breaking into her thoughts, pulling her back to the present.

It was absurd, thought Vicky as she pulled her coat more closely around herself, to be so upset at the mention of Philippe's name. That was finished, it had ended somewhere in France in 1943. Only, it never was quite finished, the tiniest thing could bring it all flooding back to her. Aunt Julia's sour remarks, for one. And her friend Sally had mentioned that she'd seen someone looking just like him walking down Bond Street. She supposed all lean dark Frenchmen with blue eyes were the same to them. To her, every speck of his being was individual and belonged to him; to others he was simply a dark, slightly foreign-looking man.

To Aunt Julia and her father, he was a threat, and so better dead.

'No good waiting for a bus, ducks,' called a woman who was

opening up a shop on the other side of the street. She gave a hacking cough. 'You'll have to walk to the tube if you want to go anywhere today.'

'I don't know that I'll find the tube station in this,' called back Vicky, lifting her scarf over her nose and mouth in an effort to filter out some of the foulness of the air.

'Keep to the kerb,' the woman said. 'Follow the kerb, and you'll be all right.'

The air in the tube was stale and the carriages smoky and stuffy, but it was nectar compared to the foggy air outside. It was with reluctance that Vicky climbed the steps back up to the surface and into the peasouper. Was it shifting slightly? Was that the touch of a breeze she could feel on her cheek? She could make out the dim shape of a tram in the centre of the road, and muffled figures on the pavement. Yes, it was definitely lifting. Now all she had to do was find the offices of Glassonby, Bassenthwaite and Hawkes.

'Your mother knew of the bequest,' Mr Hawkes told her. 'She, together with your aunt's legal adviser in France, was a trustee. It is surprising that she never told you of the terms of your late aunt's will.'

Vicky didn't find it surprising. Her mother would have told her father about it, and her father would have done everything he could to prevent his youngest daughter finding out that her maternal aunt had left her quite a large sum of money. 'Why didn't she want me to have the money until I was twenty-five?' she asked.

'My dear lady, how can I say? It is quite normal, when a legatee is not of age, to set up a trust until that person is, say, twenty-one or twenty-five, as in this case. Even thirty is not an unusual age for someone to come into an inheritance. The will was dated 1938, I believe, when you would have been fifteen years old. It is quite usual, there is nothing odd or derogatory about such testamentory dispositions. Now, we need to discuss the arrangements for the disbursements of these funds.'

Vicky pulled herself together. 'The money's in France?'

'The bulk of it is, yes, although there are some English investments.'

'If I went to France, would my aunt's lawyers give me some money?'

Mr Hawkes frowned. 'It depends what you mean. The money should be transferred to a bank account in your name. There is no trouble in arranging for these funds to be received in England. The other way round is a problem, as you may know.'

'Can I open a bank account in France?'

'It should be possible, but I think you would need to be there in person. Were you planning to go to France in the near future?'

'I wasn't, but I am now.'

'I would point out that your aunt's lawyers are in Nice, and although they will have connections with Paris firms, it would be better for you to go there.'

Vicky hesitated. 'Could you give me any money? On account, I mean? Add it to the bill?'

'Well, really . . . I don't see why not. Yes, it should be possible to advance you a sum of money. How much were you thinking of?'

'Seventy-five pounds,' said Vicky quickly.

'Oh, there would be no difficulty about that.'

Vicky had explained it to Nanny Shipton in careful detail. She would give her and Mr Hutt thirty pounds each and pay their fares from London to Calais, out in the morning, back the same evening. They would go to a restaurant in France for lunch before the two of them took the ferry back to Dover, leaving Vicky with both their allowances of francs in her pocket.

'I don't mind that,' Mrs Shipton said. 'Only not lunch in France, thank you very much, I never could do with that foreign muck. I'll make sandwiches for me and Hutt, if it's all the same to you.' Mrs Shipton would land, and go ashore and through Customs, to comply with the regulations, but no further. She was adamant about that. 'Shocking lavatories they have over there, shocking. I've been, and I know. You take care when you get to Paris, or you'll catch a disease, the germs there must be.'

★   ★   ★

So here she was, sick as a dog, and there they were, sprightly and perfectly well. Thank God they had to make the return trip, not her, complete with lukewarm tea in the thermos flask and the remains of the sandwiches to sustain them.

Mrs Shipton sailed through the formalities in the Customs shed, rigid with disapproval, Hutt, newspaper in hand, ambled peaceably along behind her, and they passed into the waiting area to sit for two hours until the return sailing. 'You get on, dear,' Mrs Shipton said to the hovering Vicky. 'You've got to catch a train, all the way to Paris.'

'It isn't a long journey.'

'Best to start early. You never know what kind of a trip you'll have; this being France, and make sure you don't talk to a soul. I still don't know why you're so set on coming to France. If you want a holiday, there's always Scotland. And they say Wales is nice.'

'I'm going to find my fate, Nanny.'

'Foreign is it, then, your fate?'

'I'm afraid so, Nanny, mostly foreign, anyway.'

'Fates come in all shapes and sizes, so you be careful. Abroad, anything can happen.'

Like what? mused Vicky, as she sat on the hard wooden seat in a train that rattled and clattered its stately way to the capital; mindful of her francs, she had bought the cheapest possible ticket. She had written to Martha, saying that she was coming to Paris, would visit when she got back from Nice. She couldn't count on staying with her. She knew that Martha would have sent her address and welcoming message to all her many friends. Martha, she had seen on the street map of Paris which she'd found in a second-hand bookshop, now lived in St-Germain-des-Prés, perfect, exactly the area she wanted to be, where all the jazz and nightlife and interesting cafés were.

The Café Etoile, she thought, her heart suddenly thumping. No, she simply mustn't allow herself to hope, not after all this time. She wrenched her mind into other channels. Madame Lafarge's restaurant, that was in St-Germain, she and Martha might go there if the prices weren't too high.

Vicky had acquired the name of an extremely cheap hotel in Paris, near the station, from an ex-boyfriend of her sister's who had just come back from a posting in the Embassy.

'If I hadn't been a diplomat, I'd have enjoyed every minute. As it was, every time there was a chance of getting about a bit, there was another crisis. Communists, de Gaulle, communists, the Marshall plan, communists, devaluation, communists, the position of Germany and communists again. I tell you, Vicky, it was completely exhausting. The only person who had any fun was the Ambassador, who's a great one for the ladies and who made the most of gay Paree. As far as the rest of us were concerned, for much of the time we might as well have been posted to Tooting.'

To a tourist arriving in Paris from the streamlined and hygienic world of middle-class America, the Hotel Crystal would have seemed seedy beyond belief. To Vicky, coming from her aunt's establishment, it was quite well-appointed. The three types of wallpaper, one on the walls, one on the ceiling and one wrapped round the pipes, didn't bother Vicky at all. Nor did the bidet on wheels under the basin, or the picture of the Blessed Virgin pinned above the bed. Even Madame Duplessis, the violently red-headed woman in her sixties who presided over this doubtful establishment, didn't alarm her.

She went down to the desk in the lobby, expressed her complete satisfaction with the room, filled in the required form, judging that it was very unlikely that it would ever be handed over to the police, paid for the night, saying that she would be leaving early the next morning, and took possession of the key to Room Six.

Chapter Two

$\longleftarrow\!\!\!\!>\!\!\circ\!\!\bullet\!\!\circ\!\!<\!\!\!\!\longrightarrow$

The names Drummond, Drummond, Dubarry and Drummond were engraved on a gleaming brass plate beside the handsome Georgian door. Years of polishing had smoothed the letters away to a shadow of their original form so that those seeking the services of the firm of solicitors had to ascend two shallow stone steps, worn in the centre by generations of well-shod clients, in order to get close enough to the plate to read the names. Satisfied, such visitors would then obey the instruction RING HERE, and press the brass bell situated to the right of the black door.

Julius Drummond, being a member of the firm, didn't. He took the two steps at a stride, gave the door a good push and passed into the austere gloom of the entrance hall. This was lit only by the traces of sunlight that shone through the elegant flight above the door and left patches of light on the black and white floor. The chequered pattern added an incongruous touch of merriment, Julius used to think, as though Drummonds and Dubarrys might emerge from their spacious chambers to play a giant game of chess.

The clerk was a tall, pale young man with very fair hair. He looked out of his cubbyhole, nodded solemnly to Julius, and went back to the racing pages of his scurrilous daily paper. Julius took the stairs two at a time to the first landing, paused to look over the wrought iron banister rail to the chess board below, and went on up another two flights. Drummond he might be, and thirty-three years old, but he was still merely a junior Drummond, not accorded the dignity of possession of the lower rooms currently occupied by his uncle and two first cousins once removed. None of these were the Drummonds and Dubarry of the brass plate, who were earlier representatives of their breed, but since the firm was still staffed by present-day members of the two families, there was no need for a new sign.

Once inside his room, Julius tossed his hat on to one of the top hooks on the hat stand behind the door and hung his coat below. Both coat and hat were better hidden from view; the black, wide-brimmed hat and flapping calf-length coat were considered very off by all the other members of the firm, whose sober suiting and bowler hats spoke of success and reliability.

'Just like his grandfather,' the elderly char who did for the firm in the early mornings claimed.

Julius's uncle, Edgar Drummond, winced when he heard her words. Not like father, he prayed silently, while remarking to his cousin that his late father had been a great dandy in his youth.

Frederick Dubarry knew quite well what else Edgar's father had been, not only in his youth, but all his life. He smiled a thin-lipped smile and hoped that Julius, like his grandfather, would have the sense to marry and have a family, whatever his personal inclinations might be.

The clerk toiled up the stairs to Julius's office. Julius was sitting back in his tilted chair, feet on the desk, studying a catalogue from a famous London auction house. 'Not work, Toby, surely?' he said, looking up as the blond head came round the door.

'Mr Edgar would like to see you if convenient,' he said. 'I believe it's to do with a foreign matter.'

'I'll be down in two ticks,' said Julius.

Pale Toby shuddered at the sight of the red socks that Julius always wore, and shut the door with a sharp click.

Edgar greeted his nephew with a frown. 'You were very late back from lunch.'

Julius looked surprised. 'Was I? I didn't notice.'

'Where did you go?'

Senior Drummonds and Dubarrys walked to their clubs in St

James's to take lunch. Julius had so far proved thoroughly unclub-bable, quite unimpressed by the efforts made to enrol him among the members of various exalted establishments. 'Join one of those stuffy places? No, thanks, Uncle, not my style.' Uncle Edward had offered to introduce him to his own club, regarded by the rest of his family as a dangerously bohemian outfit, but to Julius it was as dull as all the others.

'Nowhere you'd know, a little Italian place off Fleet Street.'

Edgar opened his mouth to try and explain to Julius, yet again, the need for an up-and-coming young solicitor to present the correct persona to the world. Who knew where or when you might meet present or future clients? He looked across the desk at Julius's face – was it those hooded eyes or the too finely moulded mouth that gave his nephew such a mocking look? – and desisted. Instead, he reached forward and picked up a letter from his desk.

'There's something come up which I want you to handle,' he began.

Up went the eyebrows. 'I? Are you sure? Is it a legal matter?'

'Of course it's a legal matter, we're lawyers. Even you are a lawyer, although you don't seem always to remember it.'

'Continue, then. What's up? A sordid divorce, which you and the rest of the firm don't want to touch, but the money's good?'

'Don't be vulgar, Julius. As you very well know, we don't handle divorce cases.'

'High time you did,' said Julius, crossing one leg over the other and smoothing the fabric of his trousers with the back of his hand. 'It's the coming thing, divorce. All those people who married in haste in the war and are now repenting in peace. And think of all the other couples driven apart by the war, men who married meek and cosy women only to find they've changed after four or five years of being in the armed services or driving ambulances or running estates or whatever. No domestic bliss for them now, so it's a quick trip to the divorce courts and off to the cattle market to find a more biddable wife.'

Edgar's face was a picture of distaste. 'You seem to have a liking for the sordid.'

'No, I just face facts. So, if it's not a divorce, what is it?'

Edgar sat back in his chair and gave it a gentle swivel. Julius regarded him with a tolerant eye, waited for him to join his fingers together at the tips, smiled when he did so, and waited.

'You speak fluent French.'

Julius sighed. It would be a business matter, he guessed, a French company looking to take over an English firm or vice versa. Not very interesting, but bound to end up in his lap, since a year spent idling in Paris after he had taken his degree had qualified him as the firm's expert on all things French.

Edgar had stopped gazing out of the window and was speaking again. 'The daughter of a client of this firm has gone to France. Our client wishes her found, and brought back to England.'

'Send whoever it is the name of a firm of private detectives.' Julius certainly wasn't interested, it sounded humdrum and quite unamusing. His mind drifted away to the end of the day. He might see if he could get a ticket for that new play at the Aldwych.

'Pay attention, please, Julius, since for once you may be able to do something to justify the salary we pay you. The young Englishwoman is believed to be in Paris. Her name,' and he shot a swift glance at Julius, 'is Victoria Hampden.'

Julius sat up, interested now. 'Hampden. Is that spelt H-A-M-P-D-E-N?'

'It is.'

'No relation to Kit Hampden, by any chance? One of his many daughters? I thought they'd all flown the coop.'

Edgar shut his eyes. 'He does indeed have several daughters, and Victoria is the youngest.'

'Victoria Hampden. The name rings a bell. Wasn't she the one . . . ?'

'Yes. She was made a Ward of Court, her name was all over the newspapers. It was altogether a disgraceful affair.'

It had been her father's own fault, thought Julius, dredging his memory for details of the case. If you were the most notorious judge on the bench, and you made your eighteen-year-old daughter a Ward of Court simply because she wanted to go out with a Frenchman . . . 'Has she finally gone to France to join up with her boyfriend? She must be of age by now. What's the problem?'

'She's twenty-five.'

Twenty-five! Julius showed his astonishment. 'If she's twenty-five she can go where she likes, her father can't stop her.'

'This Victoria has been a thorn in her father's flesh for many years. I believe there was trouble at school before she became entangled with this foreigner. If she's abroad, he feels that she may once again fall into the hands of an adventurer.'

Julius could just imagine the type of man Kit Hampden would want his daughter to marry. Why on earth hadn't she cast the paternal dust from her feet long since?

'What happened to her erstwhile boyfriend?'

'He was killed in the war, in 1943.'

'Was he an adventurer?'

'I believe her father had sound reasons for his disapproval, connected with the fellow's war work. Apart from the man's being French, of course; Hampden doesn't like foreigners. And he's particularly annoyed that she's gone away at this particular time. From what I hear, she was on the point of announcing her engagement to Douglas Fitzgerald.'

Julius raised his eyebrows. 'Ah, Duggie, the war hero.'

'Do you know him?'

'Our paths have crossed. Does old Hampden approve of him as a son-in-law?'

'Of course he does. Of good family, well off, and of course that outstanding war record. Suitable in every way.'

'Except that it seems Victoria would rather flit off to France than stay and marry him. What's she doing for money? An allowance from Daddy, I suppose.'

Edgar fiddled with his pencil. 'She has supported herself by work of an artistic nature for a while now. She studied at the Slade, I believe.'

'I would have thought that too Bohemian a place for Kit Hampden. Is she any good?'

'I have no idea. She has done the illustrations for some books. However, she has recently come into an inheritance from an aunt. Her maternal aunt.'

'A lot of money?' An erratic heiress on the loose could be difficult to find.

'A considerable sum, it seems, although since the aunt lived in France most of the money and some property also is in France. One has to consider the exchange rate when coming to any assessment of the total amount.'

What did the man expect? Twenty-five years old, inherits a pot of money in France; naturally she'd be off.

'Hasn't the girl a brother, or an uncle? Why approach us?'

'Because he knows we will be discreet. His son can hardly spare the time to go chasing round France after his sister. His other daughters have their own lives to lead, they are all married, and several of them live abroad or in remote places. Scotland, that kind of thing.'

'Dear God.'

Edgar became brisk. 'What I should like you to do is to see if you can find an address for this Victoria Hampden. You will need to go to France, contact her, and persuade her to return to England.'

Julius shook his head. 'Impossible. Sorry, Uncle, but no can do. By what possible means am I expected to persuade her to return?'

'Use your initiative, but bring her back.'

'But stop short of kidnapping. I see.' He thought about it. Maybe he shouldn't be so quick to say no. A trip to France, even on such a daft mission, might be very pleasant. 'Does anyone in her family know where she is? That would be the quickest way to get her address. If she's still in Paris, that is. When did she leave?'

'Ten days ago.'

'Ten days? Good Lord, she could be anywhere by now. Didn't they realise she'd gone?'

'She lodges with Julia Bagshot, a tiresome woman full of religious zeal. Victoria told her she was going to Scotland to stay with one of her sisters. Julia thought nothing of it, until she met this same Scottish sister by chance in Marshal and Snelgrove. The sister was spending a few days in London and said Victoria hadn't been to Scotland, nor had she been expected.'

'So how do they know about France?'

'Victoria's old nanny knew that's where she'd gone.'

'What am I to do, interrogate the nanny? I'd rather not. If she's anything like my ex-nanny, she'll chew me up into little pieces.'

'Make enquiries of Victoria's family; one of them might have some idea where she could be staying. I beg of you, Julius, be discreet. There's clearly been an estrangement, so you may have to do some detective work. On your own, there's no question of bringing a professional into this business. Discretion, Julius, must be your watchword. Is your passport up to date? Good. Then I'll ask my secretary to make arrangements with our bank for foreign currency for you. As you will be travelling to France on business, the usual government restrictions won't apply. Shall you drive?'

Julius's spirits soared. France! Paris in spring, how wonderful. Unlimited funds at his disposal, well, no, not unlimited, but a damn sight more than the measly twenty-five pounds allowed by official-dom. His languor gone, he sprang up from his chair and thanked his Uncle.

'You don't need to thank me, Julius. It's what you're paid a salary for. You're the only member of the firm who could be spared on such a matter at present. And Julius . . .'

Julius, his hand on the door handle, turned and looked question-ingly at his uncle. 'Yes?'

'Wear a sober suit, if you would be so kind. And do get your hair cut before you leave.'

Julius smiled, and shut the door behind him. He stood there for a moment, and then took off up the stairs, humming snatches of Mozart as he went. Downstairs, Toby shook his head and folded up his paper, lips pursed. Young Mr Julius would never get into the ways of Drummond, Drummond, Dubarry and Drummond; never.

Julius decided to begin with the family. Not with Victoria's father, he was far too formidable a figure, and if he had any idea where his daughter was, he wouldn't have needed Edgar's help to find her. Victoria's sisters were a better bet; his uncle had mentioned that there was a troop of sisters.

First stop, then, would be his own godmother. If anyone could advise on the Hampden family, it would be Evelyn Whistler, who sat like a glittering spider in the centre of the intricate social web of their kind. At ten to five, therefore, he was cruising round Cadogan Square looking for a place to park his Lagonda. At five to five, he was knocking at her front door.

Evelyn greeted her godson with a chilly kiss. 'Julius, shouldn't you be at the office?'

'Only for another hour, and I am still working. A client wants his daughter traced, and since you know everyone in London, I thought I'd start with you.'

She led the way up to the drawing-room on the first floor and waved him to a sofa. 'I don't know people who need to be traced. My friends and acquaintances aren't in the habit of disappearing.'

'No, but their children might be, you know how depraved modern youth is. And it's someone young I'm looking for: Victoria Hampden.'

He had succeeded in surprising her. 'Vicky Hampden? Kit's youngest daughter?'

'Yes. Unless there are two Victoria Hampdens.'

Aunt Evelyn shook her head. 'There was another, Victoria is named after her grandmother. There's no point in looking for her, she'll be in Highgate Cemetery where she's been for the last ten years. Dear me, tell me what Vicky's done now?'

'Gone to France without leaving a forwarding address.'

Evelyn Whistler gave an elegant shrug of her whippet shoulders. 'Why the urgency? Vicky will turn up in due course, those Hampdens always do.'

'Her father fears that she'll fall for an undesirable Frenchman.'

'A Frenchman? Vicky's already done that, but surely the man's dead. Sad, he was a most attractive man. She brought him here once. Perhaps Vicky doesn't believe he was killed, and has gone to find him. A pretty pointless exercise, but then the whole family are not quite sane, in my opinion.'

'That Ward of Court business. That was just to do with the Frenchman, wasn't it? It aroused a good deal of interest at the time.'

'Oh, my goodness, yes. The publicity! The scandal! So stupid of Kit to act like that, the press had a field day. And after all, Vicky was eighteen, hardly a baby.'

'What did Hampden have against him?'

'Foreign, Catholic, and he was keen on his daughter. Kit is, how

32

shall I put it, a jealous father. Particularly so where Vicky is concerned. So at the thought of her marrying anyone, let alone a Frenchman, he flew into one of his terrible rages.'

Julius wished he could have seen it. He found the English upper classes in a temper unfailingly amusing.

'You needn't look so smug, Julius. Plenty of scandals in your family.'

'Scandals? Do tell?'

'I will not. Just remember everyone's cupboard has the odd skeleton, not least yours. No one knew anything about the Frenchman, so her father had some right to be concerned. Vicky said that he was doing hush-hush work with the Free French.'

Evelyn reached out for the heavy silver cigarette box and flipped open the lid. She took out a black cigarette with a gold tip and held out the box to Julius.

He took a Sobranie and produced a pewter lighter. He lit first his aunt's cigarette, tucked now into a tortoiseshell holder, and then his own. They sat in companionable silence for a few minutes, savouring the cigarettes. Julius held the cigarette between his fingers and watched the smoke curl up from the lighted tip.

'Hampden was right in a way. Every Frenchman in London claimed to be doing hush-hush work with the Free French. Even some of the English were working for them. There was no way to check on them; de Gaulle was fearfully touchy about anything he considered interference.'

Evelyn leaned forward to tap ash into a heavy onyx ashtray on the table in front of her. Her elderly maid, who had been with her before, during and since the war, brought in the heavy silver tea tray and put it down on a table near the window, nodding at Julius whom she'd known since babyhood.

'Well, even if nobody knew what her Frenchman was up to, I could quite see why Vicky fell for him,' Evelyn went on. 'Any woman could. Now, have some tea, and tell me more.'

'Vicky Hampden's inherited a pot of money from a French aunt.'

Julius knew his godmother well. Her pale grey eyes gleamed with the curiosity that made her so well-informed about every scandal and item of gossip in her circle. 'The money must be from Belinda, although I thought she'd died a while ago.'

'There was a trust.'

'Then Vicky's gone to France to settle the legal side, very tedious it is over there. They can be so bureaucratic, as I don't need to tell you. I suppose she should have let her mother know where she'd gone, but Vicky's a strange creature. I've known her since she was a baby, and I've often wondered if she's Kit's child at all. Could be a changeling for all the likeness she has to either of her parents.' The gossipy glint shone in her eyes as she leaned closer to Julius, who was paying attention on a brocade sofa. 'Ada, that's Kit's wife, you know, has had a terrible time with Kit. That man is gothic, positively gothic, in his outlook and especially when it comes to women. Heaven help any victim of rape or molestation that comes up before him in court. In his view, if a woman's in the street alone, she's inviting all kinds of unsavoury attention.'

Julius was startled. He'd known about some of Hampden's highly dubious judgements, but hadn't realised how extreme his views were. In a fairer world, where the word justice meant what it said, he'd have been booted off the bench years before. However, since all too many of his contemporaries and colleagues shared his views, there was no reason why he shouldn't go on handing down exemplary sentences for years yet.

'Men like Kit want to put the clock back, and it can't be done, Julius, and what's more, if it could, I shouldn't welcome it.' Evelyn's voice was as sharp as her views; Julius's godmother was famous for her outspoken opinions.

She took another sip of her tea. 'Now, the Hampden daughters.' A faraway look came into her eyes. 'Let me think, who's the eldest? Muriel, that's the one. Muriel is no good to you, she married one of those depressing Scots, chieftain of his clan, the McThis of McThat, you know what I mean. All claymores and sporrans, and they live in some desolate castle in the Highlands.'

'That'll be the one Julia Bagshot bumped into in some shop.'

'Julia Bagshot! Dreadful woman. You are moving in doubtful company, Julius. Drink up your tea before it gets cold, or is there something wrong with it?'

34

Julius had forgotten his tea; he quickly took a gulp of the by-now tepid brew.

Evelyn was continuing with her round-up of the Hampden family. She had the faraway look of a Sibyl declaring an oracle as she searched her capacious memory for facts about the sisters. 'The second daughter is a possibility. Vera Rowder she is now, very smart, moves in a fast set of youngish marrieds, but underneath the glitter and the backless frocks, I think she's a pillar of respectability.'

The word in Evelyn's mouth was almost an insult. Clearly Vera wasn't a favourite.

'Next is Daphne. She's the suburban one, house in Surrey, tennis clubs, husband in the City who catches the eight-fifty to Town every morning. She might be able to help you, but she has a busy social life among her mock-tudor friends; she could be difficult to pin down. The third daughter is Gwendoline. No use to you at all, she got very religious when she was about seventeen and has become a nun in one of those suspect Anglican orders. In Yorkshire, I believe. Mind you, I can't blame her for opting for an all-female world.'

Julius's head was reeling. 'There are six of these sisters?'

'Six apart from your Vicky, so seven in all. One son, no question of a changeling there, he's the image of his father and has inherited all his unpleasant ways. Where was I? Oh, yes, Gwendoline, dear Gwendoline in her holy hideaway. Now, Gwendoline has a twin, not identical, quite different to look at, one fair, the other carroty haired. She's called Deirdre.'

'What frightful names,' said Julius.

'They are rather terrible, but poor dear Ada never had much imagination. They're all named after grandmothers and great-aunts. Deirdre is not religious, but, like Gwendoline, she gave up on men and lives with a woman friend and several dachshunds in Worcester-shire. It's perfectly obvious what their relationship is, obvious that is to everyone except Kit, who doesn't know about lesbians.'

'Oh, come, Evelyn, he had a good classical education, surely.'

'He knows about them in theory, not practice, not on his own doorstep. As far as he's concerned, the ancient Greeks got up to all kind of larks that wouldn't be tolerated in England today. Women in white robes on an island singing love poems to each other is one thing, Deirdre sharing a bed with a tweedy woman is quite another. Men like Kit never make the connection. He assumes that Deirdre is just rather keen on dogs, and that one day she'll see the light and find herself a husband.'

'Only you think not.'

'I know not. How many is that?'

'Five.'

'Five, of course.' Evelyn's eyes narrowed. 'The sixth daughter is Edith, and you couldn't forget her. She escaped her father's clutches by marrying an immensely rich American tycoon. Kit wasn't keen, he counts all Americans as foreigners and not out of the top drawer, but this man was so rich he was beyond drawers. They live in America, of course, none happier than Edith to have thousands of miles of cold grey sea between her and her papa. Long Island, and various other houses dotted around. If Vicky had her wits about her, that's where she'd have gone if she wanted to get away from Kit, but the child never did have any sense.'

'Lord,' said Julius. 'So it's Vera of the smart set or waylaying Daphne in the leafy lanes of Surrey.'

'And I'm not sure you'll get anything useful out of either of them. They aren't a loving family, and Vicky is quite a lot younger than the two eldest girls. They've never been close.'

Julius brooded with half-closed eyes, looking like a contemplative hawk. 'It isn't going to be so easy, is it? Uncle Edgar's on edge about this one, keeps on insisting I must be ultra discreet.'

'Very wise, if it's anything to do with Kit Hampden. You could try the newspapers. Some reporter may have found out about her going to France, know where she is. It's quite extraordinary the way they nose things out.'

'Why should the newspapers be interested in her?'

'They're keeping an eye on her because of the rumour that she's going to marry Duggie Fitzgerald.' Evelyn looked contemptuous. 'She'll regret it if she does, but I suppose she'd do anything to get away from her father. And she's a judge's daughter, the press like that. A pretty creature, too: auburn hair, a most unusual shade, and creamy skin.' She gave Julius a quick, sidelong glance. 'Not that it would interest you.'

36

He raised his eyebrows, and leant back against a plump grey velvet cushion. 'Not the point at issue, Evelyn. So where do I start?'

Evelyn looked into the middle distance, tapped the arm of her chair with a set of shining red nails.

Talons, thought Julius, who thought them very fetching.

'I think you should start with Vera.'

'Not the mother?'

'I'll speak to her mother on the telephone. Ada and I serve on some committees together, so I can invent a reason. I'll find out what I can, which won't be much. She decided years ago that the only way to survive was to bury her head in the sand. She did her best with those girls, but they drew the short straw having Kit Hampden for a father. Meanwhile, talk to Vera Rowder, and if she's no use, then you need to find the address of one Martha Frobisher.'

'Who is Martha Frobisher?'

'An American. She was at school with Vicky, and she lives in France, she's recently moved to Paris, I believe. If Vicky's there, she may stay with Martha.'

Julius produced an envelope from his inside pocket, smoothed it out, and wrote down *Vera Rowder* and *Martha Frobisher, school – France*. Then he folded it and tucked it back in his pocket.

Evelyn rose, stubbing out her cigarette. 'You'd better go now. I have to go upstairs and dress, I'm dining out.'

'Thank you,' Julius said at the door, kissing his godmother with genuine affection.

'Don't forget, I want to hear all about it,' she called after him.

A morning call would be best, Julius felt. The hour when busy socialites would be up and dressed, but before they embarked on their daily round of cocktails, shows, viewings, meals, dances and all the rest of the whirl that made up their empty lives.

A maid answered the door to him, looking flustered. 'Mrs Rowder? I'm not sure . . .'

'Who is it, Mary? Send them away if it's a caller, I can't possibly see anyone this morning, I'm utterly distracted.'

Julius was in the hall before Mary could stop him. He sidestepped a large trunk and righted a lacrosse stick that had fallen down. 'Mrs Rowder?' he called. 'So sorry to bother you at an inconvenient time, but it's quite important.'

A too thin, exquisitely made-up face frowned down at him from the landing. 'Who are you? I don't know you, do I?'

'Julius Drummond. I believe you know my uncle.'

Her face cleared. 'You're Edgar Drummond's nephew.'

She came down the curved staircase, and as she held out her hand to Julius he had to marvel at the polished perfection of her. Dressed in navy and cream, she was sleek from the beautifully waved hair on her head to the expensive shoes on her feet. 'We're all at sixes and sevens, my daughter goes back to school today, thank God, but the taxi hasn't come, and she doesn't seem to have half her things together.'

As she spoke, a teenage girl, bulging of limb, drab of hair and bright of cheeks, bolted through a door into the hall. 'Mummy, Nanny's being simply foul. She says I won't need my lax kit, it's the tennis term, but the silly old bag doesn't realize that we've got a match to play, the one which was postponed last term because of bad weather, and I've simply got to take everything back with me.'

Indifferent eyes fell on Julius. 'Who are you?' She didn't wait for an answer, but brushed past her mother and thundered up the stairs.

Her mother made an infuriated noise, and called up to her retreating form. 'Olivia, your manners! Never mind your games kit, it can be sent on. Mary must go out this minute and find you a taxi, or you'll miss the train.'

Olivia reappeared. 'I don't mind.'

'But I do,' said Vera Rowder, somewhat helplessly, Julius thought.

'I've come at quite the wrong time, but what I want isn't going to take a minute,' he said to Vera, whose mind was clearly not on her unexpected visitor. 'We, my firm, that is, need to find your sister Victoria. We have heard she's in Paris. Do you have an address for her?'

Now he had Vera's full attention. Her eyes narrowed. 'That girl. If Vicky's missing, all I can say is I'm very pleased to hear it. Maybe she'll give us some peace at last. I can't tell you how many times the wretched creature has dragged our name through the gutter, terrible articles in the papers, people blaming it all on poor Daddy. And now, when it's all come right and she's about to get engaged to sweet Duggie Fitzgerald, she does a flit. I've no patience with her.'

She paused, glanced at the slender gold watch on her bird-like wrist. 'Excuse me for just a moment. Olivia! You are to come down now, right now, this instant.' She turned back to Julius. 'Daughters! Do you have any children?'

'I'm not married.'

A calculating look came into her eyes, the look of a society hostess who could always do with a spare, personable young man to make up numbers or act as an escort. 'Shame,' she said, 'but on the other hand, children are such a nightmare.'

'Your sister. . . ?'

'No, I can't help you. I simply have no idea where she might be, although Mummy said France. I expect she's run off to find that dreadful man who picked her up, he was French, or pretended to be. Probably a waiter from Manchester if truth be known. We all thought he was dead, such a relief; such a pity if he isn't.'

She raised her voice again. 'Olivia, I shan't give you any money for the term if . . .'

Olivia landed with a thud at the foot of the stairs. 'Here I am, Mummy. Has Mary got me a taxi?'

Mary came in through the front door, tight-lipped. 'No taxi to be found, Madam. Shall I try telephoning again?'

While Mary and Vera were conferring, Olivia, who had crammed a hideous navy blue felt hat on her head, sidled up to Julius. She spoke out of the side of her mouth, like a character in a bad gangster movie. 'You were asking about Aunt Vicky, I heard you. I can tell you how to find her, how much is it worth?'

What a family, thought Julius, amused. 'Ten bob.'

'A pound. Come on, be quick, I've got to go.'

Julius turned to Vera Rowder. 'I've my car outside. Would it help if I ran Olivia here to the station for you? Which station does her train leave from?'

'Paddington. Oh, the relief if you would. Are you sure? I can't take her myself, I've got such a full day.'

'Is there someone who'll give me a hand with her trunk?'

'I can do that,' said Olivia with scorn, effortlessly lifting one end of the trunk. 'Come on, buck up and take the other end.'

They staggered out of the house, and heaved the trunk into the rear of Julius's Lagonda.

'Why don't you drive a more convenient car?' Olivia asked as she came out with another suitcase and armfuls of clutter. 'Take my lacrosse stick, will you, and don't drop that little suitcase, it's got a bottle of lotion in it.'

Having arranged all her possessions to her liking, she climbed into the passenger seat and gave the car door a vigorous slam.

'Aren't you going to say goodbye to your mother?' Julius asked as he slid into the driver's seat.

'I have,' said Olivia untruthfully, giving the cluster of mother, nanny and maid at the door a cursory wave. 'Step on it, or I'll miss my train.'

Julius put the car into gear as the front door of the Rowders' house shut. He was willing to bet that Vera Rowder was delighted to see the back of both of them.

'You turn right here,' said Olivia. 'That's the quickest way. Now, about that pound.'

'You speak first, and then I'll pay you.'

'How do I know you will? Once you've got the info, I haven't got a hold over you.'

'You haven't got a hold over me now, and I'm not giving you a penny until I'm sure that what you know is worth having.'

'Oh, all right then.' Her voice took on a conspiratorial tone. 'I happen to know that Aunt Vicky's got a chum called Martha Frobisher.'

'I know that.'

'Only I bet you don't know how to get hold of Martha, and I do.'

'Spit it out.'

'Aunt Vicky and Martha both went to my school. It's a dreadful place, I bet they hated it as much as I do, but one thing is, they're awfully keen on keeping tabs on old girls. I expect it's because they hope they'll marry money and support the school, when they want money for new tennis courts and things like that.'

'I see. What you're saying is that a telephone call to your school office will supply me with Martha Frobisher's present address.'

'It's the only place you'll get it from, for Martha's American and she doesn't have any family in England, there's no one you'll be able to ask.'

'Okay, here's your pound.'

'Thank you,' said Olivia, inspecting the pound note as though wary of forgeries, before folding it into a neat square. Then, to Julius's alarm, she hitched up the skirt of her hideous navy suit, and tucked the note into a pocket of a pair of stout navy school knickers.

Julius wondered by what miraculous means teenage lumps like Olivia, with no manners or discretion or modesty that he could discern, grew up into the skinny, polished elegance of a Vera. 'Will you go to finishing school when you're older?'

'They'll want me to, Mummy and Daddy, I mean, and my grandfather, who's ghastly, will insist on it, but I've got other plans.'

'Have you?'

She nodded. 'I'm going to go abroad. Travel. I want to run off with a foreigner, someone terribly unsuitable. We might live in a tent. In the desert somewhere. I'm awfully good at tents.'

Julius accelerated through an amber light. 'What time did you say your train left?'

'I didn't, but I've missed it anyhow. You'll have to take me all the way back to school. It isn't very far, you can do it in an hour.'

Julius braked and drew into the curb. 'Listen, I've got better things to do than chauffeur adolescent girls to God knows where.'

'If you don't, you won't get Martha's address.'

'You've told me how to get that.'

'Yes, only I didn't tell you that they'd never, ever, give it out to a stranger, let alone a man.'

'They'll give it to me, I'm a solicitor. What could be more respectable?'

'Doesn't matter, you're a man, you're under seventy, they won't trust you an inch. They'll tell you to write, and then they'll write to Martha, and if she says it's all right, then they'll write to you again. The speed they move at, it'll be the end of term before you get the lowdown on Martha's whereabouts.'

'So?'

'So, if you drive me back to school, I'll go to the office. They'll give it to me, I'll say Mummy wants to write to Martha.'

'Will they believe you?'

She shrugged. 'Why not? Anyhow, it's your only hope.'

Julius let in the clutch. 'If your school's so paranoid about men, aren't they going to object to your arriving back in my car?'

'No. We'll stop on the way, I'll tell you where. Then you can buy me lunch, and I'll telephone the school and tell them my cousin is taking me back. I can imitate Mummy's voice, they won't suspect a thing.'

Kit Hampden's genes were showing up in unexpected places, thought Julius, as he worked his way through London to the A40. Still, better to be a houri, which was apparently what she had in mind, than a bigot, and after his brief exposure to Olivia's powerful personality, he would be prepared to lay bets on her getting her way when the time came.

'So as well as driving you all the way there, I'm to give you lunch, am I?'

'Yup.'

Chapter Three

Vicky sniffed the air. It was chilly and damp after the brilliant spring warmth of the south, and a thin fog hung in the air, But, even so, this wasn't the chill dampness of her native city. Essence of Paris was not at all the same as essence of London. The very smell of the air was different. Probably drains, and unsavoury smells from the Seine, she told herself, wanting to be prosaic, to dampen down her feelings, not to allow her spirits to lift. It was no good. What she smelt might have a touch of drain in it, but at its heart it was the ambrosial scent of a city promising delight and adventure.

It was a new city for her, and it offered a tantalising hope of a new life. A life away from England, away from her father and away from Duggie. Was that what inheriting enough money to make you independent did to you, made you want to cast away all your old ties and affections? Before she had thought this through, with all its alarming implications, she found herself in the Rue du Dragon, a narrow, mediaeval street, dark and cobbled and very unEnglish. She peered at the name *Frobisher* inscribed against the fourth bell up, and pressed the brass button.

'Vicky.'

She looked round, then up. Martha was leaning out of one of the upper windows, and lowering a key on a long thread. Vicky was puzzled for a moment: the voice she'd heard hadn't been Martha's. It had sounded like Philippe. A prickle went up her spine, and she retreated from the door to scan the street. It was empty except for a small boy trudging home with a schoolbag on his back. It must have been Martha's voice; her imagination was playing tricks on her yet again.

The key dangled past her ear; she caught it and put it in the lock. Inside, the hall was unlit, but as she blinked in the sudden darkness, a light went on. Martha's voice echoed down the central staircase. 'Fourth floor, honey, such a long way up. I'm coming down to help with your bags.'

Then they were inside the apartment, hugging each other; Vicky had always loved the way Martha hugged her friends, without inhibition or insincerity. People in her own family weren't given to hugging. She sometimes wondered how her various sisters managed in bed, where contact was presumably unavoidable. Or perhaps, like her, they relished the closeness, only chose not to let it slide into outside life. It was a good thing their husbands weren't much given to hugs in a general way, though; imagine the horror of being embraced by Fergus with his bristling red beard, or by Vera's impeccably tailored icicle of a husband.

'Here's your room,' cried Martha, throwing open a door. 'Tiny, quite minuscule, but you won't mind. There's this cupboard in the hall, heaps of room for all your things.' She darted across the hall and gestured to other doors. 'Bathroom. Kitchen. And here's the sitting-room, make yourself at home while I put some coffee on. Don't say a word until it's ready. I long to hear every single thing that's happened, all those years to catch up on, and the surprise of your making it to France.'

Martha's sitting-room reflected its eccentric owner. A stuffed raven held pride of place on a shelf above the door, two large Greek pots with glass on top acted as tables, a Bauhaus chair was set opposite a striped Belle Epoque sofa, a round table was covered with a large many-coloured shawl with fringes quite a foot long. A Lalique lamp stood on one side of the room, and the rolltop desk on the other side was lit by a starkly modern angular lamp. Large cushions covered in Turkish rug fabric were heaped against the wall between the two windows, and Vicky settled herself amidst the reds and browns and blues, kicking her shoes off and stretching her legs as she flexed her toes.

'I've walked for miles,' she told Martha as she brought in a pot of coffee and two cups. 'I couldn't bear to disappear into the bowels of the earth, not on a day like this.'

'You could have taken a taxi, folly to lug your bags on foot.'

'They aren't especially heavy, I've not brought much with me.'

'You've come straight off the train from Calais, I suppose. Was it a bad crossing?'

'It was, but I came over several days ago. I spent a night here in Paris, in an hotel, and then caught a train to the Riviera.'

'*Riviera!* Why? And why an hotel in Paris, when there's a perfectly good room here?'

'Bless you, and here I am, but I had my head down then, I was only passing through. I just wanted to get to Nice. To collect some money, apart from anything else.'

'Are you short of money? The allowances are so restrictive, all my English friends count every penny, except those who've made arrangements, as they put it.'

'No, I'm not. At least, not now,' said Vicky. 'Firstly, because I wangled three allowances instead of one; don't ask how, since I can't bear to think of the crossing, the agony of it. And much, much better, I came into a pot of money left to me by darling Aunt Bel, and I'm fearfully sorry she died, because she was so kind to me when I was a gawky young thing, but think of me having any money of my own.'

Martha poured coffee. 'Sounds great, so she just died, and you came over to fix things?'

'No, she died quite a while ago, during the war. Heart, I think. Of course, none of us could go to her funeral, because she lived in France. That's why I've been to Nice.'

'If she died during the war, what took you so long? I'd have been over here pronto, soon as the troops were marching into Paris.'

'The money was put in trust until I was twenty-five.'

'At least you knew it was coming, then.'

'No, that's the point, I hadn't the slightest idea.'

'Didn't the lawyers get in touch with you?'

Vicky wriggled herself further into the cushions. It sounded bad, when you had to say, no, your father had dealt with the lawyers. In fact, that your father had intercepted any communications from the lawyers, and had bullied your mother, a trustee, into never saying that this money would, one day, be hers.

'You met my father, didn't you?'

Martha nodded. 'At a school speech day. He was very, very polite and looked like some ideal father out of a book, grave face, kind smile, greying hair. He seemed a real sweetie; firm but fair. Which is okay when you're a judge, isn't that what he was?'

'Is,' said Vicky. 'And he may have looked like an ideal father, and seemed kind and fair and all that, but nothing could be further from the truth. He's a tyrant on the bench and a monster at home.'

Martha raised her eyebrows. 'You sound kind of heated.'

'Kind of nothing. Just thinking about him makes me angry. Not that I want to be, I want to be cool and indifferent, and my heart not to thud and my stomach sink whenever I think about him or someone mentions his name.'

'That bad?'

'Worse.'

'How a monster at home?'

'Think about it, seven daughters, a doormat of a wife, one son in his own image. What a set-up for an overbearing, aggressive man.'

Vicky shut her eyes, remembering days which she had tried to force down beyond reach of her memory, days when one sister after another across her childhood years had stumbled out of her father's study, ashen faces and weals across back and bottom testifying to her father's warped fury. She had known just why her sisters had all been so eager to get away to school, how her mother had sent her away when she was barely seven years old, why they had been sent to the seaside or the country whenever Ada Hampden could arrange it, why her sisters had all shaken the dust of their home from their feet as soon as they could.

'He made rather a scene about your Frenchman, you never said much about it, but he didn't approve, did he?'

'No. He wouldn't let Philippe set foot in the house, he half threw him down the steps and made Mummy call the police.'

'But you went on seeing him.'

'When I could, but it was tricky. Even in the middle of a war, when he was supposed to be working fourteen hours a day in some war job, he tried to keep tabs on me.' She held her head between her hands, keeping her thoughts in order. 'You don't know what it's like to have someone going on and on and on at you. He called me all kinds of terrible names.'

'I can imagine,' said Martha.

'In the end, Philippe went away.'

'He left you to that?'

'Oh, no, it wasn't deliberate, it was work, a mission. He was going back to France, only I didn't know that then. I just knew he wouldn't be in London for several weeks, months, even. So I gave in, anything to get away from Daddy. He packed me off to cool my heels in Muriel's ghastly castle.'

'Muriel?'

'Didn't you ever meet her? My eldest sister. She's years older than I am, and married to a peculiar Scotsman who has revolutionary ideas about tossing the English out of Scotland. I told him I was with him all the way, no skin off my nose if I needed a visa to cross the border, catch me bothering. It rained all the time, and every spare moment he wasn't plotting against the Sassenachs, that's us, you know, he was out killing things. Great dead heads all over the stone walls, and I can't tell you how cold it was. Muriel seems quite happy, though, and I know why, after growing up in a house with Daddy in it, even an ancient Scottish castle with Macbeth in residence must seem like heaven.'

'So when did you hear about your Frenchman?'

'Philippe. His name's Philippe. It was dreadful, because it must have been quite a while after it happened. He'd left a message with a friend, and a keepsake to be given to me if, well, if anything happened to him. Which it did, or they said it did. The friend couldn't get in touch with me, he got the runaround from Daddy. I can just imagine that, and he couldn't get my address. He wouldn't give up, though, and in the end he persuaded one of the maids to tell him where I was.'

'Smart work.'

'Not for Rose. Daddy found out, and he sacked her. After whacking her across the mouth and breaking one of her teeth. She had nowhere to go, and no possessions or money, Daddy wouldn't let her take a thing with her.'

'But that's illegal, he could have been had up for that.'

'As Rose said, what magistrate was going to take her word against my father's? They all stick together, these people. It's their law, and it's law that's too expensive for the likes of Rose, even if she did have the courage to take them on.'

'So you got the letter and the keepsake.'

'Through the post.'

Darling Victoria. If you receive this, you will know . . .

She still couldn't bear to think of the words. She opened her handbag, and held out a slender velvet bag. 'It's in here, what he sent me.'

Martha opened it and took out a cream silk package. She slid the contents on to the palm of her hand. 'A butterfly,' she exclaimed as she opened it. 'With a painting on it. It's the crucifixion. The colours! Vicky, I never saw anything so beautiful.'

'He'd showed it to me in London. He said it had been in his family for centuries.'

'Some memento, I have to say. I suppose you realise that this is probably worth a fortune.'

Vicky shrugged. 'Perhaps. It's unimportant. It's all I've got of Philippe, so it doesn't matter to me if it's a priceless treasure or cost half a crown at Woolworths.'

'Gothic, I'd say. Do take care of it, honey. Don't flash it around. If a crook caught sight of it, you could be in real trouble.' She slid a bowl of fruit towards Vicky. 'Go on, help yourself, I know you don't get much fruit in England. I'm going to go and put some fresh coffee on.'

Vicky took an apple, and began to peel it. Her fingers were unsteady, it was infuriating how upset she still got when she thought of Philippe having the door slammed in his face by her father.

Martha came back from the kitchen. 'What happened to Rose, the maid?'

Vicky sliced off a piece of apple. 'She wasn't sorry. She was a refugee, you see, and so she couldn't be called up, that's why she was still with us. I forged a reference from my mother, and she went to work for the voluntary services. Poor Rose.'

'Poor you,' said Martha. 'Were you in Scotland for the rest of the war?'

Vicky shook her head. She was picking at the apple peelings in her plate with nervous fingers. 'Even Daddy couldn't keep me from war work. The ambulance people were a bit shirty, but he fixed them, and that meant that I turned up on some list somewhere and I was directed to appear at an office, to do with supplying uniforms it was, awfully dull. At least it was in London, and it kept me busy.'

'Jesus, you mean you went back home?'

'No. Muriel stood up for me, and insisted that I should lodge with my aunt, daddy's sister. She said that no one could object to that. Daddy wanted me back home, said he had to keep an eye on me, but Muriel didn't trust him. I moved in with my aunt, and I was really glad of the job. It was the first time I'd had money of my own, you see. I'd have done anything not to have to depend on my father for money.'

'What's your aunt like?'

Vicky was quick to catch on. 'You mean, being my father's sister? She's potty, too, but not so vicious, and of course not powerful like he is. She's ultra religious in a depressing way, big on sin and all that.'

'It makes you wonder what your grandfather must have been like.'

'Don't ask.' Vicky gloomily ate the last of her apple. 'It's a fearful inheritance. Suppose we all end up like that?'

'Perhaps you take after your mother.'

'That's not much better, she's a born victim.'

'Why didn't she leave your father years ago?'

'Women didn't, you know how the English are, and that generation gets all prissy about divorce. Also, she knew that if she left, it would be open season on us girls as far as Daddy was concerned. Like a true mother, she loved us more than she loved her own freedom.'

'I suppose she didn't have any money.'

'She had quite a lot, actually, but Daddy got his hands on it pretty smartly. He wanted her to have to beg for every penny.'

'What a bastard. Sorry, Vicky, your pa and all that, but really! I had no idea he was like that.'

'He *is* a bastard. It's a fact, not a judgement. One day he'll go too far, and find himself up to his neck in it, and then all his influence and position won't be a bit of use. I long for the day.' She stretched her arms above her head and yawned. 'Do I smell heavenly coffee, Martha? The bliss of not being in England and drinking dishwater.'

Martha gave a sudden laugh. 'Do you remember how we used to sneak into the lab and brew up over the Bunsen burners?'

Vicky's face lightened. 'I'd completely forgotten. Oh, Martha, how I hated school, and what a haven of peace and order it seems to me now.'

'I was so surprised when they took you back, after you'd run away twice already.'

'That was my sister Edith's doing. Edith is the one next to me. She spoke to the headmistress about me. I don't know what she said, probably something nasty about Daddy, and that would have gone down well with Miss Calthrop; you remember how she hated men. Edith knew that if the school didn't take me back, I'd have to have a governess or tutors at home, and I'd be at Daddy's mercy all the time.'

'It's good to know that your sisters were ready to lend a helping hand.'

'We aren't close. They only do what suits them, and that's anything to keep our name out of the newspapers. They know that one of us only has to sneeze and the press are on to it. So although they feel Daddy shouldn't get away with it, none of them wants to rock the boat.'

'Here,' said Martha, giving her a handkerchief.

Vicky blew her nose and dabbed at the wetness on her cheeks. 'It's all very dreary and rather Freudian, and I should have done something about it years ago.'

'Reported him to the cops, that kind of something?'

Vicky was horrified. 'Goodness, no. Besides, they wouldn't believe me, no one would. My mother would swear it wasn't true, and my sisters would say they didn't know what I was talking about. I'd probably end up shut away in a home.'

'This is the twentieth century, we aren't living in Dickensian times.'

'My father would be strong meat even for Dickens. Pour me some more coffee, and forget I ever spoke, please. I'm twenty-five now, hardly a baby any more.'

'The money will make a tremendous difference,' said Martha.

'Money always does. How come your Dad hasn't married you off? In fact, I read an item in a gossip column about you, not long ago. It said that your name had been romantically linked with Douglas Fitzgerald.'

'Duggie,' said Vicky, with no great enthusiasm. 'Yes, Duggie the war hero. I'm very fond of him, actually. I've known him for years, there's some family connection.'

'Very dashing and brave from what the papers say about him.'

'Yes, all that, and he has excellent prospects in banking, which is where he's making his career, and he's rich and will be even richer one way and another. Mummy adores him, and Daddy's already treating him as a son-in-law. He behaves beautifully with his sons-in-law, although I don't think Edith's husband is impressed. He's American, and I think he has a good idea of what Daddy's really like. Not that Edith will ever have said anything, she wouldn't dream of it, but I've caught a look in his eyes once or twice that makes me think he's not taken in by all the bonhomie and fine English gentleman stuff that Daddy does so well.'

'Good for him. One up to Uncle Sam, we breed them shrewd. So how do you feel about this Duggie?'

'I don't know how I feel about him. I do know that I have this creepy dream where I've woken one spring morning to find myself being hooked into an ivory silk wedding dress and being driven off to St Margaret's, Westminster to be handed over to Duggie by my father. In my worst dreams, I turn into the cake, and Duggie cuts me into elegant slices with his sword.'

'Does he have a sword?'

'He does, actually, part of his dress uniform. Don't say it, more Freud, only I don't think that's why I feel so uneasy about marrying him. I'm very fond of him. Truly.'

'Only, it isn't a wild and overwhelming passion like you had for your beloved Frenchman.'

Vicky sighed. 'It's not so much the passion, it's more that I think I'm still in love with Philippe, and maybe I always will be, and so marrying Duggie, or anyone else, is giving half-measure.'

'It passes.' Martha's voice was matter-of-fact; she knew that Vicky wouldn't be able to handle too much sympathy.

Vicky took a deep breath. 'Besides . . .'

'Besides what?'

'It's one of the reasons I've come to France. You see, I'm not sure Philippe is dead. Not one hundred per cent certain.'

'Oh, Vicky!'

'No, don't sound so exasperated. Listen. You know how it was during the war, especially with the kind of work he was doing, how can anyone be definite about what happened to him? And then, several times I've felt I've seen him, or heard his voice.'

'That's your mind playing tricks on you, you want him to be alive.'

Martha got up and looked in her bag for cigarettes and a lighter. She offered one to Vicky, who shook her head. 'I've given up, I've been trying to live on what I could earn by my drawings, and cigarettes were too expensive. So I've rather lost the habit.'

'Good for you. Foul things,' said Martha lighting up and inhaling deeply. 'If he were alive, Vicky, he'd have come and found you. Even if he'd been taken prisoner, was in some awful camp, he'd have made his way back home by now, and then the first thing he'd do would be to contact you. The war in Europe finished four years ago.'

'I know, Martha, I know all that, I've gone through all the arguments, over and over again. Only I have to be certain, completely certain. There are reasons, believe me, good reasons for my needing to know. So, I'm going to find out what did happen to him. It isn't so long ago that there won't be people around who remember him. And even if I just prove to myself that he's dead, I'll have touched his life a little. I want to go to the place where he grew up, and where he went to school, all the things he talked about. And perhaps meet his family, and here in Paris I'm going to visit his haunts from when he was a student, before the war. Is that so stupid? We loved each other so very much, he was my other self and I felt truly alive with him in a way that I never had. Then it was all ripped apart and, well, I suppose I want to tie up the loose ends as much as I can.'

'Oh, Vicky,' said Martha again, coming over to her friend to put her arms round her. 'That dreadful war, it's left so very many victims.'

'I'm not a victim,' said Vicky stoutly, disentangling herself and getting awkwardly to her feet. 'I refuse to be a victim. It was better to have loved him, just for that short time, than never to have known him. At least the war brought me that one glorious thing.'

'And took it away again.'

'That's what war does.'

She left the building where Martha had her apartment the next morning with a lightness of spirit and a bounce in her step. The London lethargy had vanished. She felt good about herself in the way she did when she was absorbed in a drawing or painting.

Duggie didn't care for it when she was like that. He resented her withdrawal into a private world. One that excluded him. How much did he care about fulfilment of an emotional or artistic kind? Forget it. Considered in that light, Duggie was a mistake.

It was startling the difference that twenty-three miles of rough grey sea and a good night's sleep could make. On the cross-Channel boat, she had vomited up the stale remnants of an existence that had weighed heavily on her for too long; had watched it disperse in the restless foam.

She waited to cross the Boulevard St-Germain. She was going to the Café Etoile. Would anyone there remember Philippe, from those faraway pre-war days? Philippe had told her about some of the regulars, and the people who worked there.

Had they survived the war? Would they answer her questions when they heard her French accent. There was no possibility that she could be taken for a Frenchwoman. Her French was of the school-and-trips-to-France variety. But why should she speak like a native? Besides, Philippe had found her English accent attractive, as attractive as English people found a broken French accent.

Martha had exclaimed at her friend's folly. 'It's madness, Vicky. You'll never find anyone who knew him. All right, he may have hung out at the Café Etoile, but that was a long time ago, before the war, and you have no idea how popular all these places on the left bank have become. It's not just the young Parisians and students up from the provinces, there are tourists, as well. You wouldn't believe how many Americans are flocking to Paris, and most of them head for St

Germain-des-Prés. How is anyone at a busy café going to remember a man called Philippe from before the war?'

'I can ask,' said Vicky. 'All I can get is the answer no, and if that's the case, I'm no worse off than before. And if there's a miracle, and I do find someone who knew him, then it's more than worth a visit to a café.'

'Just don't expect it to be like an English milk bar, that's all.'

'Goodness, I should hope not. I can't see Philippe spending two seconds in a milk bar.'

The café was filled with customers who all seemed to be talking volubly, gesticulating, shrugging. One or two sat hunched over their tables, pens in hand, scribbling away. It could have been a daunting sight to those brought up not to talk to strangers. A lot of English women wouldn't even set foot in a place like this, thick with Bohemian atmosphere, not to mention the pervading odours of cheap cigarettes, brandy and garlic.

Vicky, however, had a kick in her gallop, as her brother Charles would have said, and right now she cared nothing for behaving as a well-brought up young lady was meant to. She would have braved far worse than ranks of smoke-surrounded foreigners if it was a matter of finding someone who knew Philippe.

The only question was, where to begin. Snatches of the conversations around her began to make sense. The two men at the nearest table were planning a film, talking of shoots and shots and scenes. On the other side were a pair of dark-fringed girls, student age, almost identical in their checked shirts and American-style baseball boots that were all the range that year, deep in discussion about the pointlessness of existence.

Vicky's eyes swept round the room in search of likelier prey. No one was paying her the least attention, although in her English clothes she looked completely out of place. They were used to tourists, she supposed, come to goggle at Paris's left-bank stars. Too bad. The man behind the bar, could he have been around in Philippe's time? She edged her way through the tightly packed tables to the zinc and asked for a coffee.

'*Lucien, ça va?*' said a small man with pebble glasses as he came up to the bar beside her.

So the barman's name was Lucien. Had Philippe mentioned a Lucien, when he had lain back in bed, smoking a strong-scented cigarette and reminiscing about Paris as it had been? Lucien was a common enough name, no doubt, but it was worth a try. He gave the bespectacled customer, who was obviously a regular, his *pression*, then slid a bowl of milky coffee in front of Vicky and pushed a glass bowl of sugar towards her.

'Are you Lucien?' she asked.

'And if I am?'

'Have you worked here for long?'

'Long enough.' He was regarding her now with wary suspicion.

'I'm looking for someone who used to come in here. Before the war. Perhaps in the first year of the war.'

Lucien gave an expressive shrug and lifted his hands. 'Before the war! That is a long time ago, Mademoiselle. Many people came here before the war.'

She wasn't surprised that he, at least, had survived the war. He was the type who'd be a born survivor. She could picture him polishing glasses and setting cognac and glasses of sour red wine in front of Nazis with the same air of unconcern and indifference that he was now showing her.

'Some of them still come,' he was saying, 'Sartre and his crowd, Camus, writers, film-makers, artists, we get them all. Are you from the newspapers? Or from America, rubber-necking, isn't that what they call it?'

'I believe so, but I'm not a tourist, and nor am I American. The man I want to find is called Philippe d'Icère.'

Lucien expressed cynical disbelief in shoulders, eyes, eyebrows, mouth, before taking up a cloth and reaching for a glass to polish. 'Half the people in Paris are called Philippe. If I call out Philippe now, ten people will look up. Those who aren't called Philippe have brothers or fathers who are.'

Vicky wasn't going to give up. 'He was tall. Dark hair, a touch of grey just at the edges. Very' – she sought for the right word – 'distinguished looking.'

Lucien gestured to his customers with the cloth. 'See for yourself, many of my customers are distinguished, but they don't look it. This is not a café where distinguished-looking people come.'

'It's the way Philippe's face was made, it's nothing to do with what he was like. When I knew him, he was in uniform, one of the Free French, I don't know how he would have dressed before the war, just the same as people in here, I expect.'

'Free French, yes? Really in the Free French or one of the thousands who joined up after the war?'

'I know he was with them in nineteen forty-three.'

Lucien nodded. 'Not bad, nineteen forty-three is okay. But that's a while ago, before the war is even earlier. How long have you been looking for him?'

'I last saw him in nineteen forty-three. In London. I came here because he talked a lot about the Café Etoile. Oh, please try and remember him. He was quite tall, nothing spectacular.' Philippe, she thought, shutting her eyes at the painful clarity of her memory of him. 'He used an English soap, it had a smell of the country about it, meadows and horses . . .' Her voice tailed off. 'I'm sorry. I'm wasting your time.'

Lucien said nothing but watched her with baleful black eyes. He slotted another polished glass on to its place on the rack above his head. 'Soap,' he said finally. 'It was soap, was it? I used to wonder. I thought, some kind of cologne.'

Vicky's heart lifted. 'You do remember him.'

Cautious now, Lucien caressed the glass in his hand with the white cloth, held it up to the light, gave it another rub. 'There was a man, such as you describe. Before the war. He was called Philippe. D'Icère, you said. Yes, it was such a name, a little bit grand; old, you know. Not like his views which were very modern, very anti old everything.'

'That's Philippe,' said Vicky with absolute certainty.

Lucien turned his back on Vicky, reaching under the counter for a pile of saucers which he brought up and placed on the counter. 'Nineteen forty was the last time I saw him. He came in for a beer, went round all his friends. It seemed to me that he was saying goodbye. The Germans had just broken through the Ardennes, everything was topsy-turvy. I wondered if he'd been called up, was going to the front line, but you say he escaped to England.'

'He fought in France first,' said Vicky, anxious not to let Philippe appear a coward. 'He fled to England after the armistice, so as not to be taken prisoner. On a fishing boat, in a storm.'

'He had the luck of the devil, that Philippe.'

Vicky was jostled aside by a ferocious little man demanding a coffee. She took her own cup of coffee, a pale brown, unaromatic brew, and squeezed between the tables to set it down on a small table jammed in beside the door. Talk of existence and non-existence mingled with smoke and the drone of Americans planning their next round of shopping, the un-be-liev-able bargains there were to be had in silks, and how about those hats!

The baseball boots were now arguing about Heidegger and inauthenticity. Vicky listened with half her mind, the other half thinking about Philippe.

'. . . We live in a practical world of doing. What matters is being, not doing.'

'Acts in themselves have no meaning. They only acquire meaning when we give them one.'

Vicky left her barely touched coffee and headed for the calmer atmosphere of the street.

Martha was impressed. 'Pretty good sleuthing for a first go.'

'Lucien was cagey. Yes, he remembered Philippe all right, but he wasn't giving anything away.'

'That's the French for you. Part of it is caution; you'd have learned to watch what you said if your city had been under Nazi control. The rest is innate Gallic cussedness.

Vicky was propped up against the cushions on the floor. She pummelled one into a more comfortable shape. 'Do you know anything about Heidegger? Some girls were talking about him.'

'Best avoided,' said Martha. 'He had some nasty ideas. He told German students before the war that their being wasn't governed by rules and theories and that Hitler alone was the reality and law of Germany in the present and future. He calls himself a philosopher, but he's just a guy who's got his head where the sun never shines.'

'They seemed pretty rapt about him.'

'At that age, they are. If not Heidegger, then Sartre and the pointlessness of existence. They're middle-class kids who feel guilty about their bourgeois origins. They grow out of it.'

'They were talking about our making ourselves by our acts and remaking ourselves by further acts.'

Vicky's voice was desolate. She was remembering Philippe's down-to-earth sense of reality. He liked the world as he found it, even though he had no illusions about the war and the reasons for war. 'Behind this war there are ideas, and let it be a lesson to you, Vicky, not to get caught up in ideas. Ideas are dangerous.'

'Everything's dangerous,' she had replied. 'People are dangerous.'

He had laughed, that sudden laugh, deep in his throat. 'In your case, especially people. That mad papa of yours, for instance, he is exceptionally dangerous.'

'Oh, do you think so? Surely not. Just peculiar and inclined to lose his temper and be beastly to his family.'

'Just that?' He was serious, then. 'I tell you, as one who has met some peculiar people, be extremely careful of your father.'

Vicky could hear his laughter now, hear the warning words ring in her ears. Hell, coming to France wasn't such a good idea, not if it was going to bring back memories of Philippe with such clarity.

She stood up. 'I'd like a drink, Martha, do you mind?'

'What now?' asked Martha as she drew the cork from a bottle of wine. 'More wandering the streets of Paris, visiting Philippe's old haunts?'

'I'm going to the Languedoc.'

'Is that where he came from?'

'Yes. A village near Carcassonne.'

'I wish I could come with you. Carcassonne is supposed to be something worth seeing, a perfect walled mediaeval city.'

'Is it? How did it last so long?'

'As your café philosophers would say, it ain't what it seems. It was reconstructed in the last century by Viollet-le-Duc. Visit it while you're in the area.'

'It isn't a sight-seeing trip. I'll go soon, I think. Before my father's hounds catch up with me here in Paris.'

'You aren't serious! Are you?'

'He'll be furious that I left without telling anyone, and no forwarding address. He'll be fretting to think of my getting my hands on a pile of money, all my own, beyond his control. And he'll be raging about my appalling manners in standing up Duggie.'

'Did you miss a date with him?'

'Only a dance. Can you imagine, coming out dances are happening again?'

'I can. People like to party when the tension eases, you can't blame them. So Duggie was left looking bereft in his patent dancing pumps, was he?'

'He'll have found another partner. I didn't want to talk to him before I left. I think he might have wanted to come with me, or tried to persuade me that I should leave the legal and financial matters to my father. Until we marry, of course, when he can look after my affairs for me.'

'Christ,' said Martha.

'So don't tell anyone, and I mean anyone, where I've gone. I'll telephone if I can, or send a postcard.'

Chapter Four

Martha stood in the doorway to her apartment, her wet hair wrapped in a red towel, the turban effect and her Turkish slippers giving her a raffish Arabian Nights look. She stared at the tall man, English from his tailoring. Did she know him? Had she met him at a party, at friends'? No, he didn't have a forgettable face, she would have remembered him. 'Who are you?'

The man extended a hand. 'Julius Drummond. No, you don't know me. I've come from England. Are you Martha Frobisher?'

'That's what it says there by the bell. How did you get in here?'

'The door downstairs was open. There's a woman with a broom. She said you were in.'

'Thank you, Madame Beslay.'

'I'm looking for Victoria Hampden. I believe she's a friend of yours.'

Martha grew wary. 'Sure, I know Vicky. Are you a friend of hers?'

'No.'

'Of her sisters?'

'Not exactly.'

It was as Vicky had predicted. Her father was hunting her, and had sent this Drummond person to cajole or entice or threaten her back to England. This smooth guy was Hampden's stooge, standing there with that faint polite English smile that always made her mad. She stalled; it would be better to avoid a confrontation. 'How come you knew where to find me?'

'Your school gave me this address.'

'My *school*? They wouldn't give out any information to anyone. Are you a parent there?'

Julius laughed. 'Hardly. I'd have to have started a family unusually early. I confess that I did have an accomplice. Olivia Rowder, Victoria Hampden's niece, winkled the information out of the school office.'

'Can you beat that? How old is this kid?'

Julius thought for a moment. 'I'm not sure. Fifteen, perhaps.'

'You'd better come in.' Martha made the offer reluctantly, but she had seen the door opposite open a crack. Madame Duplessis would be standing there, ears flapping, indignation rising at the thought of Mademoiselle Frobisher entertaining a young man. That American girl wearing nothing more than a robe, she'd tell interested neighbours. The young today! Especially Americans! they'd all cluck. Hell, she could do without that.

She took Julius's hat and raincoat, nodded at the sofa. 'Sit down, would you like a coffee? Drink?'

'Coffee, please.'

Martha came out of the kitchen, a packet of coffee in her hand. 'I may as well tell you straight away that even if I knew where Vicky was, I wouldn't give you her address or phone number.' How best to fob him off? He didn't look the type who was easy to fox. 'If your story's good, and if she gets in touch with me, I might just tell her you called. Right?'

'That seems reasonable.'

'Do you always talk like that?'

'Like what?'

'Like something left over from before the war. Are you a lawyer?'

Julius looked surprised, and à little put out. 'Is it so obvious? I'm a solicitor, actually.'

'Acting for her dad?'

Julius stiffened. 'My firm is representing Sir Christopher Hampden on this matter.'

'What matter?'

'As you'll appreciate, a client's affairs are confidential.'

'Vicky's father is a very nasty piece of work.'

Martha waited for Julius to protest, get uptight, deny it. He surprised her.

62

'He has that reputation.'

'Professionally, as well as in his private life? What a son of a bitch.'

'I think that would be an apt description.'

'So why do you represent the great Sir Christopher?'

'If we only chose clients whose habits and morals we approved of, times would be lean.'

Martha handed him a cup of coffee, sat down in a chair at the table, unwound the towel from her hair and began to tease the tangles out with a comb. 'I don't think I'm going to be able to help you beyond saying that you called. If she gets in touch. Last time I saw or heard from her before this was three years ago, so don't hold your breath.'

Julius gave her a cool look, and took a sip of his coffee before putting the cup down and standing up. 'I'm sorry you don't feel inclined to help.'

'Don't get huffy, Mr Drummond. Vicky and I are friends. Would you shop a friend?'

Julius looked down at her. 'No, I don't suppose I would.'

After he'd gone, the door shutting with a click behind him, Martha paused in her combing, and looked unseeing at her reflection. He had given up too easily. He was hardly the office message boy, so his firm must consider the matter important. And he'd be expected to show some initiative, not to throw in the towel at this stage. He looked intelligent and quick-witted and resourceful. More than a match for Vicky, she was sure. He wouldn't kidnap her and whisk her back to England's shores, but a guy like that could sweet talk her into anything.

She returned her attention to her damp hair. She could do nothing until Vicky rang her. Even then, all she could do was warn her, and how much notice would Vicky take of that? People didn't change overnight. Vicky couldn't go from being her father's daughter to being an independent spirit. The money would help, but she'd need time, and if Drummond got on her heels, that's what she wouldn't have.

She felt depressed, wished she could help Vicky, knew she couldn't. And damn it, she was going to be late for her date.

★   ★   ★

63

Downstairs, Julius went in search of the concierge. What had Martha Frobisher said her name was? Madame Beslay, that was it. He didn't have far to look, she was lurking by the front door having a shrill conversation with a neighbour. He coughed, and she moved grudgingly to one side.

'Madame, a moment of your time.'

She turned to him and looked him up and down with tight, baleful eyes. 'M'sieur?'

A note crackled between his fingers. 'You may be able to help. A little information, you understand.'

'About Mademoiselle Frobisher?' She hissed the name. 'I tell you everything about that one, these Americans, the hours they keep, the men, it's a disgrace.'

The woman across the road was nodding her head in agreement. 'Sluts, all these young women these days. Ever since the war. That's when they learned to behave so badly.'

'It's a woman friend of hers I'm enquiring about.'

Her eyes snapped. 'The English one? You could tell she was English, because of the clothes she was wearing. No Frenchwoman would dress like that.'

'She is English, yes.'

'And with devil's hair?'

Julius was taken aback. 'Devil's hair?'

'Red, M'sieur. The colour of the devil. And the temper of the devil, too, I daresay. What about her? She's left. Taken her bags with her.'

'Do you happen to know where she's gone?'

A shrug, a pout of the mouth. How should she know? She wasn't the Gestapo, keeping tabs on innocent citizens. However, another note might enable her to remember which taxi had collected her, it might be someone she knew.

Money passed. Madame, with sudden energy, shrieked at a boy who was standing outside the greengrocer. 'André, André! Go to the corner, and if François is there, tell him to come. Quickly!'

The boy skipped off. Julius waited. In a few minutes, a taxi came slowly round the corner, André standing on the running board. He jumped off at the greengrocer, and the cab stopped beside Julius and Madame Beslay.

The driver looked out. He had a lugubrious face with several unshaven chins. 'Where to?'

Julius thanked the concierge, and got into the back of the taxi. He gave the driver the name of the hotel, and said that Madame had told him he had recently taken a fare from that very address. A young lady. Perhaps he would remember where he had taken her.

The taxi driver eyed Julius in his mirror, eyes bright with suspicion. 'You a *flic*?'

'Certainly not,' said Julius.

'This girl, she speaks with an English accent, copper hair, good to look at?' The driver took his hands from the wheel and carved curves in the air. 'Slim, but not skinny. A looker?'

'The hair sounds right.'

'So why do you want to know? If you aren't a *flic*.'

'I'm her family lawyer. I have a message for her. I need to get in touch with her.'

'A lawyer?' The driver lapsed into silence. The taxi rumbled over cobbles, shaking his chins. He saw the note Julius was holding up.

'Gare de Lyon. That's where I dropped her off.'

Victoria Hampden was going south, then. Perhaps to Nice, about her aunt's money. They had reached his hotel. He paid the driver, adding the note to his tip. The taxi driver folded it, and put the cab into gear. As he pulled away, he leant out of the window and called back to Julius. 'She was going to Carcassonne. The redhead.'

Julius went through the swing doors and into the small but elegant lobby of his hotel. Not Nice. Carcassonne. Why Carcassonne? She might be interested in mediaeval France, of course. It seemed unlikely, but then, he knew little about her beyond the acid comments of her sister and the unhelpful remarks of her niece, which didn't exactly give a rounded picture of her character or interests. Wait. She was an artist, had attended the Slade. Doubtless she had gone to paint the picturesque walled city.

If enquiries at hotels there proved fruitless, he merely had to walk the ramparts and she would probably be there, sitting at an easel or with a sketchbook on her lap. Carcassonne was not a large place.

He composed a telegram to his uncle. It was terse. 'VH GOING SOUTH. WILL FOLLOW.' He handed it in at the desk. It would take her the best part of a day to reach Carcassonne. If he set off early, he should be there by the afternoon of the day after tomorrow. By the evening, certainly. He went up to the stairs to change and shave before going out to dine with friends. Pity, in a way, that it was all proving so straightforward. At this rate, provided the young lady didn't prove too intractable, he might be back in England by the weekend.

On the other hand, she might indeed have the devil's temper, and refuse to return to London and Daddy. He wouldn't go back if he were in her shoes. In which case, short of kidnapping her, there was little he could do, and he would return as per previous schedule.

It all seemed so simple.

It still seemed simple the next day. Once out of Paris, there was little traffic, and his senses were alive with the pleasure of being away from his office, and instead to be cruising through the French countryside. The last time he had been here was in the war, now a world away, thank God, and with surprisingly few signs of its ugly legacy showing in the towns and villages he drove through.

He drove along straight roads, lined with poplars, the French roads of the imagination and of the tourist poster, but the reality delightful for all that. He drove through villages bustling with morning activity, with markets and shoppers and women with children. At lunchtime the action was all indoors, and the empty streets had a forlorn air. By the evening he had driven as far as Limoges, and was more than ready to stop and find a peaceful inn, a good restaurant, and to stroll by moonlight along the narrow streets between the light and dark of half-timbered houses.

The next day he set off under a sky of scudding clouds; the sun coming and going, making dancing patterns across the road. He wasn't hurrying. The empty peace of the fields and sky made haste seem unnecessary. Hurry was for cities, for London, and, as far as he was concerned, for other people. He still appreciated a life with no dramas or emergencies or sudden horrors and felt no need to pretend to an urgency he didn't think was necessary. What did it matter whether a young woman went obediently back to the bosom of her family or not? What did it matter that Victoria Hampden at her age should be able to make her own decisions and plan her own life? It was nothing to him.

Although he couldn't, when he forced himself to face up to it, feel exactly happy about Sir Christopher Hampden. Just what kind of a domestic ménage had be been running all those years? He hadn't been able to speak to Vicky's mother. The tale was that she was so upset by Vicky's taking off for France that she had retreated to the country to recover. His godmother, telephoning to enquire with her habitual nosiness – taking an interest in life, she would have called it – about his quest for the youngest Hampden girl, had said that Ada had gone to the country to get away from her husband and his impotent fury at Vicky's flight.

'Such a bad-tempered man. So controlling. So fortunate that he's a judge and can vent his rage away from his family.'

'Tough on the accused,' Julius had protested.

'Dear boy, the rest of the Hampdens have no sympathy to spare for the accused. He, or she, only has to endure it once; they have half a lifetime of him.'

'Half a lifetime for them, if he sends them down for the maximum sentence.'

'They should consider themselves fortunate to be living in these enlightened times and not in the eighteenth century; they'd all have been hanged in those days.'

'Progress is a fine thing.'

'Don't be cynical, Julius. You'll never find yourself a suitable wife if you're cynical. It's the one fault women won't put up with.'

'Dear Evelyn, I don't want a wife.'

'That's what you think.'

The landscape had changed. He had left the clouds behind, and a strong sun shone from an intensely blue sky. The light was that of the south, clear and giving its clarity to the colours of fields and crops and trees and farm buildings. He had moved from the kingdom of butter

67

to the land where the olive reigned. He was dazed by the brilliance of the sun and by the warmth, not yet the blinding heat of the summer, but the delightful glow of late spring.

He lingered over lunch taken at a roadside inn. He wondered if Victoria, too, was feeling the release and ease of the southern climate. This was where you stepped into another world, not the moment when you came ashore from the ferry. That was a transition, not a transformation. If he were in her position, he decided, he would stay, give up murky London streets and the grey tastelessness of English food and the tedium of listening to the stories of everyone else's war.

He mused on the prospects for a young solicitor ever escaping from the daily round of Drummond etc. Dreamed a life that could be led in a land where they didn't have a word for peasouper, where national bread would be impossible, where summer came every year.

Then laughed at himself for wasting time on such pointless daydreams. He paid his bill, tickled the restaurant cat between its ears, and settled into the driving seat for the final stage of the journey.

It was a preposterous place, that had always been his first thought on approaching Carcassonne. The way those crenellated walls clung to the hillside, the folly of dozens of fairytale towers, with their conical tops. Two kilometres of walls, he recalled. And an inner citadel.

He drove over the picturesque Pont Vieux, the bridge over the Aude that separated the two parts of the city. He was assuming that his quarry would be staying in the older, walled city on the hill, not in the lower city, although that was where she would have arrived on the train. It had the railway station, but the mediaeval city had the charm.

He drove through the many-arched gateway of the old city. A steep, cobbled street lay ahead of him; if he went up it, he would come to the castle at the top. There he could leave the car and set about finding a hotel.

As he got out of the car, a wave of memory came over him, of a long ago and half-forgotten love affair when he had come to Carcassonne, young and carefree and passionate, and had walked the streets of the city and sauntered between its great walls hand in hand with a woman he hadn't seen since the war started. She had gone to America, he had heard. And made a new life for herself, no doubt. Probably married with children. She'd have wanted to get married and have a family before it was too late. She'd then been the age he was now. Incredible. And here he was, ten years on and she would be forty-three and probably as beautiful as ever. More beautiful, even; Julius found women became more attractive as they got older, not less.

He had been the romantic, not her. He had imagined this city aglow with pageantry, a fortress out of time, whose walls and towers belonged to legendary days of knights and giants and adventures. The last stand of the Cathars had filled him with admiration.

Then.

Now, one war later, he knew all too well what a brutal and bloody mess even a small affray could be. The glowing vision had vanished with his youth.

A woman wiping the small tables set out in front of the bar across the road looked up and greeted him with impersonal courtesy. He crossed the road and asked for a beer. When she brought it, he enquired about hotels.

He knew so little about Victoria Hampden. How could he possibly judge her tastes? If she'd been to the lawyers in Nice already, before visiting Martha Frobisher in Paris, then she would have funds and could stay where she chose. Where would that be? Picturesque, comfortable, plain or plush?

It was a question of legwork. He would leave his bags in the car, and do the rounds of the hotels, asking at each one if Miss Hampden were staying there. Simple, possibly time-consuming, but likely to work.

It did and it didn't. He didn't have to visit many hotels. At the third one he tried he was informed that Miss Hampden, a young Englishwoman, had stayed there, but had now left. Did they have any idea of where she might have gone? Yes, indeed, for she had asked them to recommend an inn in the small town, well, large village, to be truthful, of St Aphrodise.

'St Aphrodise?' he repeated doubtfully. 'I don't know it.'

'It is named for the saint,' the stout woman at the desk informed him. 'He is the patron saint of Béziers, and legend says he spent a night at this little town, and performed some miracle.'

69

'Did you suggest an inn there?'

'Of course. Sara, one of our chambermaids, comes from St Aphrodise, and her uncle keeps a hotel, the Chameau, very clean, very convenient, very pleasant.' She had advised the young lady to stay there. She was sure that he would find Mademoiselle there.

Her eyes glistened with pleasure at a suspected amour. Julius was amused, but he couldn't tell her that he had never even set eyes on Miss Hampden. Although it really was about time he did. On being told that St Aphrodise was a mere ten kilometres away, and with a volley of directions ringing in his ears, he went back to his car. He was relieved, he realised with surprise, that he wouldn't be stopping in Carcassonne. That hotel had been the very one that they had stayed at the last time he had been here. A love affair not as forgotten as he thought; it was strange how places could bring back not only memories but also emotions. It was the emotion and not the person he felt the absence of, he knew that. It stung, the knowledge that never again would you feel quite the same way about anyone as you had then.

Ah, youth, he said to himself, and sounded his horn at a goat that had wandered on to the road.

Chapter Five

Vicky sat on a stone bench in the square. Every inch of her tingled as though she had just had an invigorating massage. She felt completely alive and utterly happy. Why? she asked herself. She hadn't found Philippe. No, but there was something of him, or at least of his family here in St Aphrodise. He might have played at this very spot under the pollarded lime trees, as a toddler, under the watchful eye of a mother or a nurse, later on as one of a gang of lively boys such as those involved in some intricate game sketched out on the sandy ground.

The fountain had the sad look of all waterless fountains, but Vicky could imagine what it must have been like here on a summer evening before the war. Gay umbrellas over tables, strolling couples, old women with yapping dogs. A band playing in the little bandstand. The fountain cooling the air with spray from dolphin mouths. Perhaps an older Philippe had sat here, dressed in cream trousers and a light jacket, wearing a panama, smoking one of those terrible cigarettes he liked, a glass of absinthe on the table in front of him. Watching the pretty girls coquetting in groups or with their beaux. Vicky felt sure Philippe had always had an eye for a pretty girl.

Of course he had. What man hadn't? No doubt there had been plenty of pretty girls. He had said she was very pretty, used to praise her vivid face and quick intelligence. Her hair, too; he said he'd always liked that colouring. 'Like a conker when it's just out of its spikes.'

She was lucky to have been blessed with a cream skin, not a pink and grey one like so many Anglo-Saxon skins. It freckled in the sun, naturally; skin like hers was bound to. Philippe had found the dusting of freckles on her shoulders and arms attractive. She didn't have many freckles on her face. He'd supposed she used protective face creams, as any Frenchwoman would, but she'd laughed, saying that the English didn't care about such things.

'Luck, then,' he'd replied.

Luck was what counted in the end, whether in beauty or battle. His luck had run out that day in nineteen forty-three. She felt in her bag, and took out the butterfly in its silk and velvet covering. She unfolded the silk and sat looking at the beautiful thing, its colours radiant in the sunlight.

Vicky could almost feel Philippe's presence as she looked at the one tangible reminder she had of him. She laid the butterfly on her lap, and went on looking at the fountain and the locals. The scene shimmered and broke up, as a new arrival broke the placid surface of the afternoon.

She sensed at once that he was a stranger, like herself. How remarkable, people would be saying to each other. Two strangers! The man was tall, dark, almost a touch of the Mephistopheles in his burnished hair and slanting eyebrows. A mobile mouth, one that suggested wit. He was English, he had to be in that jacket, the tailoring was unmistakable.

She didn't know him, but he was coming in her direction. She sat still and wary until he stood in front of her, looking down at the butterfly. Afraid and angry, she folded up the butterfly in its silk wrapping. 'I don't know who you are, but I want you to go away,' she said.

He didn't appear to be put out by this unfriendly welcome. 'Miss Victoria Hampden?' he asked. 'May I join you?' He didn't wait for an answer, but sat down beside her on the stone bench, enough of a distance between them for her not to feel uncomfortable; just the same, she edged away from him. He made her uneasy, although whether that was her certainty that he came from her father or the coincidence of his arrival just when she was thinking about Philippe, she didn't know.

He introduced himself. 'Julius Drummond.'

She looked him straight in the eyes. Give-away-nothing-eyes, she thought, dark and with only amusement in them. 'If you've come from Sir Christopher Hampden, from my father, then spare your breath. I don't want to hear what you've got to say, and I'm not, under any circumstances, going back to England. Do I make myself plain?'

'More than. So I won't say it.'

She stared at him. 'Why not?' she asked unreasonably.

'You know what your father wants. You don't intend to take any notice. End of story. Will you have dinner with me this evening? I believe we're both staying at the Auberge Chameau.'

Sneaky. He was the weasel sort, if he couldn't get what he wanted one way, there was always another to try.

'Yes,' she found herself saying, and then could have bitten her tongue out. 'I mean, no. There's no point. I've told you.'

'And I've accepted your reply. I've done what I came to do, and I can in good conscience wire my firm in London tomorrow and say "No dice."'

'No dice? What kind of firm do you work for?'

'I'm a solicitor.'

'Solicitors don't send wires saying "No dice." Your partners would have a fit. So would my father.'

'The senior partners – I'm a junior partner, of course – will merely shake their heads and wish that I would learn proper solicitorial ways. They'll refine my remark when they report to your father, that's what he pays them fat fees for.'

'He pays fat fees for you to get me back. And if you don't know it, I'd better tell you, my father doesn't like to be thwarted.'

'In which case, I can be thankful that I'm here and he's there, and there isn't much he can do about it.'

'I'm here, too, and if you think I feel out of reach of his long arm, I don't. And my wariness is justified, look, here you are. How did you find me?'

'I had Martha Frobisher's address in Paris.'

'Martha? Martha wouldn't . . . I don't believe Martha would . . . She'd never tell you where I was. Besides, she doesn't know.'

'Don't you trust your friends?'

'I don't trust anybody.' She could hear the bitterness in her own

73

voice, and didn't like it. She tried to smile. 'With a father like mine, you learn to be cautious.'

'Seven for seven–thirty?' he said. And before she could say no, he had tipped his hat to her and walked away.

Julius was down before her. He was the sort of man who would be, beautiful manners inculcated from the time he lisped his first words. The kind of manners that won admiration around the world, and made those who knew better so deeply suspicious of Englishmen. Philippe had been one of them. 'Polite phrases dripping from their lips, and an axe concealed behind the back. Such men are dangerous.'

'Isn't an axe a bit of a hefty weapon?' Vicky had said. 'Wouldn't a dagger tucked in the sock be more sinister?'

'Sock? Who carries a dagger in their socks?'

'The Scots do.'

'We aren't talking about Scots. We're talking about the English. Consider, for instance, all these fine, courteous Englishmen in SOE, supposed to be helping the French, who in reality have no interests but their own.'

'Don't you think the French look after their own interests first and foremost?'

'Yes, but we don't pretend otherwise. And sometimes, even, we feel shame. The true Englishman feels no shame. Only embarrassment if someone should let the side down or show an emotion.'

'What about Englishwomen, don't we have manners, too?'

'Englishwomen are different. They are cold and rude, but always with exquisite politeness. When they aren't cold, they are sluts, into bed with everyone they meet. Even their brothers for all I know.'

'Philippe!'

'Not you. You're a changeling. You don't truly belong to the English race. Look at your hair, your complexion. Is this English? No.'

'I had a Venetian great-grandmother. I'm supposed to take after her.'

'I knew it.'

Julius was regarding her with interest. 'Am I interrupting something?'

'What?'

'You seemed to be carrying on an interior dialogue.'

'I was. I'm sorry. Is that my drink? Thank you.'

There was a pause. 'Nice place, this inn,' he remarked.

'The camel is the emblem of the patron saint of St Aphrodise.'

'So I gather. A saint from the east, one supposes.'

'The innkeeper told me about him. He arrived on a camel, he was a missionary bishop come to save the locals from misguided pagan worship.'

'Not received with general rejoicing, once suspects.'

'No, they didn't take to his Christian message. In fact, they cut his head off.'

'A habit among the French.'

Vicky laughed. 'It didn't stop him. He went on spreading the gospel and chastising the wicked, despite his head having been severed from his body. The locals felt that showed class, and they were converted.'

'The things a man has to do to get his message across.'

Vicky speared and chewed an olive. 'Like you?'

'I delivered my message. Fortunately, I don't have my head at stake, and I don't care about conversion. The cases are not at all the same.' He rose. 'I think our good landlord is summoning us to the table.'

The dining-room of the Chameau was small and its wooden floorboards and panelled walls had the patina of age. Vicky stopped in the doorway, liking the low buzz of conversation, the chinking of knives and forks against china, the ping as one glass touched another. She heard the sound of a cork being drawn, of wine being poured into glasses, and from the kitchen to the rear of the dining-room came noises of pans and people moving about, the slam of an oven door, the sizzling of something cooking. And, best of all was the sense-stirring smell of good food. Vicky felt weak with the pleasure of it all, and weak also with hunger, as different, delectable aromas assailed her nostrils and made her mouth water.

'You like French food?' Julius asked.

*   *   *

During the meal they talked as strangers might when placed next to each other at any dinner table. Of the weather in England and France, of the crossing – 'Flat, not the whisper of a wave,' said Julius annoyingly – of London, of rationing. They discovered friends and acquaintances in common, talked about Evelyn Whistler, about art.

'Is that why you've come to these parts?' Julius asked as he laid his napkin down on the table. 'Don't you paint?'

How does he know that? Vicky asked herself. 'Yes, but it's not why I'm here.'

'Not?' He gave her a quizzical look. 'Why are you here, then? Did you assume that it was too remote and unlikely a spot for the hounds to find you?'

'If I did, I was wrong. You're here.'

'Yes, but I'm exceptional. You weren't to know that I'd be on your track. Perhaps you just decided it was a pleasant spot to spend some of your inheritance.'

'My being here has nothing to do with you, or my father, or even the money from my aunt. I suppose Daddy told you about that. He thinks it's why I came to France, I expect.'

'Wasn't it?'

'Only partly. I came to France to see my aunt's lawyers, and to St Aphrodise to look for someone.'

'Have you found him – or her?'

'No.'

'It's a small town. It shouldn't be difficult.'

'I don't think he'd be living here now. If he were alive, which he probably isn't.'

'You intrigue me.'

She gave him one of her direct looks. 'It isn't intriguing at all. It's very sad. If he's dead, he died while serving his country, this one as it happens, and I think anyone who gives his life when he's lived so little of it deserves more than to be intriguing.'

'I didn't say his death intrigued me. I said you intrigued me. You're talking in riddles, you know. Why don't you tell me about it? I might even be able to help.'

Help, indeed! He didn't want to help; he wanted to wheedle information out of her, to pass back to her father.

'Listen,' Julius said. 'As far as I'm concerned, the professional purpose of my visit to France has been achieved. I've found you. I can't persuade you to return to England against your will.'

'I don't think my father would agree with you.'

'You're an adult, you aren't in trouble, you aren't destitute, and you have reasons of your own for wanting to remain in France. I'm not going to waste time or words telling you where your duty lies. Especially,' he added, with a charming smile, 'since I think your duty lies wherever you want it to lie. If that's here in St Aphrodise, so be it. Cognac? Or do you prefer armagnac?'

He went away to order the drinks, and she sat looking out into the garden, full of the smells and rustles of night. A string of tiny lights had been hung from one tree to another; they gave off practically no illumination, but added a touch of gaiety to the scene.

What Vicky wanted was a voice to tell her, 'Trust him,' or 'Don't trust him.' Where was Philippe when he was needed?

No voices in her ear came to her aid. Julius came back with two armagnacs. 'The innkeeper, Monsieur Ribérac, tells me you've been asking about a family called d'Icère. Is this the person you're looking for?'

Vicky took the glass he was offering her. 'Were you born nosey, or did you study nosiness as part of your legal training?'

'It's an unusual name,' said Julius, sitting down and revolving his glass before tasting his drink. 'I have heard it mentioned, though I'm damned if I recall where. In England, something to do with the war. Well, everything mentioned in England is mostly to do with the war, or was until recently. Which member of the family are you especially interested in? Is this the Frenchman who so dismayed your father, caused you to be made a Ward of Court and so on and so forth? I was told he'd died in the war.'

'So was I.'

'Yet you think he might be alive.'

'It's a possibility.' She stood up, and held out her hand. 'Thank you for dinner, Mr Drummond. I expect you'll be leaving tomorrow, so I'll say goodbye.'

*　　*　　*

Julius watched her go, than sat down again. Monsieur Ribérac materialised and poured him another armangac, offered more coffee. He slid away, and Julius lit a cigarette. D'Icère, where had he heard the name?

It was in that strange state on the edge of sleep that Julius remembered where and when he'd heard the name before. He had been in a pub, sitting at a table near the bar. It was in the Flagon, he'd dropped in for a drink after work, had met a man he'd worked with in the war, Mike, his name was, he hadn't seen him to talk to for a year or so, and was pleased enough to join him and catch up on the news. Mike had returned to his own peacetime career in the law, was beginning to make a name for himself at the bar, his wife was well, expecting another baby in the autumn, two sons at prep school . . . The words came and went in Julius's drifting mind, irrelevant to d'Icère. This man had no wartime secrets that he, Julius, didn't know about. They had worked together as members of the Phantom task force in France, experts in providing up to the minute information from the action . . . No, d'Icère was nothing to do with this.

He turned over in bed, resenting the hardness of the bolster, he'd forgotten these damned French bolsters, one should bring a pillow with one. Christ, how middle-aged even to think of such a thing, amazing how he'd learned to snatch sleep in the war: jolting in the backs of trucks, bivouacking in a damp turnip field, camping out in a *pigeonnier*, bare, broken boards to lie on, bats in the rafters. Then he was suddenly back in the Flagon again, and now there was another man with them, an old school friend of Mike's, very drunk, unhappy.

'Pilot in the war,' Mike confided. 'Couple of ultra dicey missions. He gets pie-eyed from time to time, seems to relieve the strain a bit.'

And that was when the pilot had embarked on a long and rambling tale about a night landing in France. Should have been a piece of cake, wasn't. Two chaps on board, both sounded English, but could have been anything, those Johnnies who went out to France were a thoroughly mixed bunch. He was flying a Lysander, tricky work, landing in a field in the middle of God-forsaken nowhere, dump his two passengers, pick up a couple of others – an English agent, a Frenchman, someone else, he didn't know who, because as it was, he never set eyes on them.

'The English chap, he had dark hair. Dyed, I'd flown him out once before, and he'd had fair hair then. I didn't know his name, no names on that kind of deal. God, he was a bastard. Jumpy as anything, not at all the kind of man they should send out. I mean, normally they'd have parachuted in, that was what happened mostly, going into occupied territory. But you can't parachute people out, so I had to land to pick up these other types, only, like I said, I never got near them.'

Julius and his friend made appropriate noises, both of them used to hearing accounts of exploits spilling out of inebriated survivors, reliving terrible times. Perhaps it got it out of their systems, perhaps it didn't, perhaps they'd have the nightmares and the guilt for the rest of their lives.

'This bugger argued about where the pick up was to be. I had my orders, but he swore at me, told me he'd made the arrangements, and if I came down where I was planning to, all hell would break loose, I'd be landing in a den of Jerries. All codswallop, course it was, no bloody Germans out in a field in the middle of the bloody night. In the end, I thought, he seems to know, and I landed this side of the trees, instead of the other, there was a wood, you see, the landing should have been to the north of it, but no, there was the field, he insisted it was the right place.

'It wasn't. No help coming down, and it was an appalling terrain, all tufts and ruts, stupid place to land a plane. But I got her down, and they jumped out. "Where are my passengers?" I shouted, and then the silly bugger started waving his arms about and shouting that there were Germans and yelling at me to get away. So I did.'

Julius caught him as he slid off his stool.

'Sorry,' he said. 'Bit pissed tonight.'

Julius thought he and his friend should put him in a taxi, send him home.

'No, no, got to finish telling you what happened. Had to turn, into the wind, you have to take off into the wind. No Germans, no pick up, just those two. One vanishing into the bushes, the other following him. Then I heard a shot. And another one.'

'There were Germans, then,' said Julius, bored.

'No bloody Germans. I reckon he shot him.'

'Who shot who?'

'One of them shot the other one. They lost someone around then. Not supposed to know anything about it, but there was a WAAF really cut up about it, said some Frenchie had gone missing, had been going home to France. Disser, his name was. Rhymes with Pisser, I thought. Funny, that.'

At which point, he had slid to the floor and passed out.

Julius stretched out, nearly asleep now. That was why the name seemed familiar. D'Icère, Disser.

He slept.

Chapter Six

Vicky stretched her arms above her head, yawning. Then she opened her eyes.

The ceiling had once been white, but it was now a white that had seen many years' wear and tear.

A spider was making its way along one wall. Strands of past webs floated from where the ceiling met the sloping attic wall.

Vicky turned her head, this time taking in a window, open a handsbreadth, but shuttered. Light filtering through. Sunlight.

This wasn't the lumpy-mattress land of Marylebone. Where was she?

She was in St Aphrodise, in France. She was in one of the top floor bedrooms of the Auberge Chameau, named for the bishop's camel. She slid out of bed, and, still yawning, made for the window. It, and the shutters, came down to the floor. She opened windows and shutters wide, and stepped out on to a tiny terrace, terracotta tiles under her feet, several pots of brilliant flowers perched on the edge of the wall, blue sky above, with the faintest wisps of high cloud foretelling a fine day.

She leant on the wall, gazing and gazing at a scene that could have come from the Hours of the Duc de Berry; a landscape of hills and cypresses and vineyards. To her left, she could see the biscuit-coloured pantiles of numerous roofs. A bell began to ring, a single bell set in a small tower set on top of a church.

This was Philippe's country, the home of his childhood. Exactly as he had described it when they lay in the hotel bed, her head in the crook of his arm, relaxed after making love, talking as though they had a lifetime of experiences to exchange in the brief hours allowed to them before duty tore them apart.

It was strange that she'd never asked exactly where he'd come from. Except that in wartime you didn't ask anyone anything that wasn't absolutely necessary. That's what happens when you pick up men, her acid-tongued sister Vera might have said. You knew nothing of their family, their background and all those important indications of status and suitability.

Only it wasn't men, just one man. Pick up? All too literally, she had hauled him up from the road where he was sitting hunched over in apparent pain, and bundled him into the ambulance. Ignoring his protests, she had heaved him on to the stretcher, pushed his head down on the pillow, slammed the doors on him and run round to get in the front and drive to safety and shelter.

She hadn't even been on duty, she had finished an hour earlier after a bad night of attacks from the Luftwaffe. One old lady hadn't been badly hurt, and was desperate to get home to make sure her cat was all right, so Vicky had dropped her off before heading back to the depot to sign off and return home for a much needed bath and several hours of exhausted sleep before it all began again. Then the alarm had sounded, and that was when she spotted Philippe, blood all over him, sitting on the kerb.

'How was I to know you weren't hurt?' she asked, when in response to the furious thumps and bangs behind the driver's cab, she had stopped the vehicle and gone to investigate.

'You could have asked.'

'I couldn't have heard if you'd told me, it was much too noisy. If you aren't hurt, why all the blood?'

'It isn't blood. Aren't you trained to know the difference between paint and blood?'

'Not in the dark, during a raid, no. And why paint? Especially red paint, which simply isn't available these days.'

'Yes, it is. For painting stripes on poles at barriers, you know.'

'Is that what you do, paint stripes?'

'The paint was surplus to requirements, I was taking care of it for a friend.'

'A black-marketeer,' said Vicky. She frowned. 'If you weren't hurt, why were you moaning and gasping like that?'

'I tripped over something, which is how I spilt the paint over me, and I put out a hand to stop myself falling and gave my elbow a crack on something. One's funny bone, it hurts like hell, you do appreciate that?'

'Have you left paint stains inside my ambulance?'

'It's entirely your fault for putting me in there.'

'I was saving your life.'

'Perhaps you were.' The moon, which had been buried behind a curtain of heavy cloud, now floated serenely into view, and its eerie light flooded the deserted street where Vicky had halted. 'Perhaps you could add to your kindness by taking me to a place where I can remove the paint from my clothes and person.'

'Where?'

'Hop in, I'll direct you.'

Against her better judgement, Vicky found a piece of sacking and spread it on the seat next to the driver. 'Don't touch anything,' she warned as she started the engine and let the clutch in.

'Reverse, please.'

His voice was one used to command. This was no tramp or spiv she had collected in passing. He was fairly young, too, older than her, but not of a fatherly age, she decided. It was difficult to tell what he looked like, because of the paint smears on his face, but she liked the voice.

'This is the Ritz,' she said in surprise.

'Yes, they're bound to have some spare turps, I've never known them at a loss. Come on.'

'I can't leave the ambulance here,' said Vicky. 'Besides, I don't want to come with you.'

'Don't tell lies, your nose will grow, and then you won't be so ridiculously pretty any more, such a shame.'

Vicky had sat on a hard chair while an off duty porter cleaned the man up with considerable expertise. A note changed hands, the porter's face beamed, and the man beckoned to Vicky. 'Now we're respectable, we can appear in public. Have you eaten?'

Vicky recalled a wad, grey bread spread with marge and jam. 'Yes.'

'Something horrible, I see it in your face. Let's see what they can do for us here.'

'I'm off duty,' Vicky protested. 'The ambulance should have been back at the depot hours ago, and I need to get to bed, I may have to go on duty again.'

'Bed is exactly what you need,' he said gravely.

Vicky regarded him with suspicion. His eyes were dancing, crinkling at the edges, his mouth was humorous and belied his serious tone. He was the most attractive man Vicky had ever met, and she couldn't for the life of her fathom why. Her tastes ran to tall blond men, blue and grey-eyed, stern of jaw and tough of muscle. Men who treated her with kind politeness, whose embraces and kisses left her slightly stirred but quite unsatisfied, although she had never been sure why, or what it was she wanted.

Now she knew. This was what she wanted. This man with his almost black hair, his brilliant eyes, his lean, wiry frame and his absurd notions.

'Where is the depot?'

'Paddington.'

He went to the desk, where a sleepy-looking elderly man was on duty. Another note changed hands, and he came back to Vicky. 'Where are the keys?'

'Lord, I left them in the ignition. Oh, heavens, I'll get shot. I must . . .'

He said a few words over his shoulder to the man at the desk. 'There, all taken care of. Benny, whoever he may be, is used to driving ambulances, and he is driving it back to the depot for you.'

Vicky started to protest, but he simply smiled at her, and bombs, ambulances, the war, discretion, everything vanished from her mind except that she was standing in the Ritz with the most exciting man she had ever met, and she knew she couldn't tear herself away.

'Food first, or afterwards?'

'Afterwards? After what?'

Once again he didn't answer, but took her arm and escorted her firmly towards the stairs. Vicky's senses were swimming; tiredness, the thick carpet underfoot, the sudden quietness of a softly lit corridor, the proximity of this man all disoriented her, as though she had drunk a lot of champagne extremely quickly.

They stopped in front of a varnished door, and the man produced a key, put it in the lock and swung the door open, propelling her gently into the room and shutting the door behind her.

'Oh,' she said. And then, a quite different oh, as he slid his arms round her and kissed her neck. 'I don't think I should be here. I don't even know your name!'

'Philippe,' he murmured.

'I'm Vicky. Look . . .' Her voice tailed away.

A few minutes later, a last fragment of caution and reason asserted itself. 'I don't . . . I mean, I've never . . .'

'No time like the present,' Philippe said imperturbably. 'Shall we continue?'

He didn't wait for an answer.

The intensity of their passion came flooding back to Vicky now as she stood bathed in the sunlight of southern France. Wartime London seemed so far away in time and place, but the memory of their time together was a present reality.

Philippe. She whispered his name into the warm air. The leaves of the geraniums rustled, touched by a passing breeze, and the vermilion and crimson flowers swayed gently, mocking her.

She had been closer to him than to anyone she had ever known, and yet she knew next to nothing about him. She knew that he had been an only child, that he had adored his mother, who was American, had loved and respected his father.

The church bell donged again, twice, marking the half hour. She went back into her room, hungry for breakfast, wits sharpening as she wondered whether she should have persuaded Julius Drummond to stay and help her find Philippe.

He didn't need persuading. His curiosity had been aroused, and his godmother would never forgive him if he went back to London with a story only half told. Besides, he had forgotten how delightful early summer was in this part of the world, how intoxicating the scents and colours were, how vibrant the light. There was no need for him to rush back to London, what was there for him to do in England except sit with his feet on the desk, read every word of *The Times*, meet friends at the theatre or the ballet, dine out at the houses of people he didn't greatly care for?

There were rumours of a return of the season, of tennis and strawberries and girls in pretty frocks and outings to Ascot and Henley. The notion filled him with impatience. It was a world he had been born into, but one he felt there was no place for in post-war life.

He laid the thick, starched white napkin across his knees and looked with pleasure at the table in front of him. Coffee, rolls fresh from the boulangerie, croissants, pale butter, strawberry and apricot jam in small glass bowls. He looked up as Vicky came into the dining-room, rose, and pulled out a chair for her. 'Good morning.'

'Haven't you gone?' said Vicky. She gave him a sideways look from under long lashes, and Julius laughed. The charm of her; had he been susceptible to a pretty face and green eyes, or even interested at all in girls of her age, he would have been in some danger. Not that he was arrogant or foolish enough to suppose that the charm was for his *beaux yeux*.

'You want something from me,' he said as she sat down.

'Since you haven't gone, yes, perhaps you can help me. Is your French good?'

'Fluent.'

'You aren't just being modest about it, are you?' She took one of the rolls and tore it apart before spreading it with a generous layer of butter and inspecting the jams.

'Modesty doesn't come into it. I had an excellent teacher at school, and I spent a year in Paris studying international law after university.' He poured her some coffee.

'Then you can certainly help me. The innkeeper said I should speak to a lawyer here in St Aphrodise, who will be able to tell me about the d'Icère family. He doesn't speak very good English, and my French is adequate, but nothing more. It was all rather trying dealing with my aunt's lawyers in Nice, and this is much more complicated. I'm afraid of missing nuances.'

'You think there may be nuances.'

'Where there are lawyers, there are nuances.' Vicky helped herself to another croissant. 'Delicious coffee, wonderful rolls and blissful croissants. Why is French food so good, and English food so awful?'

'They take food seriously, and we don't. Food and sin are too closely connected for the English soul.'

'I don't see what food has to do with sin. It's enjoyment of anything that makes us English nervous.'

'Have you finished?' asked Julius.

'Giving you the benefit of my threadbare theory of the English psyche, or breakfast?' She looked regretfully at the basket which now only contained a few crumbs. 'Monsieur Ribérac will tell us where this lawyer is.'

'It is very easy,' the innkeeper said. 'It is off the main square, in the Rue des Récollets. Number eleven. Monsieur Lamboley will most likely be there now.'

The lawyer looked over his half-moon spectacles at the big clock ticking away on the wall opposite him. 'Will you join me for a drink? There is a bar around the corner, we can find a quiet table, and I will tell you what I know about the d'Icères. It is not so very much, because I haven't been here long. My predecessor would have been more use to you.'

'Has he retired?' asked Julius. 'Perhaps we could speak to him.'

'Unfortunately, he was killed in the war, in nineteen forty-five.' Monsieur Lamboley locked some papers in his safe and followed them out of the office and into the street.

He sat at the rickety table in the Bar Sport and tapped lean fingers on the metal table top. The waiter brought a glass of local wine for Vicky, a cognac for the French lawyer and a beer for Julius.

'Are you very busy in your office in London at present?' Monsieur Lamboley asked Julius, after a few restoring mouthfuls of cognac.

It occurred to Vicky that, although the lawyers were very different: different ages, different nationalities, one from a big London firm, the other tucked away in a small town in France, yet there was something the pair of them had in common. Not just the camaraderie of fellow-professionals, but a similarity in the way they viewed the world. Lawyers, she supposed, saw more than most of the underside of life, of quarrels and disputes. Their clients must often have suffered a loss of faith in the normal order of existence, where you rubbed along with your neighbour, got on with your fellows at work, lived more or less contentedly within the bosom of your family.

That made her want to laugh, she knew all about the bosom of the family. There again, though, when those darkest of secrets crept out into the daylight, it was the lawyers who had to deal with them.

There was a silence, as both men looked at her. They had finished swapping workloads and had realised that Vicky hadn't been listening to a word they'd been saying.

'The d'Icère family?' she said, sipping her red wine, liking its gutsy taste.

Monsieur Lamboley leant back in his chair, made some Gallic thinking noises, and then began. 'Did you notice the chateau as you came into the village? You came by train? You can see the top of it from the train. Also from the road. That is the home of the d'Icère family, they have lived here since the seventeenth century. Indeed, there is a legend that they were here centuries before that, in the days when St Aphrodise himself came to Béziers from the East.' He paused. 'You know the legend of St Aphrodise?'

They nodded.

'The d'Icères claimed that their ancestors came here with the bishop, arriving from the holy land and eventually settling here and naming the place St Aphrodise in the bishop's honour.'

'An old family, then.'

'Certainly old, although not that old.' He spoke with some asperity. 'The notion of their accompanying St Aphrodise is pure fantasy.'

'What happened to them during the French Revolution?' asked Vicky. She didn't know a great deal about French history, but she was sound on Robespierre and the Terror, which had appealed to her young imagination.

'The d'Icère family seem to have a great sense of self-preserva-

88

tion,' Monsieur Lamboley said. 'They have what almost amounts to a sixth sense of impending trouble or danger. They left France in seventeen eighty-seven, taking most of their possessions with them, and stayed in England until they felt it was safe to return in eighteen fifteen.'

'The battle of Waterloo,' said Julius.

'Napoleon's banishment to St Helena,' Monsieur Lamboley said at the same moment. He waited politely for Julius to continue, but Julius shook his head.

'Please, go on.'

'Again, in nineteen twelve, the d'Icères locked up the chateau, and went to Scotland until the war was over. The family has always had strong links with England and Scotland, many of the d'Icère brides came from those countries. This time, however, the then head of the family, Guy d'Icère, had married an American girl he met while she was visiting Edinburgh. They returned to France in nineteen nineteen, with their only child, a son, Philippe. The American wife was very cultivated, very clever. The d'Icères owned a lot of pictures, also objets d'art, sculptures, tapestries, anything rare and beautiful. Madame d'Icère took over the collection, sold many items, bought new ones more in keeping with her taste. The collection was worth a great deal of money, increasingly so as time went on. It was housed in the chateau here, although after nineteen twenty-five, the family lived in Paris and abroad and seldom came here. Monsieur d'Icère was following a diplomatic career, I understand.'

Julius was paying close attention. 'So this Philippe was born . . . when?'

'Nineteen sixteen, I believe.'

Vicky nodded her head in agreement.

'By nineteen thirty-six, the d'Icères were becoming alarmed. The American woman, you see, was a Jewess, and she wanted to return to America. However, her husband persuaded her to remain in France, since he wanted to do what he could for his country. At this time, and this is now generally known, so I'm not breaching a client's confidence, Madame d'Icère decided to have the best of her paintings expertly copied. Also bronzes, statues, jewellery, furniture. It was her intention to leave these in situ, so that the chateau should look very much the same after they had left. It was believed that she arranged for the originals to be packed up and sent to America.'

'That shows foresight,' commented Julius. 'If she hadn't done that, no doubt the gems of her collection would even now be somewhere in Germany.'

'That is another matter entirely.'

Vicky was sitting very upright, alert, interested in every detail about Philippe's family. 'Do they still live here? Did they come back after the war?'

'Unhappily, neither of them survived the war, and nor did their son. Guy d'Icère's brother now owns the chateau, but he doesn't live in it, it was wrecked by the Germans. An old housekeeper looks after the property. Bertrand d'Icère is more concerned with his land, he lives in the Corbières region.'

'You say the son died in the war?' Vicky asked.

'Yes. He was in the army, I believe, and people say he was with the Free French in London, or possibly the Resistance. Maybe both. I only came here to St Aphrodise in nineteen forty-six, you understand, and people don't talk much about the war. Not to a newcomer such as I am, in any case. It has left its scars, and it's best not to ask too many questions.'

He's warning us off, thought Vicky.

'My interest in the d'Icères is purely academic, they are an unusual family. I no longer represent them, so my information can't entirely be relied on. You would need to speak to the current head of the family, Bertrand d'Icère, or to his son, if you want to know anything more.'

'Where is the art collection from the chateau now?' Julius asked.

'None of it has ever been recovered as far as I know. It was a question that naturally arose when Bertrand d'Icère inherited.'

'How did the older d'Icères die?'

The lawyer lifted his hands. 'Mademoiselle, I do not know the details. I believe there was an accident.' He finished his drink. 'Perhaps you should get in touch with Madame Isabeau d'Icère. She is the widow of Bertrand's younger brother. I can find you her address.'

'Thank you,' said Vicky at once.

Monsieur Lamboley seemed about to speak again, then hesitated. Then he addressed Julius. 'I assume it is a professional affair that has brought you here. May I enquire why you are interested in the d'Icère family?'

'My client, Miss Hampden, has in her possession an article that belonged to Philippe d'Icère. Since she was coming to France, she wished to return it to his family.'

'It is something of value?'

'Yes,' said Vicky, looking under her brows at Julius. If he thought she was going to hand over the butterfly to some unknown uncle, he could think again.

'It must be important for you, Mademoiselle, to summon your lawyer from London to assist in your search for Philippe d'Icère's heirs.'

'Miss Hampden has recently inherited property in France from an aunt. There is a good deal of work to be done regarding the estate, you know how complicated such matters are when two countries are involved.'

Clever, thought Vicky. So nearly true, and didn't it come out pat. That was why lawyers charged their fat fees; if they were good, as Julius appeared to be, they were worth every penny.

It seemed to satisfy Monsieur Lamboley. Saying that he must now return to his office, he promised to instruct his clerk to find the address of Isabeau d'Icère and take it to their hotel.

'Thank you,' said Julius. 'We're at the Auberge Chameau.'

'I know,' said Monsieur Lamboley, smiling for the first time and looking much younger. 'Here in St Aphrodise, nothing is secret. That's why I have taken the trouble to learn a little about the d'Icère family history; Monsieur Ribérac told me that you had been asking about them.'

'Just like England, the gossip,' said Vicky. 'Places like this are so dull, you have to be interested in what the neighbours are up to, or you'd go mad. Strangers in town come as a real bonus. Bother, I meant to ask him whether the family are buried here. The chateau might have a chapel, I suppose, like big houses in England.'

'He may not know,' said Julius. 'All my French lawyer friends are paid-up atheists, and wouldn't have anything to do with the church. Why don't you go and find the church and have a look round for yourself?'

'Won't there be more than one?'

'I doubt it. Just one dedicated to St Aphrodise would be my bet. The French don't go in for religious variety, you have to remember.'

'What are you going to do?'

Julius pointed to a sign indicating La Poste. 'I want to send a telegram to London.'

Vicky stopped in her tracks. 'What about? You aren't intending to let them know where I am?'

'No. I said I wouldn't and I won't. Only I have to be in touch, they'll expect that. I'll say that I haven't been able to contact you yet, but am motoring southwards. Presently at St Aphrodise while my car is repaired.'

'You're good at lying, I see.'

'All lawyers are.'

'Will they believe you?'

'They've no reason not to. I doubt if they'll be able to find this place on the map, even. No, the trouble will come when your esteemed father starts breathing down my uncle's neck, wanting results. That won't be for a few days yet, so don't worry about it.'

Vicky did, of course. Julius didn't know her father. Within twenty-four hours he'd have been on the telephone to Julius's firm, demanding to know what had been achieved, why she hadn't already been located and returned to England.

The church was dark after the sunlight of the street, and filled with the musty smell of all old churches, mingled with incense, which Vicky wasn't sure she liked. She looked with curiosity and some alarm at the wooden confessional boxes; while the basics of the church were what she was used to, the Catholic nature of the place was utterly alien. It wasn't just the idea of the confessional, there were also the candles, and tiny side chapels with panels and paintings of saints and other holy personages. In front of one small figure of the Virgin perched on a pillar in a niche were dozens of cards thanking the blessed Mary for

92

her help in curing a child or saving a brother or ensuring a successful pregnancy and delivery.

Vicky eyed all this, and turned her attention to the altar. There was a gloomy triptych behind it, but more ominous was the glass panel in the side of the altar. She advanced to have a closer look, and was appalled to see a withered finger reposing in a gold casket.

'The finger of St Aphrodise,' said a creaky voice behind her, and she turned round to see an aged sacristan, clearly delighted to have a visitor and proud of his gruesome relic.

'Unhygienic,' she said, but in English; her French was deserting her in the face of all this idolatry. The wizened face creased into a wider smile; he clearly took it for a compliment.

Vicky turned her back on the altar. She didn't want to know what the red light glowing to one side of the altar was, nor did she want her eyes to linger on the Paschal candle. Then she took a deep breath. This was where Philippe had worshipped, and had taken his first communion. Which they did at some shockingly early age, didn't they? Long before they were old enough to understand what they were signing up for.

This might be where he was buried. She swallowed, summoned up her French and asked about the d'Icères. Nodding and beckoning, he led her to a side chapel where an ugly marble mausoleum was topped by the still figure of a bishop in mitre and with a crook at his side. The sacristan traced the letters etched round the effigy, and Vicky could just make out that these were the mortal remains of Guillaume d'Icère, who had departed this life to eternal glory in 1701.

Marble plaques on the walls and stones beneath her feet testified to many generations of d'Icères. 'Philippe d'Icère?' she said, trying to phrase an intelligible question.

'Yes, yes, here,' the man said, pointing to a marble memorial stone, much newer looking than the rest, with the gold lettering still clear and bright. There were three names on it: Guy d'Icère, departed this life on the twenty-ninth of March 1943, his wife Mathilda, died the first of April 1943 and their only son, Philippe, died January 1943.

Vicky stared at it for a long time. The sacristan, concerned by her silence, plucked at her sleeve. 'Did you know them?'

'What? Oh, yes. That is, I knew the son. Where are they buried, can you tell me?'

He could; at least, he could tell her where Philippe's parents were buried. As to Philippe, unfortunately, his body did not rest among his ancestors. It was the war, Mademoiselle would understand, people died in strange places, away from home, and were laid to rest where they fell. It was sad, but inevitable.

He didn't look sad, not with his bright, bird eyes. He was pleased at the novelty, a stranger to St Aphrodise, a visitor to the church who wanted to talk to him.

Might the priest know where Philippe had been buried? Alas, he had no idea, no idea at all. She could ask the present head of the family, he would have the details.

It felt strange to see his name cut into the memorial stone. It was somehow unexpected, not least because of his cynical lack of faith in the whole bundle of Christian teaching. She heard a whisper in her head, telling her not to be sentimental.

The sacristan looked as though he'd been here when Philippe's grandparents were alive. He had a sly look to his wizened face.

Vicky knew she was too trusting. Too confident that ultimately finding out about Philippe would be a matter of gathering information, putting facts together, and getting a clear-cut answer. How had she managed to live for twenty-five years without accepting that life wasn't like that? Even when the truth stared her in the face, she wouldn't recognise it, because the truth was muddy and partial.

And was this a pilgrimage taken in his memory, for its own sake, for his sake, or merely a tidying of the record before she married Duggie? Only she wasn't going to marry Duggie. She wasn't in love with Duggie, she was sure of that. She knew what being in love was like. Coming to France, to St Aphrodise, to this church which marked the end of a life, had brought back to her what it was like to be in love.

Was there, after all, some buried instinct that warned her, subliminally, that all was not as it seemed, and that no rosy paths to happiness would start at the church door with Duggie at her side? Was it the same instinct that had led her to ask for Julius's help?

This place was getting to her. Too many ties of the wrong kind, too much atmosphere for her to linger safely. It wasn't words that came into her head, but music, a few bars of a jaunty tune from nineteen forty-three. One they had listened to in the intervals of waiting for the bombs to fall.

'I'm sorry,' Vicky said to the sacristan. She wanted to be out of here, now, quickly, to get away from a place where her mind played such tricks on her; all this merely at the sight of his name set in stone. The sacristan was watching her. It wasn't concern for her well-being, no, he was waiting for a tip. She scrabbled in her bag for her purse, thrust some coins at him, and ran down the centre aisle and into the sunlight outside, taking gulps of fresh and non-religious air, shaking with relief.

Inside the post office, Julius queued to obtain a form, and then stood at a dusty shelf, tilted to facilitate writing, so that the writer had to hold the paper with one hand and write with the other. The inkwells at the top of the shelf were empty, stained with dried-up ink. Julius took out his fountain pen, completed his form and went back to the counter. The woman behind the glass was curvaceous and had the look of one who found much to enjoy in life. Her dark hair was drawn up into a bun so tightly that it pulled her eyes up at the corners. These eyes however, missed nothing, and she had been watching the Englishman with unconcealed interest.

Like everyone else in St Aphrodise, she knew that two strangers, foreigners, were staying at the Auberge Chameau and asking questions about the d'Icère family. Judgement was reserved as to the relationship between the English pair. Separate rooms at the hotel, they had that from Etienne Ribérac. The official line was that the man was the young woman's lawyer. So why was anyone from England interested? It must be about Philippe. He had been the one who went to school in England, he had gone to London after the fall of France. And on the subject of Philippe, the town would have nothing to tell them.

She took his telegram, checked the words – such extravagance – and gave him change for his note. Then she laid the telegram to one side; as soon as the man was out of the post office, she would telephone Lydie, who understood English, and have the meaningless words translated.

> NEWSNONE STOP FROBISHERDEADEND STOP TRACKINGHAREAPHRODISE STOP KEEPSIRKITOFFMYBACK STOP HAVING A LOVELY TIME STOP WISH YOU WERE HERE STOP

No, she'd have to wait for Lydie.

'You came out of there as though the hounds of hell were after you,' said Julius, catching up with Vicky. 'Was it a religious experience?'

'I felt very strange in there. Seeing the memorial to Philippe and his parents . . . I suppose it was a shock.'

'Anyone can carve a name on a stone.'

'The little man in black said Philippe wasn't buried here.'

'We progress, then. You look a bit shattered, if I may say so.' They had reached one of the cafés on the *place*. 'Sit here, I'll order you some brandy, and I'll go and see if Lamboley has come up with the goods.'

Monsieur Ribérac produced an envelope with a flourish. 'The address of Madame d'Icère. For you.'

Julius looked at the envelope. 'You have X-ray eyes?'

'Naturally, I asked what was the message. It might be bad news, in which case one must prepare oneself.' Guileless eyes looked up at Julius. 'It occurred to me, M'sieur, that if you wish to know about Philippe d'Icère, you could enquire at the garage.'

'The garage. Why? Will I find him there?'

'I hope not. All the world knows that Philippe is dead. But not many people in St Aphrodise will speak about him, he has a certain reputation. Everyone has the greatest respect for Monsieur Guy d'Icère, such a terrible tragedy, he and Madame. However, Marcel was close to Philippe, they were boys together, and then, when they were a little older, and Monsieur Philippe came here on vacation, then they went fishing and hunting and also out with the girls.'

'What reputation?'

Monsieur Ribérac shrugged; shoulders, arms, eyebrows, hands, all lifted. 'After the war, even during the war, there was much that was confused, who was with the Resistance, with Vichy, with the Germans, even. It was a muddled time.'

'And Philippe isn't around to speak for himself.'

'That is true. Accordingly, his reputation suffers. It is sad, but that's life.'

Julius pocketed the envelope and went to join Vicky. To his surprise, she was no longer alone, but was deep in conversation with a man Julius had never seen before. The man sprang to his feet as Julius approached.

'Julius, this is Cornelius van der Meulen,' said Vicky.

Chapter Seven

'Mr van der Meulen was kind enough to pick up my address book. I dropped it in the church,' said Vicky. 'I was rummaging in my bag for my purse, and it must have fallen out. I didn't notice it had gone, but he caught me up and gave it back to me.'

'It's nothing,' said the Dutchman.

Vicky pushed the metal chair back and stood up. She held out a hand to Mr van der Meulen. 'Thank you again. I have one or two things I want to do at the hotel.' said Vicky. 'Please don't disturb yourselves. I'll see you later, Julius.'

Julius looked after her, puzzled.

The Dutchman cleared his throat. 'May I buy you a drink? A cold beer?'

'I'm sorry,' said Julius, sitting down. 'My mind was wandering. Thank you.'

'You're worried about your friend? There is a problem of some kind? You don't wish her to be on her own? She is perfectly safe here in St Aphrodise, I feel sure of this.'

'Oh, lord, yes.'

'She is your fiancée? I would say wife, but she wears no ring.'

Julius was startled. 'No, no, we're only acquaintances.' His earlier story came back to him. 'I'm a lawyer. She's inherited some property and money from an aunt who lived in this country. It's complicated with regard to taxes and taking proceeds from one country to another.'

'Of course. The property is near here?'

'No. She has come to St Aphrodise for personal reasons, someone she knew during the war came from here.'

They sat in silence together at the small, metal-topped table. A waiter brought their beers. The Dutchman took a long pull at his drink. 'So. You may ask what I am doing here in St Aphrodise?'

'Tourism?' Julius suggested. 'Or perhaps reliving old memories?' Why had Vicky seemed nervous of this man? He didn't seem threatening, although those pale blue eyes that often went with that kind of blondness had a disconcertingly piercing look to them.

'Astonishing hair,' van der Meulen said unexpectedly. 'That was why I noticed her in the church. The sun was shining through clear glass on to her hair.'

'It's an unusual shade.'

'She was talking to the sacristan, that was when I saw the notebook fall.'

Julius drank some of his own beer. Where was all this leading?

'When I returned the little book to her, she checked in her bag to make sure that hers was missing, in case it was someone else's. In doing so, she pulled out a silk handkerchief, which she unrolled, as if to make sure that whatever was inside it was safe.'

The butterfly. Julius had watched her roll it up in the cream silk square, the first time he'd seen her.

'It caught my attention, the object in the handkerchief.'

'Yes?'

'I will tell you why it interested me.'

Julius drank some more of his beer and waited.

'I am a Dutchman, or mostly a Dutchman, as you can tell from my name.'

Julius nodded, drank some of his beer and waited.

'My mother is half German, however, and I was raised and received my education in Germany. When war broke out, I was twenty-six. I am an art historian. This is my father's field, also, and I already knew a lot before I began my studies. So I had a head start, and I was beginning to make a name for myself. Only within the limited circle of the art world, you understand.'

Julius nodded again.

'Then I was drafted into the Wehrmacht, along with all the other young men. I had German citizenship, so there was no question of my not being eligible. Naturally, my father was upset, he didn't want me joining the army which had occupied the Low Countries. My mother, though, was a loyal German. Loyal to the country, not to Hitler.'

Julius raised a quizzical eyebrow.

'I know, since the war, every German was against Hitler. But her friends were artists and intellectuals and homosexuals. These people were stigmatised, as you know, and many of them vanished into the camps and didn't survive the war.' He paused. 'She herself fell into the hands of the Gestapo, and was sent to a camp. She lived to tell the tale, although no one who knew her before the war would recognise her.'

'I'm sorry,' said Julius. 'You went on in the army, though?'

'She wasn't arrested until early in nineteen forty-five. If I had deserted, which would be my only way out of the army, she and my father would have been executed.' He held up a large hand. 'No, I don't want pity or criticism; if you choose to judge me harshly, that is your privilege and your affair, but I do not want to hear about it.'

'I thought myself a pacifist,' said Julius. 'And I joined up.'

'Our generation will have these things on our consciences until the day we die. But this is history, and not relevant to what I'm talking about. By nineteen forty-two, I had become a major, and I was serving in France. I was an assistant to a man, I prefer not to name him, whose job was to assess the quality of works of art that were confiscated from Jewish families and others, and also to keep an eye on what came on to the market.'

'Auctions, you mean?'

'Exactly. Very much the same work I had done in Berlin before the war, where I was adviser to some museums and private collectors, and would recommend that they bid for this or that item at auction. The difference in France was the number of fine works that came under the hammer, for all kinds of reasons.'

'Pictures for Goering.'

'Indeed, paintings and sculptures and bronzes and tapestries and altar pieces and anything else that was valuable or rare or pretty. The man collected art indiscriminately and with immense greed. He was, although you won't believe this, a very clever man. And charming, when he chose to be.'

'I'd heard about the charm,' said Julius. He wanted to know why the man felt he had to tell him his life story. Simply one of life's ancient mariners? He didn't think so. 'Do go on.'

'When the German occupation extended to the whole of France towards the end of nineteen forty-two, I was sent to the south to see what artistic pickings were to be had in the region. I was based in Carcassonne, but reported to Paris. Rumours reached me of a fine collection belonging to an old French family in the nearby town of St Aphrodise.'

'Ah!' said Julius.

'Yes, we come to our sheep at last.'

'Was it a fine collection?'

'It had been.'

'Do you mean it had gone?'

'Every single item was there. I had access to the family's inventory, it was handed over to me by the caretaker.'

'So why "had been"?'

'Because,' said Cornelius van der Meulen, crashing a closed fist down on the table and making the glasses wobble and Julius jump, 'because, they were fakes. The whole damn lot of them.'

'Good God,' said Julius, feigning astonishment.

'Much what I said.'

'You were sure?'

'Positive. The minute I had realised one picture was not right, a Braque as it happens, I looked harder at the rest. I did my homework, wrote back home to my former professor, wrote to my father; there was no doubt whatsoever. Excellent, first-class copies, I don't think I've ever seen better. And what a brilliant ruse! Many of these pictures had solid provenances, put the picture and the paperwork together, and you had a package that would be accepted by any auction house in the world.'

'So what was wrong with the Braque?'

'Details. Minute details. It was a picture I happened to know very well, I used it in my doctoral thesis.'

'Surely photographs, however good . . .' Julius began.

Cornelius van der Meulen shook his head. 'I had an opportunity to see the painting itself, when it was on show in an exhibition in Paris some years before the war.'

'So who had replaced the originals with copies?' Evidently, the Dutchman hadn't heard about Tilly d'Icère's cunning scheme.

'That was the question I asked myself. Forgery on such a scale, and done with such artistry, is not to be done overnight. It would take some months, I think. And not only one artist must have been involved. The man who can fake a Vermeer may not be able to copy a Monet convincingly. Bronzes and sculptures are not so difficult to copy, as moulds can be made. However, this is a different technique to that of the painter. Or the jeweller, for although I am not so expert in that field, close inspection revealed that the jewels were also copies.'

Julius's mind was running on practicalities. 'Risky, too. The artists employed would have to keep their mouths shut.'

'Indeed. And there were those around who had ways of making such men talk.'

Julius didn't care to think about such a possibility. 'What did you do about the fakes?'

'My first idea was to leave them well alone. My superior, however, demanded that I arrange to pack the whole collection and ship it back to Germany, to Goering. He said that it was only my judgement that they were fakes; I could be wrong.'

'Is this what you did?'

'I was forestalled. I sent the list to the Reichsmarschal, saying merely that this was what was in the d'Icère collection. Back came an amused note saying that I was behind the times, that many items from the collection were already in Germany, list appended. You will understand that once a painting or sculpture was in his collection, no one would dare to question its authenticity. To do so would be to suggest Goering had been hoodwinked. Not a bright idea, better to keep any suspicions to oneself.'

Julius slowly drank some more beer, anxious not to show his surprise, which was genuine this time.

Cornelius van der Meulen had drained his glass and was summoning the waiter to order another. 'For you?'

Julius had enough beer, and right now, he needed all his wits about him. A collection of paintings, all copies, then the originals turning up in Germany. 'You have no idea how or when the originals went to Germany?'

'I think that, when the copies were put on display, the genuine collection was hidden somewhere very secure, a place not likely to be found by occupying troops, nosy neighbours or art thieves.'

Is he guessing, wondered Julius, or does he know more than he's letting on? 'Only someone did discover them, and they removed them and sold them to Germany.'

'Yes.'

'Even if the substitution was made before the war, before the summer of nineteen thirty-nine, I don't suppose the originals would have been taken from their hiding place until after the summer of nineteen forty. Once the Germans were in Paris, it would be easy enough to arrange a deal.'

'It would have been very difficult before that date.'

'It has to be a member of the family. Who else would know where any hiding place was?'

'Members of the family, yes, they would know. But also servants, whoever physically helped to transport the collection, there were more than sixty paintings, you know, apart from everything else. Word gets out.'

'So you're assuming the d'Icères arranged for the copies to be made before they left for America.'

'This is so.'

'And then the hiding place of the originals was discovered, by accident, or intentionally by someone who knew where they were.'

'Exactly.'

'Tell me something,' said Julius. 'Like your war story, this is now history. In the past. Finished.'

'Over and done with, in fact.'

'So why are you here now, four years after the liberation?'

'After the war, I took up the threads of my old career, but now I live in Holland. I find I prefer it. Recently, the director of a gallery called me in; he was concerned about a painting he had been offered. A Braque, as it happens.'

'Why was he concerned?'

'This particular painting was known to be in the possession of a Swiss collector. Discreet inquiries brought the information that the picture was still hanging on the wall of his dining-room in Basle.'

'So the gallery had been offered a fake.'

'Not at all. The gallery had been offered, in my opinion, the original. Which meant that the one in Switzerland was a copy. You must understand the financial implications. Madame d'Icère probably paid two hundred pounds, to express it in English money, for her Braque. In the salerooms now, such a painting will fetch three or four thousand pounds. Maybe more.'

Julius sat back, throwing his hands in the air. 'Remind me never to buy a picture, I had no idea there were so many fakes and copies and forgeries. What had this painting to do with St Aphrodise?'

'That is what is so extremely interesting. The painting in question belonged to the d'Icère family. The copy was in the chateau, I saw it with my own eyes.'

'What did you do with the fake collection? Once you realised you'd been scooped with Goering.'

'Scooped? I'm sorry . . .'

'A newspaper term. When you knew the originals had already surfaced in Berlin, what happened to the copies here in St Aphrodise?'

'I left them where they were. The Reichsmarschal would not take kindly to my handling the copies.'

'If he'd ever found out.'

'You didn't take risks like that. Not with Goering.'

'The Germans took over the chateau. And wrecked it when they left, I believe?'

'Yes. They did a very thorough job.'

'Perhaps they removed anything that took their fancy before they left?'

'I doubt it. When the Americans and the Resistants – who were like berserks, some of them – were on your heels, well, it was best to travel light.'

'Someone must have removed the pictures before the Germans came to the chateau.'

'This is very likely.'

'So that's the source of your copy.'

'No. I myself took the Braque copy from the chateau. As a curiosity, you understand. It is still in my possession.'

'And the original is in Holland? And some Swiss fat cat has *another* copy?'

'That is so.'

Julius shook his head. 'Very confusing.' Why was van der Meulen telling him this? It didn't show him in a very good light. And it was a dangerous move, to come back to the area where he'd served as a German officer. He might so easily be recognised.

The Dutchman pulled out a cigarette case and offered Julius a cheroot.

Julius accepted it without thinking; cheroots were not something he often smoked. Cornelius leant forward with his lighter, lit both their cheroots, and sat back, his legs extended to the side of the table, one arm hooked over the back of his chair. 'So I'm here looking for art that shouldn't exist. What are you looking for?'

Julius turned the matter over in his mind as he smoked the evil-smelling cheroot. He took a strange pleasure in the sharp sourness of it, it jerked his senses into sharper focus. 'Vicky wants to know what happened to Philippe d'Icère.'

'The son of Tilly and Guy d'Icère? He is dead.'

'So everyone tells us. Do you know anything about him?'

'During the war, when I was in Carcassonne, I picked up gossip and mess talk from my fellow officers and even from the Gestapo. Although they kept themselves to themselves, they knew we didn't like them or their job. I heard that there was a man of that name, one Philippe d'Icère, who was high on their wanted list. He was a member of the Resistance, had been in charge of several daring and successful raids, especially to do with trains. He worked under the cover name of Emile. The Milice and the Gestapo were hunting for him, although I never heard that they'd caught him. They broke up one group, which was based in the hills behind St Aphrodise, but that wasn't Philippe d'Icère's cell.'

'He sounds a brave man.'

'Very courageous. Daring, and very skilful in choosing his targets.

If you disrupt the railways around there, you affect the train runnings of half of France.'

Julius felt a stab of . . . what? Resentment at the man's courage? How unworthy, he thought, disliking himself for not wanting Philippe to have been such a hero.

'And while he was living in danger and risking his neck, someone was quietly selling off his family's treasures.'

'It is not a pleasant thought,' said Cornelius van der Meulen, although he didn't, Julius noticed, look disturbed by it. 'My country-men behaved badly in the war, as did many others. But this smacks of a breaking of trust, somewhere on the way, and I find that distasteful.'

There was another silence.

'Then I saw what your friend, Miss Vicky, has in her bag. You can imagine, my eyes were riveted.'

'Is that so?'

'I think she carries around with her the gothic butterfly which was the pearl of the d'Icère collection. A priceless article, and I ask myself, is this genuine, or another copy? And how has she come by it? It is not listed among the supposed treasures left at the chateau. Yet every art historian knows of this piece and its extraordinary discovery hidden in the reliquary of a cross. Hidden for centuries, and so in perfect condition.'

'And you say this is what she's carrying around in her bag? It hardly seems likely.'

'Indeed, one would say it was extraordinary. But if it is the butterfly then it is more valuable than she can imagine. Also, I feel that Philippe d'Icère's family might want to know how she came by it. Legally, it must belong to them.'

'That's not necessarily so.'

'There speaks a lawyer. However, I feel that our interests, or Miss Hampden's and my interests may coincide. She is looking for a d'Icère; I, too, feel that the answer to my mystery will lie with the d'Icère family.'

Vicky watched the two men below as they shook hands and Julius went into the inn. She went downstairs to meet him.

'Hot,' he said, fanning his face with his hat. 'Why did you hare off like that?'

How could she best put it? She couldn't say, I heard Philippe's voice in my ear whispering, Lies, lies, he's lying. 'I don't like the look of him. I don't trust him.'

'One shouldn't judge by appearances. He seems a perfectly amiable Dutchman, with a rather sad history. Forced to serve in the German army, he told me.'

'He's a Nazi,' said Vicky at once.

'Not all Germans were Nazis.'

'I know *that*. But I bet he was. You can tell he's hiding something. What did you talk about? You've been a long time.'

'He is, by training, an art historian. And I agree with you, I'm not sure I trust him. He claims that he only wants to get to the bottom of the faked works of art that were at one time in the chateau. The originals and more than one copy of major works in the collection have been turning up at auction and in private sales. One gathers he has some anxious clients.'

'Art historian?'

'Yes. Rather unfortunately, he got a glimpse of a butterfly when he returned your notebook to you. He says it was in the d'Icère collection.'

'I expect it was.'

'He says, in which case, it belongs to the heir or heirs.'

'Nonsense.' Vicky dismissed this with a wave of her hand. 'It was Philippe's, and he gave it to me. You know that.'

'Can you prove it?'

Vicky stared at him. 'Prove it? Why ever should I?'

'Can you?'

'I have his letter, and his friend knows he wanted me to have it. The one who told me that he was dead.'

'Do you have his name? Do you know where he lives?'

How exasperating the man was. 'Never mind that. I've got it, it's mine and I'm keeping it. Now listen, the date of Philippe's death on the memorial in that church is wrong.'

'Is it? Do you know when he died?'

'Not exactly. But I know he was alive after January nineteen forty-three, because I met him in London in April nineteen forty-three. The letter and the butterfly were sent to me in June. With an accompanying note, written in a hurry by the look of it. No address, and a scrawled signature I couldn't read.'

'I wonder how many Philippe d'Icères there were.'

'What?'

'One seems to have died at the beginning of 1943, you met one in London three months later, and our friend the Dutchman was talking about one who must have been operating in the Resistance later than that.'

'How do you know?

'Van der Meulen mentioned the Milice. The Milice went back to early nineteen forty-three, but they weren't armed or properly organised until nineteen forty-four.'

Vicky stared at him. 'You're saying that for Philippe to be in the Milice, he would have to have been alive in nineteen forty-four?' She frowned, trying to take this in. Was it conceivable that, after all, Philippe wasn't dead? Or at least, hadn't died when she thought he had? This possibility brought no sense of elation, only disbelief and the old, familiar pain that Philippe, whenever he had died, or even if he had survived, was no longer part of her life. 'There might have been someone else with the same name. Or using his name. How do you know so much about the Milice?'

'It was part of my job. Do you have a photo of Philippe?'

Vicky was silent, remembering her father's appalling sortie on her room, her clothes pulled out of drawers and cupboards, her private possessions ransacked for traces of the loathed foreigner who had so threatened Kit Hampden's proprietorial control of his daughter's life.

'I had a snapshot. My father tore it up.' After jeering at her, calling her a whore, shouting that she was no better than a bitch on heat, after jabbing the offending photograph into her face.

'Unfortunate,' was all that Julius said, but she could see the compassion in his eyes. Bad-tempered father was what he must be thinking; little did he know the extent of that bad temper.

'Philippe had a photograph taken of both of us. He sent it to his parents.'

'Who were by then dead. Hadn't he heard?'

'He spoke of them as though they were alive. He can't have known. Oh, God, how sad.'

'Very.'

'But it doesn't matter. I haven't got anything to prove; I just want to know what happened to Philippe, and when.'

'Fine,' said Julius. 'And let's continue with our enquiries to that end by visiting Philippe's aunt by marriage.' He took out the envelope Monsieur Ribérac had given him from his inside pocket and opened it. 'Just as he said. Carcassonne. We'll be back for tea if we step on it.'

'Do you think she'll be a harpy?'

'From Lamboley's caginess, I should think she's going to be quite out of the common way.'

Chapter Eight

Number seven was painted in a dingy cream colour. The windows were gay with vivid geraniums planted out in window boxes, however, and the green shutters gleamed with new paint.

Julius gave a couple of loud raps with the heavy black door-knocker, and stepped back to survey the house. A head appeared above them for a moment, and then they heard footsteps from within. The door opened. A woman stood there, unmistakably British; no other people on earth could have produced the sandals, the dippy cotton frock, the grey hair arranged in an untidy bun, the half spectacles and the three chins.

Just like my Great-Aunt Josephine, thought Vicky.

The woman's faded but astute blue eyes were looking over the two of them with quite as much interest as they had shown on seeing her. Clearly she drew the same conclusion about their nationality that they had done about hers. 'Well?' she said in English.

Julius pulled himself together. 'We're looking for Madame d'Icère, I understand she lives here?'

'She does,' the woman said.

'In that case, would it be possible to talk to her? Is she in? Could she spare us a little of her time?'

'Who are you?'

Julius introduced Vicky and himself, adding that he was a lawyer. 'And you. . . ?'

'My name is Miss Wilton. I'm staying with Isabeau d'Icère. We are very old friends. A lawyer, did you say? An English lawyer? I've no time for lawyers of any nationality. You'd better come in. Mind the cats.'

Julius was used to cats, but Vicky found the pair of handsome Siameses who stalked up the stairs with them, one leading the way and the other guarding the rear, unnerving. 'Nice puss,' she tried, as they went into a sunny room with beams so low that Julius had to duck his head.

The Siamese gave her a blue glare, and with a dismissive flick of its tail, went over to be greeted by Julius, who obliged by stroking the cat's silky nose until it bit him. He withdrew his hand quickly.

'That shows she likes you,' said Miss Wilton, before vanishing through a door which she closed firmly behind her.

No one would say anything so stupid about a dog that bit you, Vicky thought. One bite and a dog would be in deep trouble, but cats could maul you to bits and nobody cared. She avoided the other cat, who was eyeing her in what she considered a vicious way, and crossed to one of the two windows. It overlooked a small courtyard, on the other side of which was the back of one of the houses in the next street.

The door on the other side of the room opened, and a woman came in. Where Miss Wilton was all solidity, Isabeau d'Icère was ethereal. Vicky had never seen anyone so thin. Her eyes were huge and watchful, her movements fluid, more like the Siamese cats than like a person of flesh and blood.

'I am Isabeau d'Icère.' Her voice was high-pitched, but not unpleasant. She offered each of them in turn a soft hand, as though a clasp would crunch her bones. Then she sat down at the huge rolltop desk. There was a large silver inkpot, with a quill pen in it. Another quill lay beside it. Each pigeon hole was stacked with papers, more papers lay in neat piles on the desk. More closely written sheets of paper, together with some large books, were on the nearby table. She picked up one of the quills and twisted it in her fingers.

One whole wall of the room was lined with shelves, filled with still more books. There was a sofa on the other side of the room, and two wicker chairs were placed opposite the sofa, adorned with fat cushions covered in squares of kelim carpet.

'Please, sit down.' Madame d'Icère waved a hand in the direction of the sofa and chairs. 'I don't know you, either of you.'

'A lawyer in St Aphrodise, Monsieur Lamboley, suggested we might talk to you.' Julius told her. 'We are trying to get news of a relation of yours. Philippe d'Icère.'

'My nephew. Did you know him?'

'I met him in London,' said Vicky. 'During the war.'

'In London? How interesting.' Her face was a blank, giving nothing away. 'He's dead. I don't really want to speak of him.'

Vicky tried again. 'I know there's a memorial to a Philippe d'Icère in the church at St Aphrodise. And I was told that he had died, by a friend of his. In England. Only the date of his death is given as January nineteen forty-three, and I met him in April of that year. So I thought perhaps the dead man is one Philippe d'Icère, and my one, I mean, the man I knew in the war, is a relation or something. With the same name. Or from a completely different family, also called d'Icère. Or that my Philippe was the one who died.'

There was a silence. Vicky looked at Julius, Julius looked at Madame d'Icère whose big eyes were expressionless. Then she spoke again, to Vicky. 'You aren't the first young woman to be taken in by good looks and charm of manner and a bundle of half-truths about secret work.' She saw the flicker of doubt in Vicky's face and pounced. 'That was his story, was it? They said that was what he was doing. I never believed it. Did this man speak good English?'

Vicky nodded.

'The d'Icères all do. It's a tradition in the family. They go to English schools or have English governesses or tutors.' Her eyes narrowed. 'The English! Nothing good ever came out of England. They betrayed us, sooner or later they betray everyone. Just as Philippe, tainted with English blood and English ways, betrayed his fellow countrymen. Englishwomen are immoral and their men have no sense of honour.'

'Betrayed his fellow countrymen?' said Vicky indignantly.

The woman's tone was biting. 'Philippe d'Icère, son of Guy d'Icère, fled to England. Then he returned to France, in the pay of the English. He joined the Resistance, therefore betraying the government of his country. Later, he betrayed his colleagues in the group, his friends. It was despicable. I don't know exactly when he died, I took no further interest in him. I can't help you. I don't want to help you. I have no time for the English.'

In which case, Vicky wondered, why was Miss Wilton there.

Julius changed the subject. 'I understand that Guy d'Icère was one of four brothers.'

This evidently touched another sore spot, for Isabeau d'Icère abandoned her Anglophobia to dive into what were clearly ancient feuds. 'Indeed he was, and he had no right to give himself airs, he was only a second son. And my Jean was older than Bertrand, who now is so important and grand. He still had to give me my widow's share,' she went on with satisfaction. 'French law is very firm about this. Of course, he claimed that many items in the collection were missing, but still, he had to come to an arrangement.'

'So who was the eldest son?' Julius asked.

'Gaston, who died before the war. Tuberculosis.

'How sad,' said Vicky. 'Was he married? Did he have any children?'

There was a moment's silence, and then an outpouring of hatred so venomous that Julius was visibly taken aback. Vicky watched his face take on the polite mask of the Englishman who is being shocked.

Madame d'Icère was talking about someone called Suzanne, who was as depraved a woman as ever existed, she would not sully their ears with the names such a woman might be called. Men had mistresses, they always had, there was nothing remarkable in that, provided the mistress knew her place. But this Suzanne . . . Well. The English whore, they used to call her. Whore was too good a name for her. Madame d'Icère finally ran out of steam, and Julius saw his chance. Was Suzanne Gaston d'Icère's mistress? Did she have children by him? Where was she now?

What did he take her for? She had avoided the woman since Gaston's death, no doubt in itself caused by neglect on the part of his mistress, and she had no wish to resume the acquaintance. If she had an idea of where she lived, it would merely be to ensure that their paths never crossed.

So she did know something. Well, perhaps, but he would do

better to leave well alone. Illegitimate children could have nothing to do with the affairs of the rest of the family.

What a bitch, thought Vicky.

Women of her type should be sterilised, not allowed to bring degenerate children into this world.

Vicky started. Where had they heard that before?

As Madame d'Icère wound down to a slower rate of words at a lower pitch, Julius tried once again to get an address.

'Nîmes,' Madame d'Icère finally and grudgingly admitted. 'I last heard of her in Nîmes. It is a place I never visit.'

'Where in Nîmes?'

She didn't know. Nor, more irritatingly, could she recall the woman's surname. Something strange, not a normal French name. But then, of course, she wasn't a Frenchwoman. The sniff said it all.

Now she turned to Vicky, her face still full of animosity. 'Why do you want to trace him, Mademoiselle, after all this time? Perhaps you have something of his you want to restore to the family. Or, no, perhaps you thought he might have left you something in his will? Put such ideas out of your mind. French people do not leave land or property or money away from the family. Did he ever give you anything? No, I thought not.'

'He gave me a butterfly,' said Vicky before she could stop herself.

The effect of this remark was electric. Isabeau d'Icère leapt to her feet and darted across the room, loomed over Vicky. 'What did you say? A butterfly? What kind of a butterfly?'

Vicky gathered her wits. 'A brooch.'

'How big?'

Julius protested. 'Madame, surely . . .'

'Be quiet. How big? What was it like?'

'A little gold brooch, with rubies and diamonds.' Vicky heard herself gabbling.

As though sensing conflict, Miss Wilton surged into the room, carrying a small tray with a glass of water and a twist of paper. 'A butterfly? An emblem of the d'Icère family,' she said, putting the tray down on the desk. 'They crop up all over the place, carved into stone fireplaces in the chateau, woven into tapestries, given as presents. I remember one vulgar jewelled affair which Guy's father gave to his wife as a birthday present. They acquired a lot of such ornamental butterflies. They used to have several of them displayed on black velvet in one of the rooms at the chateau. A hideous Braque and a Picasso on one wall, and the tasteless butterflies in ugly cases all along the opposite wall. Isabeau, my dear, you mustn't upset yourself. It's time for your powders.'

One of the Siamese cats, bored by the lack of attention being paid to it, strolled across the room and nipped Vicky's ankle.

'Ow,' cried Vicky, shooing the cat away, and rubbing her wound.

'She shouldn't be asked to remember the war. She finds it very distressing,' Miss Wilton announced.

Julius rose. 'Thank you,' he began, but Isabeau d'Icère, taking no notice of the glass of water which Miss Wilton was holding out to her, addressed herself to Vicky, fixing her with a penetrating stare.

'Take my advice, Miss Hampden, and put this man out of your mind. I suppose you went to bed with him?'

Vicky flushed, and was angry with herself for doing so.

'If you've any sense, you'll put it down to experience; if an enjoyable one, so much the better, if not, so much the worse. This Philippe of yours never existed except in your imagination. In reality, he was not a hero of the Resistance or of anything. Just a man looking out for his own interests. Like all the rest of them.'

Before Vicky could retort to this, Julius had risen from his chair. 'Time to go,' he said. 'Thank you, Madame, for seeing us.'

'I'll see you out,' said Miss Wilton. She waited while Vicky skirted round a Siamese, and then followed them out of the room and down to the front door.

Vicky was still seething. She turned on the baggy Miss Wilton. 'How come, since she hates us English so much, she puts up with you?'

Miss Wilton was unperturbed by the rudeness. 'I'm actually Scots, for one thing, and for another, you can hate a nation but like its individuals.' She had in her hand a roll of paper, and she handed this to Julius. 'I'm a genealogist. An expert on French families. I'm also a calligrapher, and I take on commissions to draw up family trees. Some I do to please myself. This was a draft of one I never finished. You may find it helpful. As well, I have written the telephone number and address of Bertrand d'Icère on there. You should visit him.'

She turned back to Vicky. 'Do you have the butterfly brooch with you?'

'Brooch? Oh, yes, the brooch. Yes. I mean, no.'

'I advise you to wear it if you have it. A pretty jewel like that should be shown off. And then everyone will know exactly what he gave you. Much safer.'

With that she hustled them through the door, bade them an abrupt, 'Good afternoon,' and shut the door behind them.

'Don't say a word,' Vicky snapped at Julius as they headed back to where they'd parked the car. 'Not one word.'

'I wasn't going to.' He opened the passenger door for her, and then went round to the other side and climbed in. He started the car. 'Where now?' he enquired.

'I don't care. What an infuriating woman, moralising away like she was some teacher at school. And that Miss Wilton, what a witch.'

'I wonder what she knows. All that stuff at the door was a trifle elliptic.'

'She knows nothing. She's pure charlatan. Warning us off like that. And those chins!'

'Put them out of your mind.'

'And that mincing woman, I can't believe she's Philippe's aunt.'

'Aunt by marriage.'

'Why has she got it in for Philippe? It was pure venom when she got going on his betrayals.'

'She probably never liked her nephew. What I want to know is why she reacted so violently when you mentioned the butterfly.'

'That was a mistake. I should have kept my mouth shut.'

'You retrieved the situation admirably. Have you got it with you?'

'Always.'

'I can't help feeling it would be better in a bank or perhaps in Monsieur Lamboley's safe.' Julian sounded worried.

'Who'd trust a bank? Or a lawyer?'

★   ★   ★

They stopped at a country inn on the way back, and lunched well, sitting out on a shady terrace under a cobweb of vines. Scallops followed by succulent slices of guinea fowl and rounded off with a raspberry sorbet improved Vicky's temper no end. Julius ate his own meal with great enjoyment, and kept his thoughts about Vicky and the true or false Philippe to himself.

'You don't have to stay in France,' Vicky said as they resumed their journey. 'If you feel it's dangerous to know a woman who carries a butterfly around with her.'

'No, but I have to get to the bottom of this mystery. Philippe is far too interesting not to find out what the truth is. For a start, I'd like to know if there is, or was, more than one Philippe d'Icère. Accounts vary so wildly. Good, bad, hero, traitor, alive, dead. The case is full of contradictions; how could I possibly go back to England leaving all this in the air?'

'Curiosity killed the cat,' Vicky said.

'You aren't intending to take Auntie d'Icère's advice?'

Vicky's hackles rose. 'I certainly am not. How could you think such a thing? I'm going to find out the truth about Philippe, and once I do find out, she and you and any other doubting Thomases will have to admit that he's not a bit like these d'Icères she's been so scathing about.'

'And what a lot of d'Icères there are.' He felt in his jacket pocket and gave Vicky the roll of paper that Miss Wilton had handed to him on the doorstep. 'Have a look at that.'

Vicky unfolded the large sheet. 'It's a family tree. Goodness, how beautifully done, all by hand in wonderful lettering. With a butterfly at the top. Oh, I see, it's the d'Icère family.'

Her eyes focused on the chart. Some of the names were written in ink, small lettering exquisitely done in a fine italic script. Others were pencilled in, and where this was the case, the handwriting was distinctly messier. Scribbles, almost. She ran her eye down the tree of the generations. Old family was right, here were d'Icères slain at Crécy, dying of wounds at Agincourt and fighting *à l'outrance* at Malplaquet. None guillotined, however; Monsieur Lamboley had been right about that. Judging by the high-ranking military titles bestowed on post-Revolutionary d'Icères, the family had quickly hitched themselves to Napoleon's star.

'Well?' said Julius, eyes on the road.

'I'm just working my way down to the present generation . . . Julius!'

Julius, imagining he was about to mow down some animal or unwary pedestrian, stood on the brakes. The car juddered, screeched, veered sideways, and came to a stop at a ninety degree angle to the road.

'What happened?' said Vicky. 'Did you hit something?'

Julius, prised his hands off the wheel. 'I? My dear Vicky . . .' He got no further. There was a loud 'crump' and an ominous crunching sound as the car jolted to one side.

Vicky stared at the wheel which had careered across the road, and now lay on its side on the edge of the ditch. Everything was suddenly very quiet, even the cicadas seemed to have stopped.

'I think that's one of our wheels,' she said finally.

'It is,' said Julius. He opened his door with some difficulty. Vicky couldn't open hers, as the door was jammed into the ground. She climbed over the driving seat and clambered out to stand beside Julius.

'Do wheels often come off your car? she asked.

The dusty road shimmered in the hot afternoon sun.

'Hardly.' Julius took off his panama hat and fanned himself with the brim. He looked up and down the long straight stretch of deserted road.

'Do you have a spare?'

Julius walked to the rear of the car. The spare wheel was held in a case on the outside of the boot. He took a look, pressed the rubber of the tyre.

'I do, but it's flat.'

'Flat? What's the point of a spare tyre if it's flat? Why is it flat?'

'Because someone has slashed it.'

'Slashed as in knife?'

'As in sharp implement of some kind, yes.'

'Deliberately?' Vicky's voice was not as steady as she would have liked.

'It couldn't have happened accidentally.'

Vicky sat down on the rough grass at the edge of the road. 'Do you suppose someone – the tyre slasher, for instance – loosened the wheel so that it came off?'

'More than likely.'

Vicky went cold. Who could have felt that much hostility towards them. 'We could have been killed.'

'Yes, but we weren't.'

'So what do we do now?' Vicky looked up and down the deserted road, stretching to a point in the distance, a geometric pattern of the road with straight lines of tarmac, ditches and trees.

'We'll have to walk, that's all.'

'Where to?'

'Let's have a look at the map.' He ducked back into the car, and stretched across to the glove compartment.

Not a single car or van or truck passed in either direction as they tried to work out where they were, calculate where the nearest village or hamlet might be. Heads bent over the map spread out on the roof of the car, they were startled by the sound of a bicycle bell just behind them.

Vicky let go of the map, which rustled to the ground. Julius tipped his hat politely to the owner and ringer of the bicycle bell, who turned out to be an urchin with spider legs and arms, mounted on a bicycle several sizes too large for him. He held the machine tilted over, brown feet firmly on the ground, a hand guarding the stick of bread in his basket. 'Your car has lost a wheel,' he informed them.

Vicky gave him an unfriendly look.

Julius, knowing that the boy might be their only saviour, smiled and asked him where they were.

The boy shrugged, his expression showing his contempt for persons who asked stupid questions. 'Here. Where else?'

Julius picked up the map. 'Can you show us?'

The boy took one look at the map and shook his head. 'No.'

Julius tried again. 'Where is the nearest village?'

The boy took his hand off the bread and jerked a thumb in the direction he had come from.

'How far is it?'

Another shrug. 'Ten minutes by bicycle?' Maybe more, he didn't have a watch, didn't know when he'd set out.

'That means a forty minute walk at least,' Julius said to Vicky.

'It won't be any use to you, that place,' the boy told them. 'There's only a few shops. No garage, no mechanic. For that you need to go the other way.'

'How far?'

He didn't know. 'Ten, fifteen minutes cycling. Perhaps less, perhaps more.'

'Is there a mechanic that way?'

This brought a gleam into the boy's eyes. There was, he told them with pride, a big garage with a fine mechanic, who just happened to be his cousin Henri.

'Could you take a message to Henri for us?'

The boy considered the question, but couldn't see any objection to it. Henri would be pleased to get the work, it would be possible to charge these mad people many, many francs, they would pay willingly whatever Henri asked. He nodded, gave the Lagonda a contemptuous look, and heaved his bicycle up. 'Next time, monsieur, drive a French car. It is safer; the wheels do not fall off.'

He pushed his bicycle into motion and rode off, wobbling violently as his legs stretched to reach the pedals.

'Will he take your message to his cousin the mechanic?' Vicky asked as she watched the cyclist vanishing into the distance.

'I don't see why not. Let's wait and see. I'd rather not set off on foot unless we have to. I suggest that we make ourselves comfortable under that tree over there. You can tell me why you let out that squawk, which had such dire consequences.'

'I simply exclaimed. I didn't expect you to slam the brakes on.'

'I thought I'd run over some wandering peasant.'

'The wheel must have been about to fall off. Lucky that you did brake. Imagine if you'd been going at fifty miles an hour when it came off.'

'Yes,' Julius agreed. 'Still, it's a pity that it happened here, in the middle of nowhere. So what was the fuss about? Did an insect sting you?'

'No,' said Vicky, going back to the car and getting the sheet with the d'Icère family tree on it. Look.' She pointed to a branch with four names on it. 'There's Guy d'Icère's older brother, Gaston, the one who died before the war.'

'Let me see that,' said Julius. 'Damn it, she's pencilled half of it in, it's impossible to read. What does this say?'

'I can't quite make it out,' said Vicky. 'The interesting bit is further down, look, doesn't that say, Phil?'

Julius seized the paper and scrutinised it, turning it this way and that to get a better light on the faint words. 'It could be Phil,' he finally admitted.

Vicky took the family tree back from him. 'What does this dotted line mean?'

'Illegitimate,' said Julius. 'And you see, the mother's name is pencilled in as well, but no *m* for married. She's a Susan someone, but I can't make out the surname. That, no doubt, is the wicked Suzanne.'

'Roll it up,' said Vicky. 'Wait until we reach civilisation, then we can get hold of a magnifying glass and have a proper look.'

It took several hours to reach what passed for civilisation, and it was late evening by the time they made it back to St Aphrodise.

'I need a bath and a drink,' said Julius.

'Which first?' asked Vicky, going round the unoccupied reception desk and swishing aside the plastic ribbons that covered the entrance to the innkeeper's quarters. 'Hello?'

'Both together,' said Julius. 'I shall lie in my bath and sip my drink.'

'Don't take too long about it,' said Vicky. 'I want dinner, and it's getting late. Bother, no sign of anyone.'

As she spoke, the plastic strips parted, and the innkeeper bustled through. 'M'sieur, Mademoiselle, I am very glad to see you.'

'Not as glad as I am to see you,' said Julius. 'I'd like a drink.'

To Julius's surprise, the innkeeper ignored his request. 'There is a woman here who has been waiting for you for some time.'

The aunt? wondered Vicky. Madame d'Icère. Who else? Horrors, surely not one of her sisters.

'I'll send up and ask her to come down.'

Could it be Martha? There was no reason for Madame d'Icère to take a room at the inn. No reason for Martha to be here, either, Vicky thought, beginning to panic

A few minutes later, there was the sound of footsteps crashing down the stone stairs.

'Olivia!' said Vicky, completely astonished.

'Dear me,' said Julius mildly. 'The schoolgirl from London.'

'Hello, Aunt Vicky,' Olivia said, jumping down the last few stairs and clasping Vicky in a bear hug. 'Oh, hello, Mr Drummond,' she added, looking over Vicky's shoulder.

'Olivia, why aren't you at school? What are you doing in France? Is Vera with you?' The last in tones of alarm.

'Calm down, Aunt Vicky. Would Mummy be here, in the season? Come *on*.'

'Well, how did you get here? Who brought you? How did you know where I was?'

'I came by train. On my own, actually. From Paris.'

'But Olivia, what were you *doing* in Paris?'

'Passing through,' Olivia said airily. 'On my way here.'

'Forgive me interrupting,' said Julius, 'but from what I remember, May is not a month for school holidays.'

'Too right,' said Olivia. 'We've an Australian girl at school, and that's what she always says. No, it's term time all right, only not for me. Not any longer. I've run away.'

Chapter Nine

Vicky panicked.

'I must phone Vera immediately. Olivia, you'll have to go back to London. At once. Now, this very minute. I wonder if we can get you a seat on a plane.' She noticed for the first time that Olivia had what seemed to be a school raincoat wrapped round her. 'Do take that mac off, you must be frightfully hot.'

'Boiling,' agreed Olivia. 'There's a slight problem, though. You see I nipped off from school on my way to games.'

'On your way to games?' It took a moment or two for Vicky to realise the implications of this. 'Olivia, no!'

'Yes,' said Olivia, removing her coat.

The innkeeper made several very Gallic noises, lifted his eyes to heaven and fled.

'Good God,' said Julius recoiling. 'What a dreadful garment. Put your coat back on at once. You can't be seen like that, you'll frighten the natives.'

'She already has, poor Monsieur Ribérac,' said Vicky. 'Isn't it ghastly? Oh, it does take me back.' She assumed the haughtily refined tones of a catwalk commentator. 'Olivia is modelling the romper suit, suitable for all summer games.'

'Romper suit?'

'Note the rubber buttons and the Peter Pan collar. Her hat is this season's model of the traditional dust bonnet.'

Olivia produced a hat from her pocket and twirled it in the air.

'And that white floppy hat is actually called a dust bonnet? I don't believe it.'

'Don't you have any sisters?' Olivia said, absent-mindedly scratching a mosquito bite on her knee. 'Didn't they go to boarding schools and wear horrible uniform?'

'I have no sisters, and I'm glad, when I look at you. Thankfully, no member of my family went around looking like that. Good heavens, what is the school thinking of?'

'It goes back a long way, this outfit,' said Olivia confidingly. 'I think they wore it in Victorian times, when the school was founded.'

'It's quite practical,' Vicky said. 'Julius, stop fretting about how Olivia is dressed. The post office will be shut by now. I'd better go and charm Monsieur Ribérac into letting me use the phone. Oh, Olivia, you are a pest. How did you know I was here, by the way?'

'Ways and means.'

'Don't be evasive.'

'From Martha Frobisher, then.'

'*Martha?*'

Olivia spoke as though to a not very bright child. 'When I got to Paris, I went to Martha's apartment. I had wormed her address out of the school, to give to Mr Drummond here, and, naturally, I copied it down for myself. I thought it might come in handy, and you see it has.'

'And Martha told you where I was, and allowed you to catch the train?'

'No, actually, Martha was pretty beastly, she said I had to go straight back to England. No need for you to go phoning Mummy, in fact, because that was the first thing Martha did. Mummy was out, of course, as always, but Martha left a message, and then she got on to the school. Officious, I call it. And do you know what that awful old crow in the school office said to her? "Run away, has she? That family seems to make a habit of it." See what kind of a reputation you've left behind you, dear Aunt Vicky.'

Vicky was stung. 'How very unfair. I was the only one of us who ran away, at least I think I was.' Doubt struck her, as vague memories drifted up into her mind of first Muriel and then Daphne appearing in the house when they should have been at school. On each occasion, Vicky hadn't been allowed to speak to them, and she had been too young then to think much about it or put two and two together.

'There's no point in the school making a stink about it,' Olivia was saying. 'Girls are always running away.'

'Nevertheless,' began Vicky.

'I hate people who say, "Nevertheless." It always means they're going to come out with something horrible. I say, is there anywhere I can eat? I'm starving. I didn't have many francs, only what I got from Martha.'

'In a minute,' said Vicky. 'I just want to get this Martha business straight. If she was doing all this ringing round, and wanted you to go home at once, how come she told you where I was?'

Olivia looked shifty. 'She didn't exactly *tell* me. I found out.'

'Snooped,' said Julius.

'She had a pad beside the phone, and there it was. So I borrowed some francs . . .'

'Which Martha had left lying around,' said Vicky resignedly, knowing that it was Martha's habit to put notes and coins down in the oddest places, coming across little treasure troves of cash weeks later.

'A fugitive, a spy and a thief,' said Julius. 'It's good to know that our English schools are turning out such fine specimens of womanhood, an honour to their country.'

'It's all very well you being sarky, you never had to put up with my school. Or my parents. Or my grandfather.'

'We each have our burdens in life.'

'I'm too young to have burdens. I want to enjoy myself, and I can't do that at school, it isn't allowed. I can't do it at home, because I've got such stuffy parents, and they treat me like a child. So I've made a bolt for freedom.'

'Exactly how old are you?' Julius enquired.

'Fifteen. Old enough to leave school, I would point out.'

'Old enough to know better,' said Vicky.

She looked at Olivia in a most unfriendly way. All she wanted to do was wash, change, and then sit down with Julius over a good meal and find out how she could trace Gaston d'Icère's offspring. What a nuisance Olivia was. She was brought back to the here and now by

Olivia's aggrieved tones. 'You haven't been listening to a word I've been saying.'

'No, I haven't. I've got my own problems, thank you, and the last thing I need is having to sort you out.'

'I don't need sorting out. I need feeding.'

'A telegram for Monsieur Drummond,' announced the innkeeper as he came importantly out into the garden. 'Marked urgent, so Madame Caziot, the postmistress, who is very conscientious about such matters, has sent her son round with it. He is waiting in case there should be a reply.'

Julius had opened the telegram and read it. 'It's from my uncle. He says that Christopher Hampden intends to instruct a firm of private detectives to find you, Vicky, and persuade you to return to England.'

'Oh, God, I wish he wouldn't do things like that. Why won't he understand that I can do what I like and live where I want to. Does that mean that you've been taken off the job?'

'Looks like it,' said Julius.

'No bill to present to my father any more,' said Vicky. 'Those six shillings and eightpences mount up.'

'I'm tying up loose ends here in France. I'm here at Sir Christopher's request. He'll get billed all right, our clerk will see to that.'

Vicky drummed her fingers on the reception counter. 'I'll retain you. And pay you, of course.'

'What for?'

'To find out what happened to Philippe d'Icère.'

'I didn't realise solicitors were human bloodhounds,' commented Olivia. 'The next thing, someone will be asking you to find me.'

'It's only a matter of time,' said Julius. 'I wonder why my uncle's allowed Hampden to push him around like this? I'm rather surprised he ever agreed to send me over here.'

'I expect they're members of the same club. You scratch my back. You know.'

'They do go to the same club, I will admit.'

'So what are you going to do?'

'Send a telegram back, tomorrow morning, there's no need for any urgency, saying that I am now acting for you.'

'Will that keep them quiet? Persuade my father to leave me alone? Vicky was doubtful. She knew her father too well to be optimistic.

'If Grandpa doesn't get his way, he'll go off on one of his roars,' Olivia said. 'And can't you just imagine the kind of private detectives he'd know. Keen on the scent, no expense spared, Pinkertons always get their man. Or find their woman, in this case.'

'They can find me all they want, they can't make me go back to England, can they, Julius?'

'I think the only way you could be forced to return to England would be if you had committed an extraditable offence. As I'm not up on the laws governing extradition in France, I can't speculate on what sort of a crime you would have had to have committed to allow such a process.'

'Murder,' said Olivia with relish. 'The big one. Grandpa could bump someone off. He'd love to do that, some beastly wog or wop or one of his other pet hates. Then he can fix it so that Aunt Vicky is the chief suspect, and *voilà!*'

'You have a very fanciful mind,' said Julius severely.

'Olivia,' Vicky protested. The fact that she had more than once wondered if her father might be capable of murder didn't mean that she wanted such a thought raised in anyone else's mind. 'He's a lawyer, a judge. People like him don't go round killing people.'

Olivia took no notice. 'Or, he could send a couple of tough guys over, to kidnap you, Vicky, and hustle you back to England. Drugged,' added Olivia with relish. 'In a bundle in the boot of a powerful black motor. All done at arm's length, by minions. The real perpetrator, that is, Grandpa, would never be caught.'

'Oh, do shut up, Olivia,' said Vicky. 'You watch too many gangster films.' The prospect of private investigators on her trail made her more alarmed than she was going to admit in front of her niece. 'He's more likely to send a posse out to find *you*,' she added, going on the attack. 'He'll force your father to have you made a Ward of Court. He has a passion for doing that, please note, and then we'll all be in the soup.'

Why couldn't her father just leave them alone? She was twenty-five, and Olivia was Rowder's responsibility, not her grandfather's.

He'd messed up his daughters' lives, now he seemed to be intent on doing the same to his grand-daughter. It was odd that, though, that Vera, ultra normal in her roles of wife and society hostess, should have a daughter like Olivia, who was showing signs of not caring tuppence for the family's rigid rules.

'It's the post-war generation,' Olivia said as though she had been reading Vicky's thoughts. 'We aren't prepared to put up with being pushed around. Our childhoods were passed in trauma and distress, so naturally we are rebellious. And we have no time for old types like Grandpa, stuffed full of complexes. My goodness, he ought to see a psychoanalyst. Seven years it takes, that would stop him making trouble all over the place.'

'Have you been studying the subject?' Julius was amused.

'There's a girl at school whose father's a whiz psychoanalyst, her whole family came over from Vienna when things got nasty. The Nazis, you know, and so on. She knows all about psychology, and she's got copies of Freud's books that she lends to us less fortunate ones. It's all to do with sex, you see. That's why Grandpa's so keen on whips, he really needs help.'

'Olivia!'

'Now, come on, Aunt Vicky. You must be more modern in your outlook.'

'I don't think Mr Drummond wants to hear about our family.'

'He won't blab, he's paid not to. Besides, you can't have secrets from your lawyer, it always leads to trouble. If he doesn't understand that Grandpa's nuts, he might be bamboozled into doing what he wants.'

'I'm not so easily bamboozled,' said Julius. 'We are now going to stop talking about families, and have dinner. We shall then decide what to do about you.'

'You aren't going to do anything about me.'

'In that case, you'll have to stay in those ridiculous garments.'

'Oh, *clothes*. I thought you meant about me going back to England.'

'First things first.'

*   *   *

Vicky woke with a heavy, throbbing head. Too much of the local wine last night. Had she really drunk that much?

Then she remembered. Olivia. Olivia was a headache, and no mistake. She'd have to go back, however much she didn't want to. Only how? If she refused to go, she could hardly be heaved bodily on to a plane or train. And if she were persuaded to board a train, she, Vicky, would have to go with her, trains to Paris and on to Calais, boat across the Channel to Dover, another train to Charing Cross and finally a taxi, all the way to Vera's immaculate front door. And that would be her, Vicky, back in the lion's den.

If she didn't go with her, Olivia would be out of the train at the next station, and off God knows where.

Could she blame her?

No.

In fact, she secretly admired her niece. She had guts. Her own running away efforts hadn't been half so efficient. She had been picked up the first time by the school before she'd managed to get on a train. The second time, she'd boarded the train and hidden successfully in the lav all the way to Paddington, only to find her mother and a large policeman waiting at the ticket barrier.

She wondered how Olivia had managed to slip through all the nets. And to get across the Channel, and then down to the south of France. You had to hand it to her, she was a smooth operator, and also, what was it the Americans said? A tough cookie, that was it.

There was a knock on Vicky's door, and a tousled head looked in. It was the tough cookie. 'Oh, good, you're awake.'

Vicky shut her eyes. Large Olivia, crammed into one of her aunt's nighties, was a sight horrible to behold. What muscles the girl had, and surely none of her sisters had been that tall at her age. How had the girl's slender mother and her ectomorph of a father produced this Valkyrie?

'You look very fit,' she said feebly.

Olivia flexed a bicep or two. 'Self-defence classes and lots of work in the gym,' she explained. 'The school's aim is to enable us to look after ourselves, however threatening the situation.'

'Are you supposed to strongarm your husbands?'

'Miss Calthrop, as you know, isn't interested in husbands, and doesn't a bit want us to be wives and mothers. She fosters a spirit of independence and adventure. She wants her old girls to cross the Sahara on a camel, or climb Kilimanjaro or swim the Bosphorus, not to settle down to domesticity.'

'This is not what it says in the school prospectus. She must have got much worse since our day; she never approved of men and marriage, we all knew that, but she wasn't actively encouraging us to break out.'

'Anyone who believes all the rot they put in school prospectuses deserves what they get.'

Vicky felt the bed sag as Olivia sat down. No, there was no question of frogmarching Olivia on to plane or train. The way she looked, she could probably pick her and Julius up, one under each arm and carry them out of the airport or railway station.

But what did the girl want to do with herself in France?

'Live,' said Olivia ecstatically. 'And I can learn French, think how useful. Mummy and Daddy were going to send me off to some frightful finishing school in Switzerland in a year or so. Not at all what Miss Calthrop approves of. Look at all the money I'll save them.'

'Where are you going to live? And on what?'

'Don't be such a wet blanket, Aunt Vicky. I shall have to find a job, that's all.'

'Oh, Olivia, what kind of job? Who would employ you?'

'To start with, a family, I can look after their little ones and teach them the English language and English manners. Sophie, a French girl at school, says the French are very keen on English etiquette.'

'Etiquette indeed, where do you pick up these ideas? And who would employ you to look after their children? The French are very fond of their children. Haven't you noticed how they don't send them away to boarding school? They wouldn't entrust them to a total stranger, and please remember, you've got no references, no experience. It wouldn't work, Olivia.'

'A spot of forgery and a few white lies should do the trick. We used to make up references about each other at school. For fun, you understand. Like one girl would pretend she was applying to be a stand-in for some queen or other, and another one up for a vacancy as one of Louis XIV's mistresses.'

Vicky shut her eyes and wished she hadn't asked.

'Or do you think Mr Drummond might be persuaded to write me a reference? That would be impressive, solicitors are so solid and respectable.'

Julius was feeling far from solid and respectable.

Like Vicky, he had awoken to a certain sense of oppression, which soon crystallised into the problem of what they were to do about Olivia. He didn't imagine for a moment that they might put her on a train or find a flight for her. This teenager was clearly very used to having things her own way, and he blanched, as might a stronger man than he, at the thought of insisting that she take herself back to London.

And, he reminded himself, it was nothing to do with him. He could wash his hands of the whole Hampden family, much the wisest course. Then he could leave at once, take himself back to his placid life in a solicitor's office, dealing in a leisurely way with the trusts and wills and property dealings of the English middle classes.

Two factors weighed against this. No, three. First, he couldn't walk away and leave Vicky to cope with Olivia on her own. Chivalry was not that dead. Second, he was damned if he was going to give up on the Philippe d'Icère hunt. That was a mystery he wanted to see solved. Not, he had to acknowledge, because he thought that Vicky deserved or was at all likely to find her lover alive; he was too realistic to believe that. It was more that his curiosity had been thoroughly stirred, and he couldn't bear not to go on until it was satisfied. The third reason, which he wasn't keen to admit to himself, was that the grey skies of a chilly English summer and humdrum work of his career in London weren't exactly beckoning. He had tasted the temptation of freedom, and it was proving a fruit hard to resist.

By the time they met at the breakfast table, he and Vicky had come to much the same conclusion about Olivia. Which was, to do nothing. Vicky would send a telegram to Vera, saying that Olivia was with her, and safe and well. Julius would send the telegram he had already drafted, advising his firm of his new client, and adding that his uncle should have prevented Christopher Hampden from employing detectives.

'Let my sister and brother-in-law decide what to do,' said Vicky. 'I shall be elusive if they manage to track me down or find out the telephone number of the inn. If I don't get into a conversation, I can't be bullied or threatened into doing what I don't want to.'

'They'll probably send Nanny over to get me,' said Olivia, her mouth full of croissant.

Julius averted his eyes.

'That's a grim thought,' said Vicky, 'but she wouldn't come. Not if she's anything like our old nanny. I bet she thinks the French are brothers under the skin to Martians.'

'Your father might come,' suggested Julius.

Olivia thought about that as she buttered a roll. 'Nope. He's too busy, and besides, travel makes him bilious. Mummy can't come, her diary bulges with parties, dinners, dances and ghastly things like that, and when she's not out at social functions, she's at the hairdresser or the dressmaker or beautician. And then every Friday to Monday she and Daddy dash off to the country to stay with more friends.'

'Don't worry about it, Vicky,' Julius said. 'It's up to them to coax Olivia home, not you.'

While Vicky took the raincoated Olivia to the shops, hoping that she would find some clothes to fit Olivia's very unFrench size, Julius went to the post office to send the telegrams. At the counter, he found himself standing next to the lawyer, Monsieur Lamboley, who was having what sounded like a lengthy chat with Madame Caziot, dressed this morning in a tight scarlet jumper.

Monsieur Lamboley lifted his hat, said *Bonjour*, and gestured for Julius to take his place.

Julius demurred. He was in no hurry. He had all the time in the world. In fact, he had just thought of an alteration he needed to make in one of his telegrams.

He went back to the sloping shelf and busied himself by doodling on a form for reclaiming postal charges on returned items. He didn't want Lamboley listening to his telegrams as Madame slowly read out every word. The telegraphese might seem nonsensical, but the nonsense might arouse Lamboley's interest. One didn't trouble to put innocent facts in code, even to save money.

On his own part, he strained to catch the conversation, now drawing to a close, that was going on at the counter. News was being exchanged, exclaimed about, noted, he was sure of that. He certainly caught the words *Anglais* and *Anglaise* more than one once, and no doubt his and Vicky's antics were the subject of much interest in the town.

Better discreet than sorry, he decided, and he pocketed the telegram he had written out to send to London. He would send Vicky's telegram to her sister, but he would telephone his office and speak directly to his uncle.

Monsieur Lamboley was on his way out. He paused to speak to Julius. 'Any luck yesterday with Madame d'Icère? I hear you went to Carcassonne.'

'We did, and it was helpful. We were advised to talk to Monsieur Bertrand d'Icère.'

The lawyer made clucking noises. 'Not an easy man to talk to. I warn you that he may be awkward. But certainly, as I advised, he should be able to answer many of your questions. Whether he will choose to do so . . .' He shrugged, lifted his hat once more and made for the door.

There he stopped and turned round, as though a thought had just occurred to him. 'I understand that your car needs further repairs after your accident yesterday. If you want to speak to Marcel, this is the time to do it. You will want to hire a car while the work is being done, and Marcel works at the garage. He won't want to talk while he's working, but you will find him at noon at the Restaurant le Languedoc. It's owned by his cousin, and he always eats there.'

Julius's next decision was where to telephone from. At the post office, the obvious place, Madame Caziot would monitor every word and even though she probably didn't speak a word of English, he wasn't going to risk it. At the inn, Monsieur Ribérac would consider it his duty to listen to a conversation to England, especially if it was about the hot news item of the moment. It was better not to request the use of the lawyer's phone. Julius knew too much about his own profession to trust any fellow member of it.

A bar might have a telephone, and possibly offer some privacy. At this time of the morning, the proprietor would be cleaning and checking supplies and taking deliveries. It was worth a try. And here, just across the road, was the Bar des Cathares.

It looked good, Julius thought as he went in. He appeared to be the only customer. He approached the well-polished wooden counter, with rows of bottles behind it, some suspended upside down, some on shelves. His eye ran along the names of the drinks: Pernod, armagnacs and cognacs, anise, Dubonnet. A large coffee machine stood on the end of the bar, chrome work gleaming.

What was missing was any human being serving behind the bar. From the noises in the yard behind the kitchens, he judged that some heavy shifting was going on. He tapped on the bar with a coin. After a few minutes and a loud shout for Jacques from the area at the back, a young boy slid along behind the bar.

'M'sieur?'

Julius ordered a coffee and asked if there was a telephone that he could use to telephone England. At the word telephone, Jacques nodded energetically, and pointed to a small cabin in the corner. At the mention of England his face clouded. 'One moment,' he said, and vanished. Julius waited. The *patron* appeared, stout-bellied and amiable. No, it would not be possible for him to call England from the coin telephone. However, he could arrange it on the other telephone, only did M'sieur appreciate that it would be expensive? And also, there would be a delay, perhaps a considerable delay.

Julius assured him that he didn't mind waiting. He wrote down the telephone number, handed over a note as proof of his goodwill, and took his coffee over to a table near the counter. Behind the counter, the *patron* was speaking into a receiver on the end of a long wire.

Julius put down his coffee and beside it the copy of the newspaper he had bought on the way.

There would be a wait of some forty-five minutes, the *patron* informed him. Julius nodded, reached for his coffee and opened his paper. The *patron* disappeared into the back rooms again.

The telephone rang, a shrill sound that made Julius put down his paper and brought the *patron* to the bar. He picked up the receiver and beckoned to Julius. He held his hand over the mouthpiece. 'At the end of the call, the operator will tell you the cost.' Then he vanished again.

Edgar Drummond's voice echoed down the line. He sounded annoyed. Julius listened for a few minutes and then broke in. 'Just as you like, but Miss Hampden is now my client. No, there is no conflict of interest. We represent several members of any number of families all of whom are at each other's throats; it's never bothered you before.'

No, he disagreed, they weren't strictly speaking Hampden's solicitors, he was with Atkinson and Arkwright. By going after this hare-brained scheme to hire detectives, he had absolved them of any responsibility towards him. No, he wasn't coming back just yet. If his uncle wanted to do that, it was fine by him, he would take it as part of his holiday. He *was* being reasonable. Yes, and Miss Hampden was perfectly reasonable in her desire to trace Philippe d'Icère. He had given her an extremely valuable present, and she was uncertain whether to keep it, to return it to the family or to the man himself, should he in fact still be alive.

Edgar's voice, although oddly distorted, was quite clear now. 'Take it from me, Julius, Philippe d'Icère is dead. It is a fact. No, I can't tell you how I know, but I do. You have no idea of how much trouble your ferreting around could cause.'

'Trouble for whom?'

'Dear boy, for every one of us. There are wider implications; we could land in a very nasty mess. I beg of you, Julius, not as your senior partner, but as your uncle, to drop this affair. Leave the girl in France, let her make a new life for herself by all means, if she can escape the people Hampden's sending out. But don't get involved, don't let your curiosity get the better of you.'

He was pleading. Julius held the receiver away from his ear and looked at it in disbelief. He had never, not once, known his uncle to plead for anything. The phone quacked at him. He interrupted. 'Just tell me how you know d'Icère is dead. Do you know when he died? Or how?'

'Julius, I'm warning you, you're out of your depth. Leave for England. Now. Before it's too late.'

The operator cut in to say that their time was up, did he want a further three minutes. 'Run out of time, Uncle, sorry,' said Julius, and hung up.

Vicky had managed to equip her niece with an ill-fitting pale blue blouse and navy skirt. A wide-brimmed straw hat lay on the seat beside her.

Julius was startled by the change in her appearance. 'You look quite different.'

At breakfast she had been a large schoolgirl, now a tall young woman sat composedly at the ironwork table under an umbrella, sipping a noxious coloured drink.

'It's the hairdo,' said Vicky helpfully. 'I spotted a hairdresser, and whipped her in for a quick cut and shampoo and set. Doesn't it make a difference? And the woman at the shop is altering a couple of frocks for her.'

Yes, it was the hair that made the difference. Formerly, it had looked lank and straggly, but now it framed her face in sleek blonde waves.

Vicky saw his surprise, and laughed. You would have known about his lack of sisters. Here was a man who'd never noticed the extraordinary transformation that happened to girls in their middle teens as soon as they got away from school clothes and the watchful eyes of teachers and mothers.

Julius addressed Olivia in a firm voice, the sort he used to elderly ladies dithering about their wills. 'Vicky and I are lunching at a restaurant in the town. Alone, because we want to ask someone a few questions.'

'Still on about the missing lover?' said Olivia, giving her aunt a pert look.

'Olivia . . .'

'You, Olivia, are staying here and eating the no doubt excellent lunch that Monsieur Ribérac will provide.'

'Boring.'

'We shan't be long.'

Olivia's blue eyes were mutinous. Vicky had a brainwave. 'Have your lunch, and then go back to the beautician and have a manicure. On me.'

Olivia's eyes gleamed. 'Nail polish? Red polish? And on my toes?'

'Yes,' said Vicky recklessly. 'Whatever you like, and then come back here and wait for us.'

'I'll do that,' said Olivia, spreading out her hands with their neat but plain fingernails. 'Mummy never lets me wear polish. She says it's tarty on a girl my age.'

Julius took Vicky's arm and led her out of the inn before she could change her mind. 'What the hell do a few red nails matter; no one she knows is going to see her.'

Vicky reflected on this. 'True.'

'And you aren't actually responsible for her.'

'I feel responsible. Where are we going? I assume there is a reason for abandoning Olivia and it's not just that you can't bear another sight of her table manners?'

'There is that, but no. We're going to talk to an old friend of Philippe d'Icère's.'

They found Marcel Vosges without difficulty. He was sitting at a corner table of the restaurant alone, a whippet of a man, who chewed his food quickly and thoroughly as he listened to what Julius had to say. Vicky, whose French had improved dramatically during her time in France, found his bursts of rapid speech hard to follow, but Julius was managing.

Marcel took a gulp of wine, wiped his mouth and shook his head. 'We spent a lot of time together as lads, Philippe and I. It's sad to think he's gone. Like so many others. One is grateful, Monsieur Drummond, simply to be alive.'

'You're sure he's dead?'

'Oh, yes. His uncle wouldn't have his feet tucked in under the ancestral table if he wasn't sure that Philippe was dead. And I reckon if he'd survived he'd have been back to see his old friends. Mind you, I can't tell you exactly when he died, or how, or even where he's buried.'

'Don't you find that strange?'

Marcel paused, then forked some salad into his mouth. 'In wartime, so much is strange. It began with a rumour, people talk, you know. Then, it would be in the summer of nineteen forty-three, Bertrand d'Icère put up that plaque in the church. I haven't seen it, I never set foot in the place, but my wife goes, and she told me about it. That settled it. You wouldn't catch Philippe's uncle spending money on an engraver if he weren't certain that Philippe wasn't going to come along after the war.'

'Yet I've heard of a man in the Resistance, called Philippe d'Icère, a brave man, a hero you might say. That was later than nineteen forty-three.'

Marcel was unimpressed. 'Another man of the same name, some distant relation, these grand families have tentacles like so many squids. I heard that a Philippe d'Icère had been a collaborator, turned his friends over to the Gestapo. Some people think that was Philippe from here. It wasn't. Take it from me. I knew Philippe from when he still wet his bed at night. He wouldn't betray his friends.'

'Do you suppose the police might have any information about him? Records from the war?

'In the war, if a man was said to be dead, you take it from me, you didn't expect to see him again. Bertrand had the correct papers, I suppose, or all the legal business wouldn't have happened so smoothly and quickly.'

'So the police wouldn't have been involved?'

Marcel laughed. 'The police! Have you seen the police in St Aphrodise? One old officer who's on the verge of retirement and will do anything for a quiet life, and a gendarme who's wet behind the ears. There's no point in telling them anything, and if you were stupid enough to go to headquarters in Carcassonne, they'd send you off pretty smartly with a flea in your ear. 'Have you made this enquiry at your local gendarmerie? No? Then there is nothing we can do, the correct procedures must be followed.' They're as bad as those bloody Nazis, they were great ones for correct procedures. When it suited them, that was.'

Vicky touched Julius's hand. 'What's the French for mole?'

'Mole?' said Julius, his mind running on little furry creatures.

'On your skin. You know. Ask him if Philippe had a mole anywhere on his body. A big one, in a place where you wouldn't ordinarily see it.'

Julius raised his eyebrows, but asked the question. Marcel gave a knowing laugh. 'Mademoiselle must have been very friendly indeed with Philippe if she'd seen that mole. Certainly he had a mole, in a very private place.'

Vicky persisted. 'At the top of his leg? Almost in his groin?'

'Yes, Mademoiselle, he did,' Marcel said. He waited to see if any more details might be asked for, then accepted a cognac from Julius, recommended the *poulet à la creme* to them and went back to his garage.

'Marcel's Philippe must have been the man you knew in England,' said Julius.

'Has to be,' agreed Vicky.

'It doesn't sound too good.'

'It sounds thoroughly fishy, although it's a relief to know for sure that the Philippe everyone knew here was my Philippe. One can't help wondering a little, when the circumstances surrounding his death are so confused. I know it was in the war, and everything's different in wartime, but there's still a mystery to be cleared up. After all, Bertrand certainly lied about the date of his death. Why?'

'You're sure about Bertrand lying, are you? Could you prove that whenever Philippe died, it wasn't when Bertrand claims?'

'Can I provide evidence to satisfy a lawyer, you mean? Documentary evidence that Philippe was alive in the January of nineteen forty-three? Yes, if necessary. Shall we eat here? If that's the *poulet* I can smell, I'll have some.'

Julius looked round and spotted the waiter, who was leaning up against the counter in front of the door to the kitchen smoking a noxious cigarette. He beckoned to him, had a brief conversation about the menu and ordered lunch for them both. The waiter went back to the counter, picked up his cigarette, which was still alight, called the order through to the kitchen, and set about opening a bottle of wine.

Vicky sipped her cold white wine and fingered the slice of bread she had taken from the basket.

'Do stop torturing that bread,' said Julius, who was watching her intently. 'Here comes the food.' He sat back as Marcel's cousin Sophie, the buxom teenage daughter of the proprietors, put their plates in front of them. She wished them *bon appétit* and vanished back into the kitchen. 'Never mind another Philippe, I'm almost ready to believe we've strayed into a parallel universe, and there's another Victoria Hampden who met another Philippe d'Icère.'

'I assure you, I'm the only one.'

'Apart from your grandmother in Highgate cemetery, of course.'

Vicky laughed. 'How do you know about her?'

'Never mind. I refuse to add the ghost of your no doubt respectable grandmother to this muddle.'

'No, we can do without any more ghosts.'

'Which brings me back to what's haunting you, Vicky. You were married to Philippe, weren't you?'

Vicky put down her glass and stared at him. 'Why do you think that?'

'Oh, come on. Loyalty and lasting attachments are all very well, but you've gone to a lot of trouble over a man if there was no more to it than a passionate but brief love affair six years ago. I understand sentiment, and undying love and so forth, but however romantic and devoted you were, you wouldn't be doing this if Philippe weren't your husband. Nor would he have sent you the butterfly; such a beautiful heirloom, for an heirloom is what it is, is a gift made to a wife, not a mistress. You're considering marrying again, isn't that so? And therefore you have to be absolutely sure you are a widow, and free to marry.'

'It would hardly be fair on Duggie not to make sure,' said Vicky. She didn't look at Julius.

'Ah, yes, Duggie. We haven't talked much about Duggie, have we?'

'There's no need.'

'In due course you'll have to. I'm your lawyer, remember.' His voice was mocking. 'Remember Olivia's advice; don't keep secrets from your lawyer. It's always a mistake.'

Chapter Ten

Olivia flew to meet them. 'There's a ferocious Frenchman waiting to see you. He says his name's d'Icère.

Vicky's heart lifted.

'Not your young man, Aunt Vicky,' said Olivia blithely. 'This one's much too old, and honestly, you wouldn't want him as a lover. No one would.'

'Olivia!' said Vicky, and then bit her tongue, she sounded just like her own mother.

'Bertrand d'Icère, I expect,' said Julius.

Vicky hung back. 'He's not going to want to see me.'

'I don't care what he wants.' Julius went into the inn. After a moment's hesitation, Vicky followed, hissing at Olivia to wait outside or go and sit in the garden. Olivia protested.

'Please, Olivia. You know how stuffy people of that generation can be.'

Olivia took this as an apology and agreed to wait in the garden, with the proviso that Vicky was to tell her all about it when the French guy had taken himself off.

Fingers crossed behind her back, Vicky agreed.

Inside, a tall man with a sallow complexion and dark hair streaked with grey was eyeing Julius without enthusiasm.

He came over to Vicky, took her hand, and bowed over it, his lips kissing the air an inch above her flesh. Cold, almost black eyes looked her up and down. He spoke in a slightly gravelly voice, very slowly. 'Mademoiselle Hampden? I am enchanted to meet you.'

Liar, thought Vicky, managing a smile.

'I welcome you to St Aphrodise as a one-time friend of my unfortunate nephew, Philippe.'

'Thank you,' said Vicky, after a long pause realising that some response was expected from her. Vicky's face was curiously blank. Bertrand didn't seem to notice it, or he took it for her normal expression. Vicky wasn't concerned with what Bertrand was thinking. She was listening to a familiar voice ringing in her ears. Surely this time, if she turned round very slowly, she would see him standing there, eyes dancing with impatience.

'No, Vicky, don't waste time on that. Listen. Listen to me. Don't trust Bertrand, don't believe what he says. Don't take his denials at face value. He's a tricky man.'

Bertrand was talking, smoothly and with authority. 'It seems that you have been misled about the date of my nephew's death, indeed about the very fact of his death. However, I can assure you that my nephew, if he was indeed the man you met, is, sadly, dead. He died in January nineteen forty-three. I received information to this effect from the authorities. The necessary paperwork was forthcoming, and I'm afraid any efforts on your part to challenge this will meet with disappointment.'

'Oh, I don't want to challenge anything,' said Vicky. 'I came to France because I wanted to find out exactly what did happen to him. How did he die, for instance?'

'He died in an incident. Involving the Germans. A very common occurrence, sad to say. Many headstrong young men lost their lives in this way.'

'I knew him in England. Do you know why he came back to France?'

'He was always a hothead and a risk-taker. He felt he could serve his country by returning in some secrecy to take up the threads of his old life and to work with the Resistance which was becoming stronger in the area. But he was an amateur, and he ran into an ambush. He never had a chance.'

'He was shot just like that?'

'It was normal.'

Vicky pressed him. 'No time to talk? To plead for mercy?'

'If they were under threat, the Germans shot first and asked questions afterwards.'

'How did you hear about it? Did it happen locally, this incident?'

Bertrand looked at Julius. 'And you are?'

'Julius Drummond. Miss Hampden's lawyer.'

'I heard she had an Englishman with her. Naturally, you have no rights in France. And our law is different from yours, we have the Code Napoléon. Your knowledge of law will be of no use here.'

'I appreciate that English law is not the same as French law. I am looking after Miss Hampden's interests with regard to an inheritance from her aunt, who lived in this country.'

Vicky noticed the flicker of relief in Bertrand's eyes.

'You were telling us about the incident, Monsieur d'Icère.'

'Ah, yes. It happened a few kilometres from here. A man brought me the news. The sad news.'

'His body?' asked Vicky.

Bertrand looked pained, as though it was unseemly for a young woman to mention bodies.

'The German authorities removed his remains. They will have buried him in Carcassonne.'

'Do you have the details? Exactly where?'

'My dear Mademoiselle, the Germans were not in the habit of telling us where they had disposed of those they had shot. You in England have no idea of what life under Occupation was like. We suffered while you dined and danced and made merry in London. Having betrayed us in nineteen forty, you were not interested in our sufferings in the long years of the rest of the war.'

Vicky opened her mouth to make a vigorous rebuttal, caught Julius's eye, and shut it, contenting herself with a contemptuous twist of her lip.

Bertrand took this for a smile. 'You may be light-hearted about it, but for us, for France, it lies heavy on our hearts.'

'Naturally,' said Julius. 'Weren't the formalities a problem? No body, nothing to prove that Philippe was dead except a stranger's word?'

'The man who brought the news wasn't a stranger. Everything

was arranged. It was all different in the war.' Bertrand was looking at Julius now with real dislike. 'You wouldn't understand.'

'No, I dare say I wouldn't.'

Bertrand gave Vicky a foxy smile. 'And now, I come to the real purpose of my visit. I gather that you have in your possession an item that you claim Philippe gave to you. A butterfly, very large, very beautiful? Also very old and very valuable. It is an heirloom of our house, and I assume that part of the reason for your visit to St Aphrodise is to restore this to his family. You have it with you?'

Julius stepped in. 'Miss Drummond has in her possession a butterfly ornament given to her by Philippe d'Icère. She is under no obligation to return such a gift.'

'I think differently. If it were a trinket, a mere token from a lover, then we would all wish that Mademoiselle could keep it to remind her of a past amour. One sympathises.'

One patronises, thought Vicky. She smarted at the contempt in his voice, the casual offence of his words.

'Mademoiselle?' His voice was sharper now.

'No. What Philippe gave me, he meant me to keep.'

'To keep such a valuable object exposes you to suspicion. If it were not given as you say, it could be considered theft.'

Vicky drew herself up, cast Bertrand a withering look and stalked out.

'That's your answer,' said Julius. 'My advice is that you don't pursue the butterfly. It could cause you more trouble than it's worth.'

'I think, Mr Drummond, that you have little idea of the value of this piece.'

'I know that the entire d'Icère collection is of great value. All yours now, I suppose. I should be content with that, Monsieur d'Icère.'

'He left in a hurry,' said Olivia, as Bertrand's car roared away down the street. 'Temper, I'd say.'

'Where's Vicky?'

'Stamping about upstairs. More temper. I thought the years

brought self-control, but I see this isn't so. Do you like my nails?' She flourished ten vivid nails.

'Bright.'

'Sexy, I think. What do we do this afternoon?'

Julius wondered if he could suggest she might like to sit in the garden with a book, then decided against it. 'We're going to Toulouse.'

'Are we? Good. Is it far?'

'Not very.'

'Is your car ready?'

'I shouldn't think so, but I'm sure we can rent one.' He hailed the innkeeper, who had just come in, full of curiosity about Bertrand d'Icère's rapid departure. Julius cut short the crablike enquiries about their interview with Bertrand and demanded to know what kind of a car might be available for hire in St Aphrodise.

Monsieur Ribérac pursed his lips. 'It is difficult now, after the war, there are not so many cars, and always trouble with spare parts, it is hard to keep a car on the road. And the cost of petrol, it is a scandal. Maybe . . . You could ask Marcel at the garage. Did you make his acquaintance? He has a car that he rents out when he doesn't need it. And, while you are there, you can make further enquiries about your own motor.'

'We met Marcel today.'

The innkeeper's eyes shone with inquisitive delight. 'And he told you about Philippe d'Icère? As I said, they were very good friends.'

Clearly the townspeople's tongues had been wagging. 'We went to his cousin's restaurant for lunch.'

'Excellent, excellent. If you had asked my advice, that is the very place I would have recommended. I hope M'sieur didn't have the fish? I would not advise the fish.'

'Where is the garage?' Julius wrenched the conversation away from kitchen rivalries.

'Beyond the restaurant, there is a road to the left. You will see his workshop, there is a big Michelin sign, you can't miss it.'

★　　★　　★

149

Vicky raised no objections to a visit to Toulouse, merely nodding when Julius said he needed to visit a library. 'I think we ought to be out and about, just in case any plug uglies hired by my father turn up.'

Julius blanched. 'I do hope you're joking.'

'Nobody jokes about my grandfather,' said Olivia, cramming her hat on her head. '*On y va*, only where?'

'It's a *Deux Chevaux*,' Vicky said, as Olivia took one look at the car and burst out laughing.

'Not what you are used to, Monsieur Drummond,' said Marcel with a foxy grin. 'But reliable, and very economical on fuel.'

Julius regarded it doubtfully. He couldn't see himself driving it, and he certainly couldn't see that Olivia would fit in the back.

Marcel was rhapsodising on the glories of the car's two-stroke engine. Julius walked round the car, his right hand supporting his other elbow, his left hand fingers tapping his mouth. He nudged the running board with a polished brown shoe. 'I suppose we could catch a train.'

'Trains are infrequent,' Marcel assured him. 'And besides, stations are never in the centre. There's always a long walk. People could get heatstroke on such a walk in this sun.'

'No,' said Julius. 'I'm afraid it won't do. Is there another establishment where we can rent a car?'

Marcel wasn't letting business walk out of his garage just like that. 'Over the road is a bar. You and the young ladies go and have a beer, a coffee, a soft drink. Very pleasant, very peaceful, I assure you. My aunt owns the bar. Then, in ten, perhaps fifteen minutes, I will return with another car. A more suitable car. He looked sorrowful. 'Naturally, it will also be a more expensive car.'

'Never mind. Just get it.'

Marcel had come to an arrangement with a rival establishment, and with great pride, he drove a black Peugeot out of the garage. 'M'sieur could drive to Africa in this,' he cried. 'The comfort! The style! Much more suitable for M'sieur and the ladies!'

'Not a lot of leg room in the back,' commented Olivia as she clambered in. 'Vicky, since my legs are longer than yours, don't you think I should sit in front?'

'No,' said Vicky. As the youngest she had had years of being crammed into the back of saloons and the bucket seat of sports cars. There was no way she was now going to give up a privilege of age, no matter how cramped Olivia was. Suffering was good for the young, her family had always said.

Julius tossed a map into the back. 'Can you read a map?'

'I can,' said Olivia, unfolding it with care. 'Whether what I read and what's happening out there on the road is the same, I'm not so sure about.'

'Concentrate,' said Julius, letting in the clutch, and tooting a brisk fanfare on his horn as he turned into the street.

'What exactly do you want to look up in the library in Toulouse?' asked Vicky. 'You're being very mysterious.'

'Not at all. There are merely a few legal points I want to clarify.'

'I hope that means you've thought of something to trip up that odious Bertrand. There was no love lost between him and Philippe, you know. I remember Philippe talking about him.' She laughed. 'He called him the Moscow man, said he was very left wing. I can't believe it, hardly very communistic to be as grabby as he is.'

'Are there good shops in Toulouse?' asked Olivia.

'Bound to be,' said Julius.

'And, if we're lucky, freedom from any watching eyes,' said Vicky. 'Not to mention sudden loss of a wheel.'

Julius looked at her. 'You feel a need to be wary?'

'Impossible not to. You didn't tell old Ribérac where we were going, did you?'

'Indeed I did. I said we were going to be tourists in Béziers. That ought to throw any interested parties off the track.'

'You're dotty,' said Olivia with good-humoured scorn. 'I'm not serious about Grandpa coming after us with a parcel of thugs.'

Julius and Vicky exchanged glances.

'Better safe than sorry,' said Vicky. 'After all, Bertrand might have called out his henchmen.' She wound up the car window. Although the sky was still a clear blue, a wind had blown up that carried more than a hint of ice.

'From the Pyrenees,' the innkeeper had told them. 'It blows for two, three days, everybody shivers a little, and then back comes summer.'

Julius had winced when Olivia had gone thundering upstairs to fetch her school raincoat over her arm. 'She'll stick out like a sore thumb in that.'

'Why shouldn't I stick out? I don't care.'

'We don't want to attract attention, that's all.'

'Oh, you're on about stupid old private eyes coming to get us,' said Olivia scornfully. She had refused to leave the mac behind, and now she sat with it dragged over her like a blanket.

'How can it be so hot one minute and so cold the next?' she complained. 'Perhaps if Julius shut his window, we could get the car a bit warm.'

Julius sighed and rolled up his window. He hated driving with the windows up, in fact he hated driving in closed cars. He put up with all kinds of weather driving in his Lagonda, judging it a fair price to pay for the freedom of an open car. Now he put his foot down on the accelerator, forcing the Peugeot into a speed beyond its comfortable range.

The engine emitted rattles and strange noises.

'Julius, don't go so fast,' said Vicky. 'This isn't a racing car.'

He slowed down. 'The faster I go, the less time I have to spend cooped up in a metal can.'

'That's all very well, but the engine sounds as though it's about to blow up. We don't want another accident.'

'Endangering our lives, just because of your fads,' said Olivia. 'If you want to know, I think the car you drove me to school in is a terrific show off. And you drive it much too fast. I noticed that at the time. I think it's good for you to appreciate what the rest of the world has to put up with.'

Sitting in the back, she felt out of reach of retribution, and so added a few more of her thoughts on the matter. 'Melanie, she's the one I told you about, who knows psychology, says that men who drive open, sporty cars, especially if they speed, are escaping

152

symbolically from aspects of their lives where they feel hemmed in. It'll be sex, mostly, it always is when it comes to the unconscious.'

Before Julius could gather his wits and breath to utter a withering retort, Vicky had rounded on Olivia. 'It's naive in the extreme to make remarks like that, apart from being incredibly rude. I wouldn't blame Julius if he stopped and tipped you out on to the verge. You should be grateful to him for not hounding you back to England. Do try not to be unpleasant.'

Olivia looked out of the window, her face defiant. 'I hate being grateful,' she muttered unrepentantly.

Julius, slowing down even more as the road narrowed and a van coming the other way threatened to push him off the road, had time to regain his sang froid. 'Sticks and stones,' he said. 'Leave the girl alone. She's at a difficult age.'

Olivia didn't say another word. When they reached Toulouse and found a parking place in a shady street, she got out and walked defiantly past Julius, nose in the air.

'Which will teach me such a lesson,' Julius murmured to Vicky, as they followed the outraged Olivia across a wide square. 'You go and speak soothing words to the absurd child. I'll buy a map and find out where the main library is.'

He caught up with them a few minutes later, map in hand, and Olivia, although still haughty, seemed mollified. A proposal that they should buy ices brought a definite gleam to her eyes.

They chose a table inside the café, since the sharp wind was still blowing and made it too chilly to consider sitting outside. Julius showed Vicky where the library was on the map. 'Not far from here, luckily. We'll meet in an hour and a half. Here if you like, it isn't far to the library.'

The library was quiet, almost deserted. An aged scholar with dry precise features and half-glasses sat at the big central table, barricaded in by large leather-bound tomes. A middle-aged woman in a dark dress with a white collar was half way up a stepladder, rearranging books on one of the higher shelves. The librarian sat behind a large desk, pen in hand, consulting some papers. He looked like a lizard, with hooded eyes and a reptilian stillness about him.

Hardly a hive of industry, thought Julius, as he approached the librarian's desk. His name was inscribed on a wooden bar at the front of the desk, Dr F. Duhamel. He didn't look up, and Julius gave a cough.

A precise finger marked a word on the paper before him, and the librarian took his eyes from his work to look at Julius. 'M'sieur?' he asked in a weary voice.

Julius explained what he was looking for. A dry sigh greeted his request. The librarian pushed back his chair, lined it up with the desk with mathematical precision and walked in quick, shorts steps over to the ladder. He spoke rapidly and inaudibly to the woman, who began her descent, one hand holding her skirt to preserve her modesty. She reached the floor, nodded to the librarian, and then walked briskly towards a counter by the door, her brown, laced shoes squeaking on the parquet floor. She pulled out a big ledger and placed it on the counter, before opening it with both hands.

She made little clicking noises with her tongue as she ran her finger down a list of numbers and names. 'Please take a seat, and I will bring what is available to your table.'

A fly droned against the window. It was hot in here, with the sun beating down on the glass panels in the dome. Julius could hear the wind buffeting about the dome, and making the windows rattle, but there were no cooling breezes in the library. A man seated at the central table gave a series of dry sniffs, and then two explosive sneezes. They cannonaded round the library, but he was unconcerned, merely pulling out a very large purple handkerchief and dabbing at his nose.

Julius stretched his legs out and waited. The woman wasn't hurrying. She placed one volume on the counter beside the ledger and then went in search of another. Clearly she didn't intend to hand them over piecemeal. Julius began to feel bored. He ran his eye over the books on the shelf nearest to him. Statutes and regulations for each year of the last century. Not what he felt like dipping into. This was beginning to remind him of the hours he had spent in the law library at university, forcing himself to work, fighting a daily renewed battle against a rising sense of tedium.

He had stuck it out, got his degree, spent an agreeable year in France, endured more hours of torment at law college, and had qualified. Thus entitling him to spend more hours lost in wordy phrases and large, dull tomes. When had he last had a case that interested him? He didn't even get cases, he told himself. Only careful, painstaking trust work, drawing up and executing wills, arranging for the conveyancing of this and that property.

All low-key affairs. When the juicy numbers came up, for even the best families squabbled over wills and land, his uncle or one of his cousins took charge. He supposed they regarded such matters as dangerously exciting for a young solicitor. He wondered when he would stop being young Mr Julius. Presumably when all the older men had retired and he was sitting at his desk wound about with cobwebs, white-haired and thinking of nothing but his club.

Some daring firms were employing women. Not only as clerks, that had been inevitable for many firms during the war, but actual solicitors. But those were the modern practices, firms that dealt with divorce and libel suits, who had actors and film stars among their clients. Worldly firms, who thought nothing of centuries of respectable tradition.

He could move, he supposed. There were openings in more go-ahead establishments, and he had friends working at such firms, and by all appearances flourishing, despite the shaken heads and pursed lips of their elders. But it would distress his uncle beyond measure, and he would feel disloyal. No, there was no way out within his profession that he could see.

Way out! Look at him, doing it again, brooding about his London life in this ridiculous fashion. What had that wretched Olivia said? Hemmed in? Damn the girl and her phony psychology.

The woman was standing beside him, holding a pile of books and with her eyes fixed on his red socks. 'M'sieur,' she said coldly, laying the books down on the table and marching off before he could say thank you. Didn't care for my socks, he thought with amusement. And then, Lord help him if Olivia started analysing his reasons for wearing red socks.

He pushed such frivolous thoughts aside and swung the books round so that he could look at their titles. He moved his chair into a more comfortable position. It made a vile squeal on the floor, earning him a beady lizard look from the librarian. He selected a volume, pulled out a notebook and settled down.

He had to concentrate. It was slow work, reading the precise, formal French, finding his way through unfamiliar territory. He became so absorbed that when a voice spoke behind him, he didn't pay any heed.

The voice spoke again, a little more loudly. 'I beg your pardon.'

Julius looked up, frowning, a finger marking his place in the text. Why would anybody here be speaking to him in English? He swung round. There stood the Dutchman, Cornelius van der Meulen.

'I think we may be able to be of assistance to one another,' the Dutchman said.

Olivia had cheerfully borrowed as much money from Vicky as she could, and had bought herself a new-look summer skirt and a blouse to go with it, designed to be tied in a knot at the waist. Rope-soled shoes completed her ensemble, which she insisted on wearing at once; looking very glamorous and about ten years older than her age, she waltzed out into the street entirely pleased with herself.

'I hope that's it,' said Vicky. She knew that Vera would be horrified by Olivia's sophisticated appearance if she could see it, but she couldn't, and Olivia's eventual and inevitable return to England and her family was too remote a prospect to bother about.

'You haven't bought a single thing,' said Olivia reprovingly.

Normally, Vicky loved clothes, and especially so when she had money to spend as she now did, thanks to her late aunt. But today her mind was elsewhere, and she hadn't felt tempted to buy anything.

'Not one pretty thing, to wear when you have dinner with Julius?'

'With *Julius*? Why should I make any effort for Julius?'

'I don't see why not. There you are, thrown into each other's company, it's very romantic. And anyhow, when Grandpa finds out where you are, and that you've been with Julius all this time, and staying in the same hotel, he'll go bananas and Duggie will challenge

Julius to a duel. A fight to the death!' She made a dramatic flourish with an imaginary sword.

'Olivia, you do say the stupidest things. And how Victorian you are. There's nothing improper about Julius and me working together to find Philippe. And even if I was doing something quite scandalous and wicked, which I'm not, I'm twenty-five, and neither Duggie nor my father have any authority over me.'

'Grandpa,' said Olivia with great earnestness, 'has authority over everyone.'

'Not me. Not any more. I go where I choose, live where I choose, and spend my time with whomever I please.'

'No need to snap my head off.'

'You make me very angry, Olivia, saying things like that. Thinking them, even. Concentrate on your own life, which is, I would point out, full of problems.'

'You're frightfully touchy. Okay, I won't mention it again. Only you *would* be wise to think about how Grandpa's going to react to your escapade here. And Duggie. He has an evil temper, Duggie has. You may not have noticed, wrapped up in dreams of nuptial happiness.'

'What do you mean?'

'I once saw Duggie kick a cat. I mean, he may be a dog person, well, bound to be, he's that sort, but even so. A man who'd harm a defenceless animal might do anything. I just thought I'd mention it. Forewarned is forearmed, after all.'

'Thank you,' said Vicky.

'Mind you, it's probably no good you getting keen on Julius,' she went on irrepressibly. 'Not with his complicated love life. And there's no need to look at me in that way, for it's hardly a secret. Everyone knows about it.'

'Such as who?'

'Well, Annabel Patmore, whose stepmother used to be Julius's mistress, told me . . .'

Vicky, dying of curiosity, but determined to win this battle, forced herself to keep cool. 'Who is Annabel Patmore?' she interrupted 'No, don't tell me, a friend at school.'

'She is. Do you know her?'

'I don't. I must say, we didn't have such strange girls as you seem to know when I was at school.'

'That was because you aren't the post-war generation. We're different, I keep on telling you. We have a totally modern approach to life.'

'I hope this Annabel is making more of a go of her school career than you are, that's all,' said Vicky blightingly. 'And no more gossip about Julius, please, it all smacks of the more vulgar newspapers.'

'You sound just like my mother. Stuffy!'

'Too bad. It's called being grown-up, which you aren't. Now, it's getting late, is there anything else you want to do or buy?'

Olivia was easily distracted. Her face lit up. 'I long for a smart handbag, and look, they have them over there, lovely ones in the window. On sale, it says; that means cheap. I've got some money left, do let's go and see.'

They weren't far from the café, and it was nearly five o'clock. 'They'll be closing,' warned Vicky, who didn't want to be dragged round yet another shop. 'I'll go on. You do your shopping, then come and join me at the café, it's just round the corner at the end of this street.'

Olivia plunged across the street, narrowly avoiding a collision with a man on a bicycle, who shook a fist at her, and vanished into the shop of her choice. Vicky, feeling unwarrantably old, walked quickly on to the café, trying not to wonder about the identity of Annabel Patmore's stepmother, and rather hoping that Julius might have finished before the library closing time and be there already. She heard the roar of a car engine behind her, and ducked into a shop doorway. She was just in time, as the powerful motor, going much too fast, shot past, two wheels on the pavement. It reached the end of the street and took the corner with a squeal of tyres.

If this were a film, she thought, that would have been a deliberate attempt to run me down. But no, it was nothing more than careless French driving.

Julius wasn't yet at the café. Disappointed, but resigned, she ordered a *thé* and sipped the weak brew slowly as she watched the citizens of Toulouse passing to and fro. Women with children, teenagers in baseball boots, older women with loaves of bread stopping to gossip with friends, businessmen hurrying home, brief-cases in hand. Dogs were being exercised, a group of boys were teaching one of their number to ride a bike, with many shrieks and much shouted advice.

Vicky had found a table outside in a sheltered spot that was in the sun and out of the wind. It gave her a better view of approaching pedestrians, without her appearing anxious as she would inside, obviously watching everyone who came through the swing doors.

She looked at her watch, slightly puzzled. Twenty past five. No reason to expect Julius yet, he was clearly staying at the library for as long as he could. But where was Olivia? She'd better go and see. Leaving the bag with Olivia's cast-off clothes on one of the chairs at her table, she promised the waiter she would return shortly and set off back towards the shop where she had left Olivia.

The shop was closed, as were all the others around it, and the street was quiet and empty of people. Certainly empty of Olivia, who was hard to miss. Drat the girl, where was she? What a time to pick to go off, doubtless she hadn't found what she wanted in that shop, and had gone back to one she'd spotted earlier. She must have realised that all the shops would have closed by now.

A little further down the street, something caught her eye. She walked over to the object lying on the pavement. It was a leather purse. Brown leather, quite worn.

It was Olivia's purse.

There was Julius at last, oh, thank God. She ran towards him, holding out the purse, incoherent in her explanations.

'Vicky, calm down. Yes, I believe you, it's Olivia's purse, but she's simply dropped it, in fact, she's probably gone off to look for it, not knowing where she last had it.'

Vicky shook her head. Julius was talking sense, it was a reasonable assumption, but she knew it wasn't so. She controlled her panic, spoke carefully. 'She should have come straight on to the café. If she found she hadn't got her purse, I'm sure she would have come and told me, asked me to help look for it. Julius, it's twenty to six. It's nearly an hour she's been gone. She's only fifteen, after all, and in a strange city . . . Anything might have happened to her.'

Van der Meulen, who had been listening to all this with alert attention, spoke for the first time. 'I think your young friend may simply be lost. The streets in the centre of Toulouse all look very alike, these small ones around here especially.'

Julius saw the distress in Vicky's face, and her fear.

'We'll go and find her,' he said. 'Which way?'

They retraced Vicky's steps and knocked on the window and door of the closed-up shop. A peeved looking woman opened the door a crack to explain that they were shut, would be open at eight-thirty the next morning.

Julius put his foot in the door, and asked about Olivia.

Yes, yes, she had had such a young lady in the shop, shortly before closing. A tall English girl. She had bought a handbag, very chic, very good value. Had she her purse with her? Of course, she took the money to pay out of her purse, yes, it was a purse just such as M'sieur was holding.

Her curiosity was aroused by this, and she opened the door a fraction wider. 'You have lost her?' Truly, that was a matter for concern. Only fifteen? *Zut*, she would not have believed her to be so young, but what was a well-brought up girl of that age doing out by herself? She agreed with the blond man, Mademoiselle had undoubt-edly taken a wrong turning, very easy to do in a city such as Toulouse. It had been some minutes after five that the young lady had left the shop. She hoped that they would very quickly be reunited with her, she was sure that they would be.

An hour later, this optimism was proving unfounded. They had returned to the café, where she was most likely to turn up, and left a message with the staff for her to stay there until they came. Julius suggested that Vicky could wait at the café while he and the Dutchman searched. Vicky was vehement in her refusal, how could she stay and fret, while she could be looking for Olivia? And whose niece was she, anyway?

They traced all the streets that Olivia might have gone down, and drew a blank. They stopped people in the street and asked if they had seen Olivia. The result was shrugs and sympathetic shakes of the head.

Olivia had vanished.

'Right,' said Julius, after they had checked back at the café yet again: no Olivia. 'It's the police station next.'

Vicky didn't argue, although she felt that the police would be no use at all. She had a growing conviction that Olivia wasn't lost, that she had been forcibly removed from the street. She saw her grand-father's hand in this, and felt that the police would be able to do nothing, that even now, Olivia would be in some hired heavy's car, probably with a woman private detective in attendance, her grand-father was nice in such matters, heading for the coast and a port and a boat back to England.

Only, she remembered suddenly, they couldn't do that. She had Olivia's passport in her room at the inn. Olivia had given it to her for safekeeping.

Julius, when she put forward her theory about her father's likely involvement in an abduction of Olivia, gave it as his opinion that the lack of a passport wouldn't be a problem. All it needed was for one of the people involved to have a passport with his or her family included, Vicky would know how cursory was the inspection of passports at the French end, and by the time they got to England it wouldn't matter. 'Your father will have had her made a Ward of Court by now.'

Vicky laughed; she was close to hysteria by now.

Mr van der Meulen was doubtful. 'What you say may be right, but has this young lady no spirit? Would she not fight her abductors, cause a rumpus, attract attention? At the port, if not before?'

'I dare say they'll have given her a Mickey Finn,' said Julius.

Vicky winced. Would her father go that far? She didn't know. The further she got from her father, the more she wondered at his nature and his approach to life's problems, the more she feared that his actions and reactions went beyond those of an irascible eccentric with a partiality for lashing his daughters.

The waiter at the café, who with the rest of the staff was taking a keen interest in the missing English girl, gave them directions to the police station. 'It is not far. No, quicker to walk there, than to fetch your car.'

They walked quickly, Vicky breaking into a run from time to time in order to keep up.

'That's it,' said Julius, pointing across the road to an impressive building. Guards were on duty at the gate and the French flag flew from a large flagpole in the centre of the courtyard. A black Citroën was drawn up by the entrance, and smartly dressed gendarmes in their kepis came and went.

After a brief tussle at the gate, the gendarme on duty reluctantly allowed them to enter, and pointed the way to enquiries. 'Where we'll have to wait for hours,' said Vicky.

'I think not,' said the Dutchman.

'No, we won't,' said Julius. 'This has the makings of an international incident; I think you'll find we get seen by someone very senior very quickly.'

'An Englishman prepared to make a fuss,' said Cornelius van der Meulen. 'And abroad, too. I think this is most remarkable!'

The police were polite but completely uninterested in Julius's tale of a lost tourist. People were always losing themselves in Toulouse, especially the English. They should be less mean with their money and provide themselves with city maps such as were on sale at every kiosk. Julius and his friends should go back to the café to await the fourth member of their party, who would doubtless be impatiently waiting for them.

The missing person was only fifteen? A shrug, a curl of the lip, what did M'sieur expect if he let a girl of this age wander about a strange city on her own?

Julius moved in for the kill. This wasn't any fifteen-year-old. This was the grand-daughter of one of the most important men in England, a top judge, no less, at whose command the whole of Scotland Yard would leap into action. Did the officer really want to be the one who had washed his hands of the affair? Did he not have the wit to imagine the headlines in the world's press, the straining of the *entente cordiale*, the likely reaction of the hordes of American tourists with all those wonderful dollars, if an innocent young girl came to any harm in broad daylight in a French city?

And how would such a case affect tourism to France? If an English teenager could vanish without the police being in the least concerned with her recovery, then how safe would Mr and Mrs John Doe from Boston feel about that planned trip to France, Europe?

The officer's face went pale. Two colleagues who had been passing through and had heard most of this spirited attack, were shaking their heads and looking very alarmed. The police officer behind the desk whacked his hand down on a bell, doors opened, more men appeared, orders were shouted in loud, rapid French.

'That's stirred them up a bit,' said Julius with satisfaction.

'Oh, never mind scoring points,' said Vicky. 'Will it work? Will they find Olivia?'

A gendarme materialised at Julius's shoulder. 'What?' he said. 'See Monsieur l'Inspecteur? Indeed I will.'

As Julius followed the gendarme out into the passage, the Dutchman took Olivia's arm. 'I think that after Mr Drummond's masterly résumé of the situation, they will do everything possible to recover your niece. They now feel that not only their jobs and the international reputation of the French police are at stake, but also the honour of France.'

'I'm glad to hear it,' said Vicky.

Chapter Eleven

The car had drawn up beside Olivia as she walked away from the bag shop.

The driver leant out of the window and called to attract her attention. He had dark hair, was wearing a suit and tie; he looked just like any other businessman on his way to somewhere in Toulouse. Except, perhaps for the opaque sunglasses. He held an open map in his hand, and as she went towards him to say that she was a stranger in the city, and could be of no assistance, a man and a woman leapt out of the back and pounced.

In the ensuing scuffle, Olivia, kicking out and struggling furiously, dropped her purse. She was about to exclaim about this, when it occurred to her frantic mind that it was better to leave it, pray to God Vicky would recognise it, know that something had happened to her.

By the time she had thought this out, she found herself, despite her protests, wedged in the back seat of a car, with a scarf covering her mouth. The car, which had threaded a rapid and sure path through the warren of streets in the centre, now came to a wider road, a boulevard, Olivia noticed, with pollarded trees down either side.

The gag was getting damp where it had been pulled into her mouth, and she felt sick. She might be sick, and then she would choke in her own vomit, and what then? No, she wasn't going to be sick. She wasn't going to show a hint of weakness, she was going to show them, and her grandfather, just how far from a pushover she was.

The driver kept his eyes on the road and his foot on the

accelerator. The man and woman in the back didn't say a word, but their grip on Olivia never slackened.

If they're planning to drive me like this all the way to Calais or wherever, they can plan again, thought Olivia. The words of the gym instructor, the sergeant who had taught them self-defence at school, came back to her. *Keep calm, think, watch. Wait for your opportunity, it will come.*

That was all very well in theory. And indeed, it was easy in practice, when you were in the school gym. In reality, when you were walking along a shopping street in Toulouse, with a new handbag in your hand, going to meet your aunt in a café, you didn't expect to be attacked and abducted.

More of the sergeant's words echoed in her ears. *Always expect the unexpected.*

And, after all, she should have expected this, she knew what her grandfather was like. Damn him, damn him, damn him. Here she was, under the power of a perverted old grandfather, whose lust for control over every member of his family seemed to become more extreme with every passing year.

Olivia made herself breathe more slowly. She met the woman's eyes; she was looking at Olivia, and Olivia was taken aback by the anger and contempt in her face. That wasn't the expression of a woman doing a job she had been paid to do. For the first time, fear washed through Olivia. Were they doing this on her grandfather's orders? Or were they something quite different. Kidnappers? Her grandfather was a very rich man, not that you'd know it, for he was also extremely mean. Her father came from a wealthy family, could be expected to raise a lot of money to save a beloved daughter.

She was hazy on the subject of kidnaps, but she had an idea that gangs in that line of work spent months watching their quarry before they made the snatch. Had these people or their associates been watching her for months?

Not very likely. Her school kept a vigilant guard against intruders, watchers and lurkers. In the headmistress's opinion, a large institution containing over four hundred girls presented a tempting target for men, who as a species were unreliable, immoral and tiresome. So Miss Calthrop's precautions were thorough, and her suspicions boundless.

Anyone on the lookout for a kidnap victim would very soon find themselves in the local police station.

Without turning round, the driver said something in low, fast French. Olivia caught the word eyes, and then another scarf was tied over her eyes. The woman was doing the tying, and she pulled it so tight that Olivia let out a muffled squawk of pain. How dare they cover her eyes. It made her feel even more uncomfortable, and, to her annoyance, more frightened. As they drove on, still in the same silence, her anger intensified rather than diminished, and she settled down to make a plan. She would co-operate and not resist physically, although they needn't think she was going to get into conversation with them. She'd behave like a zombie, lull them into carelessness, and then might come a chance to practise her muscular skills.

Not yet believing that anything serious had happened to the English girl, the placid, pipe-smoking Inspecteur took notes of everything Julius told him, dictated a description of Olivia, Vicky having provided details of her new outfit, and arranged for police stations and officers across the city to be alerted. He sent out extra patrols. Then, just in case, he summoned those whose job it was to keep tabs on the underworld and organised crime networks of Toulouse and told them to meet or talk to their contacts.

'Soon,' he said, tamping the tobacco into the bowl of his pipe with a wide finger, 'we will have some news!'

They did, but not news that brought any pleasure to Julius or satisfaction to the Inspecteur. Vicky had gone back to the café with Mr van der Meulen, fretting at her inability to do anything. Just as well, thought Julius as he listened frowningly to the reports coming in.

No officer on the beat had seen Olivia, nor been able to find a single person who had seen her since the shopkeeper had closed the shop door behind her last customer of the day. The word coming back from the criminal fraternity was negative, combined with a sense of outrage that maybe some outside gang had dared to make a snatch on their territory. Besides, many of the underworld bosses had daughters, they didn't like innocent young girls being abducted, what was the world coming to when such a thing could be allowed to happen?

Other officers, with a sigh, set about hunting through the records kept on known perverts. 'Better that the young lady's aunt doesn't know about this side of the enquiry,' the Inspecteur told Julius with a sigh and several puffs of his pipe. It was regrettable, but there were unsavoury types in Toulouse, just as there were in the countryside and in communities everywhere. Mr Drummond, being a lawyer, would know about such cases.

Julius knew about them all too well, but Olivia didn't strike him as the type likely to be a target for such an attacker. He explained this to the Inspecteur. She was too tall, too big, too strong-looking.

The Inspecteur nodded his head in understanding. These English girls, with their hockey and many other outdoor activities, they were formidable, he knew all about them. He tended to agree with Julius, she did not, on the face of it, seem a likely victim. And, judging by what Julius and Vicky had said, there was little point in their hunting down the names of the child molesters. Some girls of fifteen were little more than children. Miss Rowder, by all accounts, was more likely to pass for an adult.

Julius wasn't too sure about this, but the Inspecteur had taken more notice of Vicky's words. A woman of sense, that one, keeping her head, even though worried and alarmed. Indeed, if her niece had the same admirable English phlegm and sang froid, then her chances were good.

Chances of what? thought Julius. Being found alive? Escaping from the clutches of some captor or captors?

'And of course, although our confidence that she had merely lost her way was misplaced, it seems that the most likely explanation is some action on the part of her grandfather. Unnecessary action,' added the Inspecteur severely. 'Arrangements for the return of Miss Rowder to her family in England could have been made with the willing assistance of the French police had the no-doubt distinguished judge been a little less hasty in his reaction to her running away.'

'He is a man possessed of a strong family feeling,' said Julius carefully.

The Inspecteur regarded him through clouds of tobacco smoke.

'Just so.' He paused, taking another deep puff at his pipe. 'It is a matter of some delicacy, one imagines. I have requested a senior colleague in Paris to contact Scotland Yard, to allow discreet enquiries to be made as to whether the judge has indeed employed some firm of over-zealous private operators to bring his grand-daughter back to London. If this was the case, doubtless further information would be forth-coming, to enable those involved to be traced.'

'If not?' said Julius.

'If not, then in addition to having you and Mademoiselle Hampden expressing your concern, we shall doubtless have Sir Hampden to reckon with as well.'

Julius covered his eyes with his hand. That was all he needed, Christopher Hampden in one of his famous furies, converging on the French police, on Vicky and on him. Probably with the ambassador, a bigwig from Interpol and Inspector Maigret in tow.

'One moment,' said the Inspecteur as a uniformed man came in with a message in his hand. He took it, read it, and looked across his desk at Julius with raised eyebrows.

'It seems that Scotland Yard are even keener on discretion where this judge is concerned than we are. Tactful enquiries made by them have elicited the information that Sir Hampden is in Scotland, at the home of his eldest daughter. On a fishing holiday. Monsieur and Madame Rowder have not yet informed the judge that Mademoiselle Olivia Rowder is missing from school. They hoped that they could get her back home, and indeed back to school before he finds out. If he did find out, it was their intention to inform him that she is on a school visit to France. The head teacher of the school is said to be willing to verify such a story.'

'Oh,' was all Julius could find to say. He pulled himself together. 'I'm not surprised they haven't told him. It shows great good sense.'

'It is apparent that very many otherwise truthful people are prepared to tell several lies in order for this girl's unauthorised trip to France to be kept secret.'

'In the circumstances, and knowing the people involved, all I can say is that I'm not surprised.'

'Nor am I, Mr Drummond The perfidy and deviousness of the English has long been common knowledge among the French.

However, this changes matters, and if a serious crime has been committed, as now seems possible, then I regret that secrecy may not be possible for very much longer. If you would be so good as to wait in the outer office, I will leave you for a while. It is now necessary for me to arrange the facts of this case, inasmuch as there are any facts, so that the matter may be laid before the Juge d'Instruction.'

'Oh, lord,' said Julius.

Unaware of all this activity on her behalf, Olivia was feeling more and more cramped and uncomfortable tied up in the back of the car. It was with great relief that she felt the car stopping.

A door slammed; the driver's door, she thought. Then the man beside her opened his door and slid out, still holding on to her arm. Then she found herself being pulled across the seat and out of the car and hauled over someone's shoulder.

Whoever it was staggered under her weight, and Olivia braced herself for a fall. She was spared the bruises, as other hands lifted her off, and lowered her to the ground. A voice spoke close to her ear. 'If we untie your ankles, will you walk in a sensible manner between us?'

Olivia thought rapidly. This was not the time to make a bid for freedom, not while her legs were numb and her mouth and eyes covered. She nodded, a hand grasped her under each elbow, and propelled her, stumbling, forward. 'Step,' hissed the voice. They were going through a front door, thought Olivia. The floor here was tiled, she could tell from the sound their shoes made. She heard a door open, and then she was on the move again.

They guided her to a chair and sat down, finally releasing her arms. Her hands flew up to the scarves, and she tugged the blindfold off before they could stop her. The man from the back of the car cursed and started forward as she sat blinking in the light, but the driver restrained him.

'Take the gag from her mouth,' he ordered.

Olivia rubbed her ankles, then her eyes, and then waggled her jaw experimentally. Her teeth felt as though she'd been biting on a horseshoe, and her mouth was dry. 'I'd like a drink of water, please,' she said in a croaky voice.

The woman advanced towards her. She was very short, Olivia now saw, petite would be the word for her. And very trim and chic, with elegantly cut hair and a well-made up face. Old, of course, thought Olivia. At least thirty-five. The backseat man, as she thought of him, was about the same age, or perhaps older, with grey flecks in his receding brown hair and a thin mouth beneath the broken nose. The boss of the operation seemed younger than the other two, although as he still had his sunglasses on, it was hard to judge. Certainly there was no trace of grey in his thick, almost black hair.

The woman was hurling abuse, demanding to know why she should be given a glass of water, a whore like her, whose accursed lover had caused the death of so many good men and women.

This was lost on Olivia, whose French was nowhere near good enough to understand the very explicit language the woman was using. 'I'm thirsty,' she said in English. 'You'd be if you'd had your mouth gagged like that. And the scarf tasted disgusting, I just hope it isn't poisonous, what I've been swallowing.'

The man in sunglasses snapped his finger at the second man, who left the room and returned a few minutes later with a glass of water, which he handed to Olivia. She thanked him, took the glass with a steady hand, and drank it all. She put the empty glass on the table beside her and looked around the room.

It appeared to be a study: there was a desk set under the window, outside which she could glimpse some kind of formal garden. She was sitting on a polished wooden chair with a narrow, straight back. There was a more comfortable wooden chair drawn up to the desk, and an armchair in the opposite corner of the room. The whole room was lined with books. The floor was tiled in pinky marble, with a cream rug in front of the armchair.

Olivia was puzzled by all this, although she kept her face expressionless. *Never give away what you're thinking*, had been the gym sergeant's maxim.

Her knowledge of criminals, culled from the more lurid popular detective stories by English and American authors, hadn't led her to expect cultured kidnappers. Dark glasses, who seemed most at home here, must therefore be a Moriarty, one of the suave, urbane nasties who ruled their underlings with sarcasm and literary allusions.

171

Moriarty sat down on the desk chair. 'We've brought you here to answer some questions,' he began.

Questions? This was it. Questions about her family, about their wealth, about how best to contact them with ransom demands. Olivia's lips tightened. She wasn't going to say a word.

'We want you to tell us, Mademoiselle Victoria Hampden, everything you know about Philippe d'Icère.'

Vicky spent a terrible night, frantic with worry during many wakeful hours; tossing and turning when she did eventually fall asleep.

Scenario after terrible scenario passed through her whirling brain. Rapists, psychopaths, white slavers and cruel kidnappers stalked through her dreams. When her fears receded for a while, their place was taken by guilt and inward-turned rage. She was the one responsible for this. She had set a pattern by running away from school. At twenty-five, she had run away again. What an example to set an impressionable teenage girl. How was she to tell Vera, how to face her own mother and worst of all, father? God, what a mess she'd got herself and Olivia into.

The marks of the night showed in her shadowed eyes as she went downstairs to breakfast. Julius glanced up at her, saw her pale face, and frowned. He was in the lobby, propped up against the desk, talking to someone on Monsieur Ribérac's telephone.

The innkeeper himself was hovering in the background, beaming.

Beaming? Was the man mad?

He pointed towards Julius. Her eyes followed the innkeeper's fat and triumphant forefinger; and her heart leapt. Julius was making a thumbs up sign with his right hand.

'They've found her?' she asked the innkeeper.

'Yes, but yes, Mademoiselle! The police, so efficient, our French police, have rung to say she is safe and well. Monsieur Drummond is speaking even now to the Inspecteur from Toulouse.'

Wild with impatience, Vicky could hardly bear to wait for Julius to finish his conversation. She wanted details. She wanted to know exactly where Olivia was, what had happened to her, to be assured that she was indeed safe.

Julius finally rang off. For a moment, Vicky thought he had been going to hug her, he looked so pleased. He didn't, however, but smiled at her instead. 'Calm down,' he said. 'She's fine. Now, come and sit down, and the good Monsieur Ribérac will bring us coffee and rolls and croissants, and I'll tell you what the Inspecteur said.'

'Breakfast? We can't wait for breakfast. We must go at once.'

'Go where?'

'Toulouse, of course. Is she at the police station?'

'Ah, yes. I understand your keenness, but unfortunately she isn't at the police station. They don't actually know where she is. Now, don't make a scene, I tell you, she's in no danger, she's quite safe, and no one's hurt her in any way.'

Vicky sat down in her chair with a thump, and opened her mouth.

'Listen,' said Julius firmly. 'I will explain. The police heard this morning from a contact, a go-between merely, not anyone involved. She said that it was a case of mistaken identity.'

'Mistaken identity?' Vicky's words came out in a high-pitched shriek.

Julius spoke slowly and deliberately. 'Olivia was taken because they thought she was someone else.'

'I don't believe it. Come on, Julius, there just aren't people like Olivia around, not in this part of the world. How can you mistake a hulking English schoolgirl for anyone else? Or is this some gang that makes a point of abducting adolescents? And if she isn't at the police station, where is she? Why haven't they gone to get her?'

Julius gave her a quizzical look. 'Olivia sent a message to us, two words, the Inspecteur said. He was very puzzled by them.'

'What two words?'

'Romper suit.'

'Romper suit? Romper suit! Then it *is* Olivia.'

'I told you it was. The reason there's no point in going to Toulouse is simply that she isn't there. The police only know that she's safe, apparently perfectly happy, and that she will ask her captors to drop her off in St Aphrodise later today. That's what her message to the police said.'

Vicky was rendered totally speechless. She sat bolt upright, staring at Julius in utter astonishment.

He began to laugh. 'Does that make you more sure that she's all right?'

'Oh! Oh, wait till I get my hands on her.'

'This is the girl you've been worrying yourself sick about all night, remember that. By the way, and she said the reason that she didn't get them, whoever them may be, to send a message last night was that she thought it was rather late, and you'd probably be in bed.'

It took at least ten minutes for Vicky to be restored to something like equilibrium. Julius poured her a cup of coffee and waited for the questions that Vicky would ask now that the shock was over.

She drank her coffee, absent-mindedly ate a roll and jam, then looked up at Julius. 'Nothing to do with my father, then? He still doesn't know anything about her running away from school?'

'Not as far as we know. The Rowders have been told that Olivia is safe and sound, and all they've said is please could you get her to Paris and they'll make arrangements for her to finish her education here in France. Sounds like they've washed their hands of her.'

'They like their children not to be at home. They cramp their social life, and also, the more the offspring are away, the less my father can have to do with them. Yes, don't say it, what a strange family.'

'Not surprising, with a man like your father at the head of it.'

Vicky thought about it as she ate a croissant. 'Do you admire my father? As a lawyer, I mean, and considering him professionally as a judge?'

'If you want the truth, no. I think he's a menace, his sentencing is erratic and often cruel, and his summings-up can be amazingly partial. I'm only surprised his verdicts aren't overturned more often.'

'The unjust judge, in fact. I suppose he gets away with it because he's one of the gang, and better cruel than getting soft with the criminal classes. Mummy longs for him to retire. The only time he's more or less human is when he's fishing. If he retired from the bench, he could fish all day and sleep exhaustedly all night. Personally, and speaking as an unnatural daughter, I agree with Olivia, I think he's slightly crazy. Lots of people are, of course, and it doesn't matter very much. It's only because he's what he is that it becomes a problem.

And as no one will admit there's a problem, he can go on doing exactly as he likes. And as I've got older, and can think about it almost coldly, I ask myself just how crazy he is.'

'Makes you wonder about our wonderful legal system,' said Julius.

'Quite.'

Julius got up. 'I suppose you'll want to stay here at the inn today, for when Olivia comes back.'

'I do not, I don't want to see or think about the wretched girl until several hours have passed and I've lost all desire to throttle her. What I want to do is carry on with my search for Philippe.' She paused, and then said with more passion than Julius had seen in her before, 'Oh, I do miss him. I do so wish he weren't dead. He's the only person I've ever felt completely and utterly happy with. And, do you know, I don't care any longer whether he was the brave *resistant*, or the cunning traitor to his country and his friends; I just wish he hadn't died.'

Julius looked away, unable to bear the heart-rending tone of her voice and the look of desolation on her face. 'I'm sorry,' was all he could find to say.

Chapter Twelve

———◦◦◦———

Vicky knew it was time she pulled herself away from the past. It was all dreadfully sad, but she and Philippe would never meet again on this earth, and therefore she, who was still alive, must look to the future, not dwell in the past. Philippe had never had any time for might-have-beens. She admitted, for the first time, that it would have been easier for her if she'd put it all behind her, kept her secret marriage to herself, started a new life.

If only the man she wanted to marry, or thought she wanted to marry had been anyone but Duggie. She caught sight of a man turning the corner of a street in Toulouse, and for a moment she'd thought it was Duggie, had almost called out his name in surprise. Her feeling had been one of panic, alarm; not the delight one should feel about a man she was thinking of spending the rest of her life with.

Julius's voice broke in on her thoughts. 'I'm going to call in on Monsieur Lamboley. Then I'll go to the Bar des Cathares, where there is what passes here for a private telephone, and try to get through to London, to find out if there's any news at their end.'

'Why should there be?'

'Oh, one never knows,' he said vaguely.

The lawyer was happy to talk to Julius, and was unsuspicious when Julius skilfully brought the conversation round to some legal points he was unsure about. Monsieur Lamboley congratulated him on his grasp of French law.

'This isn't exactly my field,' said Julius, 'but I studied international law in Paris for a year.'

The French lawyer approved, said it was untrue what people said about the insularity of the English. And had he got any further in his efforts to uncover more about Philippe d'Icère.

'Not really. His aunt believes him to have been a member of the Resistance, but not a loyal one. She says he betrayed his country.'

Monsieur Lamboley was cynical. 'Everyone in France was a member of the Resistance at liberation. And I dare say Madame d'Icère was not an enthusiast for the Resistance, at the time or now. She holds strong anti-communist views, and was very much in favour of fascism. It is a right-wing point of view,' he added, almost apologetically, 'not uncommon in France. It is not precisely that such people wish the Germans had won the war, but . . .'

'I understand,' said Julius, taking pity on the man. 'We have them in England, too, I assure you.'

The lawyer shuffled papers about on his desk. 'Mademoiselle Hampden is well, I trust? Not distressed by the unfortunate matter of her niece going missing?'

How the devil did he know about it, Julius wondered. 'No. She was worried, naturally, but the girl is safe and well. Miss Hampden is at the beauty parlour.'

The lawyer nodded his head several times. 'My wife is the same. After an upset, she must go and have her hair done, or her face. This will be relaxing for her, and of course one is happy that the English girl is not, after all, lost.'

Julius left the lawyer's office and walked across the square and down the narrow street with its high, shuttered buildings on either side. The sun was nearly overhead, and on one side, the houses were bathed in sunshine, while the opposite side was still in shadow. A line of sunlight shone across the cobbles at his feet; a lean tabby cat came out of a doorway and flopped down in the strip of sunshine, shutting its eyes and washing its paws with the disdain of its kind.

Julius glanced up at the bright flowers tumbling down from window boxes. He took deep breaths of the air, carrying a whisper of drains and cypresses with it. Then he thought of London, pulled a face at the cat, and went into the Bar des Cathares.

It had more customers this morning. Two men, wrinkled and practically toothless, looked up from their dominoes to give him a rheumy once-over before returning to the game. A stout woman with a string bag containing an enormous cabbage on the seat beside her sat very upright, sipping a colourless drink from a small tulip-shaped glass.

Jacques was nowhere to be seen. As Julius ordered a *pression* from the ample-bellied *patron*, he could hear a woman's voice chastising the unfortunate boy somewhere in the rear. He took his drink to the same table he had occupied on the previous occasion and set it down on a cork mat advertising Marlboro cigarettes. Another man came in, and approached the bar, laying his hat down on the stool next to him.

Julius instantly knew him for an Englishman, that blazer could only have been made in England, and only an Englishman would wear it, reduced as it was to a faded facsimile of its original dark blue splendour. The man gave his order, and waited with one foot resting on the brass rail beneath the bar. Then he turned and looked casually round the bar, not apparently expecting to see anyone he knew, not looking as though he planned to meet anyone, merely with the indifferent gaze of the Englishman abroad.

When his eyes reached Julius, however, the cool look vanished. He let out a yelp of surprise and abandoning hat and drink, strode over to Julius's table.

'Julius Drummond, by all that's wonderful. Quite the last person I would expect to run across in a back street bar in St Aphrodise, of all places. Julius, dear boy, what are you doing in these parts?'

'Have a seat,' offered Julius. He had stood up at the other man's approach, holding his hand out to be wrung. Nursing his knuckles, he sat down again and waited while the man went back to the bar to gather up his glass and hat.

'Never mind me, Adrian, what brings you here?'

'Damn it all, Julius, I live here! Well, not at St Aphrodise, but not far off, my place is a few kilometres to the south.'

'You live here? What about your career?'

'Climbing the ladder of the civil service? Couldn't face it, Julius, and that's a fact. Don't think they really wanted me, either, to be perfectly truthful. They weren't too keen on us johnnies after the war, you know the ones who'd been working in my field. Thought we might have learned some naughty tricks, felt we weren't respectful enough of red tape. Perfectly correct, of course. We had been spoiled for ordinary work. Not many of us could really settle down to it, and I didn't even try.'

Julius was nodding in agreement. He had too many friends, had heard of too many people, who had been unable to adapt to work in peacetime offices. Danger and cutting corners and finding incredible solutions to impossible problems didn't equip men for a life rising steadily through the ranks to become Chief this or Head of that for a few years before they had to retire.

'My uncle popped off in forty-four and he left me his nest egg. No, no; no need for sympathy, it was nothing to do with the war, just cussedness and a dodgy ticker, that was what took him off. I'd never seen much of him, he was much older than my guv'nor, but he was my godfather, and he never married, so I came into a nice round sum. That was that. I told a grateful country I was happy to have my services dispensed with, packed my bags, rolled up my carpets, and off I went.'

He sat back and took a long and appreciative pull at his beer. 'Tell you what, Julius, people come out here, friends and family, you know, and they moan about the beer. Can't see it myself, I like it light and cold, peps one up no end.'

Julius looked at his old friend's face, his fair skin reddened by the sun, his slightly snub nose sprinkled with freckles, his sandy-coloured hair sleeked down in a semblance of order. Julius knew very well how much effort Adrian had to put into quelling his unruly hair.

'So you're lotus-eating, are you?'

'Good heavens no, that wouldn't do for me. No, no. I got a bit of land with the house, and I'm trying my hand at a spot of farming. Grapes, you know. Grow like weeds around here, vines can, only the wine tends to taste like it comes from weeds. Ugh!' He grimaced horribly. 'I've got an idea that if one goes for quality, not quantity, and if I can plant the right types, there's bound to be a market for it.

It's never going to be anything grand, but good medium-priced wine is where the market is going to be, and that's where I think I can score. Come up and have a look at what I'm doing. Peggy would be thrilled to see you. How long are you here, or are you only passing through?'

'I'm staying in St Aphrodise, tying up the loose ends on a case. You know.'

'Still beavering away in Drummond, Drummond, Dubarry and Drummond, Julius? You're wasted there, I tell you. A family firm's a fine thing, but it don't suit everyone, and that's a fact.'

'A lot of people would be glad of a job like mine.'

'A lot of people would be damned glad for any job at all. I tell you, England's a miserable place right now. It isn't only the God-awful weather, we're all used to that, although living over here does make it seem worse. But everyone's so miserable, they look half-starved, they're freezing because there isn't enough fuel. The shops are empty, it's a hell of a bleak situation.'

Julius felt roused to defend England. 'Rationing hurts, but at least everyone suffers equally.'

'It's the strong pound that's crippling the country. There's no good in us behaving like a number one world power when it just ain't so any more. I tell you, there's no rationing in France, and the franc is as weak as can be. What's the result? Hard times, yes, but the factories are beginning to recover, which means more jobs, and the shops are bulging with food. Americans are flooding in, spreading their dollars around, that's good for business, and it all filters down to Monsieur and Madame Average. I tell you, I wouldn't live under Attlee's government for anything. Austerity's all very well, but one's got to feed one's family.'

Julius recalled that Adrian had children. He enquired after them.

'Still young enough to be fun. They go to a French school, amazing how they pick up the language. I suppose they'll have to go back to England to boarding school in due course, but I must say, I don't like to think about it.' He shot a shrewd glance at Julius. 'What about you, Julius? I haven't heard any scandalous rumours about you recently, had your wrists slapped once too often, heh? That firm of yours must keep you on a tight rein, it doesn't do for a Drummond to break out the way you're inclined to. Don't tell me you've got a wife and a couple of babies in the nursery, for I won't believe it.'

'No, I won't stretch your credulity that far, Adrian. I'm not married.'

'And no one in your eye? Damn it, Julius, I believe there is.'

Julius wished, not for the first time, that his old friend from childhood, school and university, wasn't so perspicacious. The breezy manner concealed a sharp mind, and he had a genius for picking up what hadn't been said. Mind-reading, his colleagues used to call it. It had earned Adrian the nickname of The Alien, and certainly, his knack of touching the spot was uncanny.

'Lay off, Adrian,' he said. 'Let me get you another beer, I've a feeling you may be able to help me with a knotty problem.'

'Anything I can do, dear boy.'

His affability vanished, to be replaced by a wary look when Julius returned with the two beers and came straight to the point.

'You were working for SOE, during the war.'

Adrian revolved his glass in his hands, inspecting the patterns his fingers had made on the cold condensation. 'I was involved with SOE, yes.'

'Did you ever come across a man, reputedly working for the Free French, could be English, could be French, by the name of d'Icère?'

'D'Icère, you say?'

Julius watched his friend as he held his glass of beer up to the beam of sunlight that came in through the window above the entrance. Playing for time, he thought.

'You know, dear boy, there were an awful lot of chaps involved in the French end of things during the war. There was de Gaulle and his ill-disciplined rabble, I can't tell you the trouble they caused us. Then C's lot had fingers in umpteen French pies. SOE was really a picker-up of pieces. We briefed the fellows, and women too, dreadful thing that, and sent them out to parachute into France or Holland or wherever. Half the time, you weren't too sure what anyone was called. Secrecy, don't you know, one never asked too many questions.'

'Don't prevaricate, Adrian. The war's over now, and I don't want you to have to dredge up any grim memories. All I want is a simple answer, does the name d'Icère ring any bells?'

There was another silence, while Adrian slowly drank some more beer, and Julian sat back, arms folded, watching him.

Adrian put his glass down, wiped traces of foam from his lip with the back of his hand. 'I'll tell you how it is, Julius. And this is strictly *entre nous*, right?'

'Right.'

'Like I said, we sent agents in by air, sometimes by sub. They met up with the locals, helped get them organised, provided radio links to London, taught them how to use explosives, you get the picture.'

'Adrian, I know all this.'

'Patience, dear boy. That's the famous part, those are the agents, jolly brave, all of them, that they make the films about. The other sort, well, we don't mention them, and they mostly just want to go home and forget about the war. The ones that lasted, that is. Most of them didn't.'

'I know, Adrian. I do know, and I'm sorry to rake it all up.'

Adrian tugged his ear lobe. 'Yes, well, that's all right. So, in late nineteen-forty, when there was no Resistance to speak of, just a few cells operating in Paris and some other big cities, we slid a good few agents in under cover to work in the more rural areas. Had to be careful, of course, because cells were often communist run, and those bods owed allegiance first to Moscow and only second to France. Sounds bad, but it was so. I suppose they felt it was the only hope for a better France, all that kind of thing. The fashion was to find some actual Frenchman who'd left France when the Germans moved in, and send them back.'

He drained his glass; Julius got up and went to the bar to get him another.

'Thanks.'

'Go on.'

'Philippe d'Icère was one of those. He'd nipped across the Channel when the Germans were rolling the French army up. We sent him back pretty smartish, a delay might have been suspicious. He did first-rate work for us, made plenty of contacts, set up one group in particular which was excellent. He was brought back for a briefing in early nineteen forty-three, and then flown back. Then he bought it. I reckon the Jerries were waiting for him. The chap who was with him managed to get away, and when he came back, he had all d'Icère's papers with him.'

'Neat, to be able to keep hold of his papers.'

'Terrifically risky thing to do. Clear against the rules. Well, stands to reason. If you were picked up and you had two sets of papers, the plod didn't have to be Einstein to work out there was something fishy about you. So, to cut a long story short, we used them. Mind you, it's a risk, because you never know when some old chum is going to come bobbing up and say, "Hullo, hullo, you aren't Jules or Henri, I've known him for years, and you don't look a bit like him." On the other hand, they had to seem local, from the same region, because otherwise the chaps he needed to recruit and brief wouldn't trust him.'

'No women, then?'

'None. The Lord knows, they were brave enough, both our agents and the women who joined the Resistance, tougher and more efficient than the men half of those French *resistantes* were. Only for that kind of undercover work, it had to be men. They had to have an aura of authority, and be able to go into bars, hang round the docks and so on. The French are all terrified of their wives and mothers, same as the rest of us, but they don't take orders from any other woman, and that's a fact. Does it matter? This guy you're looking for isn't actually a woman, is he? Nothing like that?'

Julius laughed. 'I get your point. So you kept the identity belonging to one Philippe d'Icère, who'd died in France in nineteen forty-three, and you gave it to one of your agents.'

Adrian opened his mouth, then shut it again, and shook his head. 'That's the trouble with you, Julius, always hitting the bullseye. That was about it. We chose a man who was English, but had been educated in France, gave him an intensive briefing on the language and ways of the area he'd be going to, and smuggled him in as one Philippe d'Icère.'

'Only not around here.'

'No. We knew all we needed to about this guy d'Icère. The original one, that is. We sent the agent to a town the other side of Carcassonne. His code name was Emile, I remember. He took on the role of a bookseller, which happened to be something he knew about, and opened a little shop. Said he'd been living in Paris, and had left to get away from the Germans. It was good cover, plenty of reason for people to come and go to a shop like that. He did excellent work right through to late nineteen forty-four, when we got word the Gestapo were on to him. He made for the hills, joined up with a gang of Maquis, and proceeded to beat merry hell out of the Fritzes until liberation.'

'And then?'

'Home to his wife and young children. Exhausted, with a mind full of horrors and a crippled hand, courtesy of the time the Germans caught up with him.'

'How on earth did he get away from them?'

'Slippery as an eel, Jamie Wright was. A good sort, and has been doing his best to make a go of things since the end of the war. It's not been easy for him, though.'

'I can imagine,' said Julius, thinking how straightforward and lacking in risk his own wartime work had been in comparison. 'What you're saying is that this Jamie Wright pretended to be d'Icère for two years of the war.'

'That's about it.'

'You said d'Icère had a reception party waiting for him when he landed. Who was with him? Who brought the news and the papers back?'

Adrian fidgeted with his glass. 'It isn't a state secret, I don't suppose. It was Duggie Fitzgerald. Brave as they come, Duggie.'

'Who was Duggie's boss?'

'Lord, I'm not sure.' Adrian laughed and gave Julius a friendly but painful jab in the ribs. 'Tell you who the big white chief was, though. You'll never guess.'

'Who?'

'Why, your uncle. Edgar Drummond. Sits behind his big desk now, raking in the six-and-eights, but he was one of our lot during the war. Didn't you know?'

'One tended not to know what anyone else was up to.'

'You're right there. For instance, I haven't a clue what you did, although I bet it was brainy stuff.' He paused, musing over the past. 'Tell you what, I've got a snapshot of Philippe d'Icère. The real one.

He came to my and Peggy's wedding, I've got a picture of all of us who were there. If I can lay my hands on it, I'll send it to you.'

'Would you? I'm at the Chameau here in St Aphrodise for the moment.'

'Tell me, Adrian, what made you choose this part of France?'

Adrian looked a bit sheepish. 'It was Philippe, actually. The way he used to talk about it, it sounded just the job. The kind of place I like. I'm not so keen on green country lanes, to tell you the truth.'

In the end, Julius didn't ring his office in London. In the light of what Adrian had had to say, his questions were irrelevant. After Adrian had finished his beer, looked at his watch, exclaimed that Peggy, who had been to the market, would have his guts for garters, and left the bar in a rush, Julius simply sat and thought.

He ran both hands through his hair, pushing it back with his fingers. Had Adrian solved the mystery, or simply deepened it?

Three Philippe d'Icères. One genuine. One going under a false name. Both brave men, risking their necks for their countries. And another, shadowy one, who had been a liar and a traitor. Could he have been one of the other two? Or might it have been Gaston's illegitimate son? Not strictly entitled to the name, but with some cause to use it.

Was what lay behind all this fear and treachery and greed? Perhaps, despite what his sister-in-law had said, Gaston had married his English mistress. If that Philippe were legitimate, then the chateau and the collection would belong to him rather than to Bertrand. Or so he might have thought, unaware as he was of Vicky's existence.

He picked up his hat, paid for his and Adrian's beer, and went out into the brilliantly sunny street. The cat had gone.

Chapter Thirteen

Vicky spotted Cornelius van der Meulen as she came out of the beauty parlour. He was sitting on the surround to the fountain. It was working today, albeit rather half-heartedly, more dribble than gush. Perhaps because it was market day, she thought. She edged her way past busy shoppers and stalls offering everything from parrot food to lace undies, and touched him lightly on the shoulder. 'Good morning, Mr van der Meulen.'

He jumped up and visibly relaxed when he saw who it was. 'Miss Hampden,' he said, holding out his hand.

And why are you so jumpy? wondered Vicky as he expressed his delight at the safe return of her niece.

'Isn't she with you?' he asked.

'She's coming back sometime this afternoon, if you please. It seems that one of the people who swept her off is bringing her back.'

His eyes narrowed, and he gave a low whistle as he fell into step beside her. 'And the police permitted this? They aren't questioning these people, charging them?'

'Julius says not. I find it very fishy, but then I don't know much about the way the French police operate. Perhaps because she's come to no harm, they prefer to close the case without any further fuss or publicity.'

'They must have a very strong reason for doing so! Who are these people? Are they Masons? What strings are they pulling?'

Vicky had to laugh at the Dutchman's indignation. 'Maybe Olivia will throw some light on the affair when she deigns to come back.'

'I confess, I am eager to meet this English schoolgirl who is so nonchalant about being abducted. She was abducted? It's not a question of a pick-up?'

'Don't be absurd! She's only fifteen, she wouldn't know where to begin.'

'My apologies if I offend you, but you must know that some girls of fifteen are very grown-up, in all kinds of ways.'

'Not Olivia.' Vicky was definite. It wasn't that she was shocked by the suggestion, although Cornelius van der Meulen probably thought she was. She knew all about teenage houris. There was Lauren, at school with her, who had slipped out after dark to assignations with men at the nearby air force base. Gertie, a fellow ambulance driver's younger sister, who'd had to be forcibly hauled off her patch in Soho some months short of her fifteenth birthday. Maisie, her sixteen-year-old cousin who'd run away to Scotland with a man twice her age.

'And the police know it's not the case. No, she was taken off against her will. Once they realised they didn't have the right woman, they clearly set about soothing her. To great effect, as we see.' She stopped to look at a stall selling baskets, held up a raffia bag with leather handles to test its strength.

'Who was the woman they were after?'

Vicky made an impatient noise. 'They won't tell us that, I don't suppose, and anyway, what does it matter?'

'Does it not occur to you that they may have mistaken one Englishwoman for another?'

Vicky put down the bag, and took out her purse to pay for it. Then she went over to a stall selling honey, and browsed among the glass jars. 'Do you prefer set honey? Or clear? Runny honey, as we used to call it in the nursery. I think the world divides into set and clear types. Like big and little enders in Swift, you know.'

The Dutchman looked surprised, then laughed. 'You're putting me in my place, in that astonishing way the English do.'

'I wouldn't dream of being so rude.' Vicky selected three jars of honey, paid for them, and stowed them away in her newly bought bag. 'For my friend in Paris. She adores honey. Do you suppose there are so many Englishwomen in Toulouse, waiting to be carried off?'

'It will have occurred to you and also to Mr Drummond that these people may have wanted to grab you.'

'Julius mentioned that,' said Vicky. 'I have a troublesome and possessive father, you see, who's quite capable of paying people to haul me back to England. Only if he has let loose any hounds, he'll have given them photographs of me. So no, they didn't mistake Olivia for me. I'm meeting Julius for lunch at the inn. Won't you join us?'

The Dutchman bowed. 'I should be delighted.'

Vicky found it a difficult meal. The innkeeper had set a table for them on his terrace, under a lattice of vines. They had fish, and drank a local white wine. It should have been a delightful meal, but she still felt uncomfortable in van der Meulen's company.

Julius seemed troubled about something, but was cagey when questioned. He told them the police were taking an interest in the fake pictures from the d'Icère collection. Paris wanted them to make some enquiries. In particular, they were anxious to know where a gothic butterfly was. 'It sounded like the one you described to me, Mr van der Meulen.'

'Please, Cornelius. And I may call you Julius? Thank you. An enamel work, with a crucifixion scene. A very famous piece, but missing for several years.'

Vicky kept her head down and ate her strawberries and ice-cream as slowly as possible.

'A butterfly has turned up, they told me on the telephone this morning. Diamonds and gold with lapis lazuli.'

Not my butterfly, or a copy of it, Vicky thought with relief.

'It has to be ascertained if this is the one they are looking for. It seems the d'Icère collection included several butterflies.'

'Monsieur Lamboley has this in his office?' asked the Dutchman.

'It has been sent to Carcassonne.'

'Ah.'

'Wouldn't the police there let you see it if you wanted to?' asked Vicky, finishing the last of the strawberries.

'I prefer not to go to Carcassonne. It has unfortunate memories for me, and I fear my presence there might arouse strong feelings if I were recognised.'

Vicky was just about to ask why, but Julius forestalled her. 'Van der Meulen was posted there, as an officer in the Wehrmacht, during the war.'

'I am not reluctant to return there because I was guilty of atrocities, this is not the case. However, one is guilty by association, and must tread carefully. I am pretty sure this butterfly, although doubtless made with genuine diamonds and lapis and gold, is a copy. It is known as the Lindburgh butterfly, and the original is in a museum in Antwerp. They acquired it shortly after the war, with money given by an American benefactor. The butterfly was made by a Flemish craftsman, you understand.'

'I don't understand anything,' said Vicky. 'Julius told me about the collection now in the chateau being nothing but copies, and that the originals and further copies are turning up in the market. It makes no sense.'

'Tell us about the more famous butterfly, the one they're looking for, the gothic butterfly,' said Julius.

Vicky glanced at him, but his face showed nothing but polite interest. Under the table, his foot nudged hers. She assumed a look of intelligent interest. 'Yes, do.'

The Dutchman produced his cheroots, the innkeeper hurried away for ashtrays.

'So,' van der Meulen said, tilting his head back and blowing several expert smoke rings. 'It is France, in the province of Languedoc, some time in the first half of the fourteenth century. A master goldsmith whose name is unknown, depicts a scene of the crucifixion in the shape of a butterfly. The butterfly is a beautiful creature, light and fragile, that lives for a short time. It is mysterious, also, the transformation from the ugly, earthbound caterpillar into the static chrysalis into this ethereal insect. It is a symbol of the soul, the psyche if you like.'

'And of the death and resurrection, hence the crucifixion,' said Julius.

'Just so. It is also a transformation of another kind, the impermanence of the butterfly captured in the permanence of gold. Technically, the work is superb, with the colours glowing through the translucent enamel. It was a reliquary, of course, fit for a prince, and probably worn by a prince of the church. Two ancestors of the d'Icère family, who owned the butterfly, were cardinals. The family, although French for many generations, was originally Italian. It would remind the cleric of his mortality and of eternal life, and the jewel and its relic would protect the wearer from evil.'

'The colours of the original must surely have faded over six hundred years.' Julius remembered the brilliant colours of Vicky's butterfly.

Van der Meulen shook his head and blew out two streams of strong-scented smoke through his nostrils. 'No, no. The butterfly reliquary was designed to fit into the hollow head of a crucifix. The crucifix hung in the private chapel of this family until the Revolution. Then it was hidden away, and later hung in the village church. The butterfly inside was only revealed when a workman dropped the crucifix while doing some repairs in nineteen thirty-four. The family was delighted, the art world very excited, and it was displayed, at the family's request, in a special case.'

'In the church?'

'Exactly so. I saw it there at the end of nineteen forty-two.'

'Sizing it up for Goering's collection?'

'You have a poor opinion of your fellow men, my friend. Not all Germans are so bad, you know. I advised the priest to hide it, and helped him replace it in the hollow cross where it had been kept safely for so many centuries. Some time later, a report came in that the butterfly had gone. An investigation was carried out, and the conclusion was that, in this case, German soldiers were not responsible.'

'Very convenient.'

'And true. No one believed this, naturally. None the less, it was true. The destruction to the interior of the church was gross and unnecessary, and even I, not a good Christian by any means, would say that it was sacrilegious, what was done and left there. The priest, who had been brutally beaten in the attack, recovered, but had no memory of the attack or the time leading up to it. It is often so. The crime remained on the books of the police, unsolved.'

'Terrible,' said Julius.

'Awful,' said Vicky.

It was with a sense of relief that she heard the sounds of a car drawing up outside the inn and, hearing voices, knew that Olivia had arrived.

She flew out of the inn to gather a startled Olivia into her arms. As much of her as she could, that was, for Olivia was some three inches taller than she was.

'Wretched girl,' she said into Olivia's blonde hair. 'I could murder you.'

'Why?' said Olivia. 'Here I am, safe and sound. Aren't you pleased? And Aunt Vicky, this is Jean-Luc.'

Vicky blinked. However she had imagined Olivia's abductor, she hadn't visualised him as some six foot of extraordinary good looks, with dark, dashing eyes, a mobile and sexy mouth, and a smile that would turn any girl's head. Christ, Olivia, what have you got yourself into? she asked herself as she looked at Olivia, who had eyes for no one but Jean-Luc.

'I shan't thank you,' she said to him as coldly as she could manage, 'for as far as I'm concerned, you're a criminal, and should be treated as such.'

'Aunt Vicky!' cried Olivia.

'Be quiet. What this man did was wicked. It caused very great worry and distress for me and your parents, and a lot of work for the police.'

'Mademoiselle, you are right. There is nothing I can say in my defence, although I am very happy indeed to have made the acquaintance of Mademoiselle Rowder.'

All this, and a voice like Guinness, thought Vicky inconsequentially. 'It would be better if you hadn't. Is it a habit of yours, snatching girls from the pavement?'

'Mademoiselle!'

'I can only assume that you and your friends were drunk or suffering from some mental disorder. Nothing else can account for such behaviour.'

I sound exactly like one of my aunts, thought Vicky, appalled. I'm only ten years older than Olivia, and probably much the same age as this Jean-Luc, and I've turned into an Edwardian great-aunt. She felt she would never forgive Olivia for this, worry and fear would pass, but aunty attitudes might stay with her for good.

'Olivia, I think it best if you go up to your room.'

'Oh, Aunt Vicky, don't come over all heavy-handed. Look, if . . .'

Vicky felt the situation slipping out of her control. Why should Olivia take herself off? She wasn't a child, to be sent away while the grown-ups conferred. Vicky parried with the last threat remaining to her. 'Be careful, Olivia, or I shall send a telegram to your grandfather.'

'I quake,' said Jean-Luc, his eyes full of laughter. 'Is he as terrifying and formidable as you, this grandfather?'

'I'm an amateur,' said Vicky with spirit. 'He's had a lifetime of practice.'

'Attagirl,' said Julius, who had been watching the scene with appreciation from the rear of the room. He came forward and introduced himself to Jean-Luc. His voice was cold, and he didn't hold out his hand to the other man, Vicky noticed. Jean-Luc's own extended hand dropped to his side. His expression was rueful but wary.

'We need to talk,' Julius said. 'Out on the terrace, I think.'

Julius looked Jean-Luc up and down as they faced each other under the vine. Tall though the Frenchman was, Julius had the advantage of him in height. He also had several more years under his belt, although he didn't care to think what this unexpected young man might have done during the war. He could make a good guess at it, though.

'You were in the Maquis?' he asked, and had the gratification of seeing that he had startled Jean-Luc.

'I was, but this is none of your business.'

'I decide what is and isn't my business. I'm Miss Hampden's lawyer and she's Miss Rowder's aunt and therefore her niece, being only fifteen, is in her charge.'

Jean-Luc hit back. 'What did you do in the war then, Mistaire Drummond?' He rolled his Rs very deliberately.

'Among other jobs, I was an interrogator in army intelligence,' said Julius.

Jean-Luc was silent.

'I assume that you abducted Miss Rowder in the mistaken belief that it was Miss Hampden you were snatching?'

'You're very quick.'

'What did you want of Miss Hampden?'

Jean-Luc's eyes darkened, and his chin went out. 'What I still want, M'sieur, information. Information about a man called Philippe d'Icère, who is a dishonour to his country, a traitor, in fact. Also a thief and a murderer. Is that sufficient reason for what I did? Miss Hampden has been asking questions about him all over St Aphrodise. I heard that she had a very, what shall I call it, warm regard, for this man.' His scorn was evident.

'I've been looking for Philippe d'Icère, also. You made no attempt to snatch me.'

'No, you're too big. Of course we wouldn't have taken Mademoiselle Olivia if we had known she was only fifteen. She didn't – doesn't – look fifteen, you must confess. And well brought up young ladies of such an age don't customarily wander around by themselves.'

Olivia, who hadn't taken her eyes off Jean-Luc's face, flared into indignant speech. 'I wasn't wandering. I was shopping.'

'She was,' said Vicky. 'In broad daylight, in the afternoon. You make France sound like Spain in the days of the *duenna*. And why go to the lengths of kidnapping anyone? Why didn't you come to the inn and ask to speak to me?'

'None of us were sure of the game you were playing. A little quiet questioning seemed the most efficient way to bring quick results. But tell me now, if you would be so kind, why exactly are you here in France, searching for a man who betrayed his companions and his country? Are there no traitors in England for you to run after?'

'I think you've said enough.' Julius spoke quietly, but firmly. 'You aren't aware of it, I suppose, but you're speaking to the man's wife, so watch your tongue.'

There was a squeak of astonishment from Olivia. Jean-Luc turned to Vicky in astonishment. 'You were married to Philippe d'Icère? You are Madame d'Icère?'

Vicky nodded.

'Then I wish you joy of such a husband, and be very sure not to cross him, because your husband is a man who kills anyone who gets in his way.'

For all Jean-Luc's contemptuous words, Julius, couldn't help liking this young man. 'I think you are probably mistaken in your harsh opinion of Philippe d'Icère. We have heard all kinds of stories about him, and there is certainly a lot of uncertainty about whether he was the villain you describe. Oh, sit down, do.' He pulled out a chair for Vicky, and looked questioningly at Olivia. She was installed on the broad stone top of the crumbling balustrade that edged the terrace, and she shook her head, happy to stay where she was and gaze at Jean-Luc.

'Let's ask fat Laurent there to bring us something to drink,' said Jean-Luc.

'You know the innkeeper?'

'I know everybody.'

They waited while the innkeeper was summoned, and he came back swiftly with a tray of drinks, his beady eyes shining with unselfconscious nosiness. Vicky frowned at him as he hovered in the entrance after putting the drinks on the table, and he reluctantly slid back into the inn.

'I'd be grateful,' Vicky said, 'to hear your story about Philippe. I've come to France to find the truth about him, and about his death.'

'You have reason to believe him dead?' said Jean-Luc at once. 'Let me tell you that the memorial to him in the church here is nothing to go by. Bertrand d'Icère would put up a memorial to himself if he saw any profit in it. He is the kind of man that if he said, "Today is Tuesday," you would look at the calendar to make sure.'

'Philippe didn't take after his Uncle,' said Vicky coldly. 'I trusted him, and I never had reason not to.'

'Very fine, but now you ask for the truth,' said Jean-Luc. 'I warn you, you will find the truth deeply unpleasant. Anyone would, and for you, with an attachment to this man . . .'

'Carry on,' said Vicky.

Jean-Luc half closed his eyes, and began to speak in the soft voice of the born storyteller.

'In nineteen-forty, I was made a prisoner of war, along with tens of thousands of other Frenchman. I was sent back to Germany, to a camp, from which I escaped. They put me in another camp, and I escaped again. I cannot bear to be caged, it is something in my temperament.'

Vicky nodded, thinking with a flash of humour that Jean-Luc and Olivia had that in common, they both liked running away.

'I made my way back to France, where I had become one of the absent.'

'Absent?' asked Vicky, puzzled.

'But yes, Madame. For us, under the Occupation, the war was all about absences. Friends from schooldays or from the café were, from one day to the next, not there. Their apartments would be empty, or have only a grieving mother or wife or husband to tell you they didn't know where your friend had gone. Then, many, many people had left Paris before the Germans marched in. More absences, you see. In the country, there were those absent because, like me, they were prisoners in Germany. Later, people were no longer there because of the laws made by the occupiers, and enforced, I am ashamed to say, by Frenchmen in the Milice, forcing every man from seventeen to sixty to enroll for compulsory work, either in France on the coastal defences, or in Germany. Boys and men and even grandfathers removed themselves, melted into the country, went to other towns, became nomads.

'Finally, groups of us came together, determined to make an end of this German oppression. We were the Maquis.' He spoke the name with great pride, and Julius, who had been looking at a tree at the edge of the garden, flashed him a quick look.

'We lived rough,' Jean-Luc went on, 'persuaded people to give us food and other essentials, or stole them, preferably from the Germans and from collabos.'

'You must have been very young for all that,' remarked Julius.

The fire of memory of those days was burning in Jean-Luc's eyes. 'In wartime, boys become men very quickly. Mine was a good group, we had some training, we were supplied with explosives. I can tell you, we gave those Fritzes merry hell. Others joined us, we were careful, mind you, we didn't take just anyone. One mistake was one too many. And we made a very bad mistake the day we welcomed Philippe d'Icère as one of us.'

Vicky moved in her chair. She sat forward, very tense, her hands cupping her jaw. 'And?' she said, as Jean-Luc fell silent.

'He arrived one night, flown in from England. He was in a bad way, something had gone wrong, he said, and his companion, a man code-named Raoul, had been shot. Was lying there, dead. We went to investigate, and yes, there was a body there. Although we were a little puzzled. If the Germans shot a man, they usually took his body away. Also, there had been no information about German patrols in that area. D'Icère's family is an old one, with long connections in this part of France. We did not know him, we hadn't worked with him before, but we saw no reason to mistrust him. He stayed with us for three weeks, long enough to learn enough about us to condemn us all, and then one night he slipped away and ran to the Germans.'

'I don't believe it,' said Vicky.

'There's no doubt about it. He took with him all the details of our next attack. Because of this treachery, fifteen of us were captured. Three of us managed to escape before being sent to camps in Germany. None of the others survived. Some of the women the Germans dealt with on the hillside, before our eyes. I will spare you the details, the whole world now knows how the Germans were.'

Vicky had gone completely white. 'I . . .' she began, and then shook her head. 'There's nothing I can say.'

'There is,' said Jean-Luc sharply. 'You can tell me where Philippe d'Icère is. Have you seen him since nineteen forty-three? Do you know where he is?'

Vicky was white-faced. 'He's dead. He died in the summer of nineteen forty-three.'

'I don't believe so.'

Vicky shook her head, holding back her tears. 'I told you, that's why I came to France: to find out how he died, to visit his grave.'

Julius took her hand and gave it a squeeze.

'And according to you, he was a traitor.' For the present, her feelings had gone quite numb. She had taken in Jean-Luc's words and the substance of what he was saying, but the meaning and consequences of it were beyond her.

'There is, you know,' said Julius in a conversational tone, 'another Philippe d'Icère who joined the Resistance.'

Vicky stared at him. '*Another* Philippe? Which one this time?'

'An a.k.a.' said Julius.

'A.k.a?' Jean-Luc was puzzled. 'What do you mean?'

'Also known as. He used the name as an alias.'

'Who is this man?' asked Jean-Luc, ultra alert now. 'A Frenchman?'

'English,' said Julius, and he told them about Jamie Wright.

'How long have you known about this?' Vicky asked.

'Since this morning. I ran into an old friend, who was with SOE during the war. He told me.'

'You might have said.'

'I've hardly had the chance.'

'SOE?' said Jean-Luc. 'I know all about SOE, dipping in and out of France, bossing us about, failing to deliver the arms and equipment we needed. If this man pretending to be d'Icère was English and SOE, then he was probably carried by his group. Men like that did more harm than good.'

'Don't make assumptions until you have the facts,' said Vicky angrily. 'All Frenchmen aren't war heroes, and a lot of English people lost their lives trying to help you. Ask around, see if this Jamie alias Philippe was really a dud before you condemn him.'

Jean-Luc raised his eyebrows. 'You express your opinion very forcefully.'

'For a woman, you mean?' Handsome was as handsome did, thought Vicky. Julius might be infuriating at times, but at least he didn't trample all over her with the arrogance of a Jean-Luc. He might think like Jean-Luc, it was impossible to know just what was going on in Julius's agile mind. Only, if awash with masculine superiority, he had the grace to keep it hidden.

'There's no point getting into an argument over it.' Julius's voice was cool and unemotional. 'Time for you to be going, I think.' He stood up and waited for Jean-Luc to rise.

Jean-Luc got up, laughing. 'Ah, that English coolness. But before I go, I must say goodbye to Olivia.'

Olivia jumped down from her stone seat, and smiled up into Jean-Luc's face. 'Goodbye, Mr Kidnapper.'

'*Au revoir*, Olivia.'

Olivia flashed him a last, brilliant look, and dashed into the inn. They heard her thundering up the stairs.

Julius gestured for Jean-Luc to go on ahead. He escorted him to the entrance to the inn and stood on the step to watch the Frenchman get into his car.

He still didn't shake hands with him, Vicky noticed. 'Why not?' she asked him as he came back in.

'I don't care to. However charming he is, however brave and daring he was in the war, he still snatched a fifteen-year-old girl in the street.'

'He explained that it was a mistake.'

'Ah, it would be all right if he had snatched you as he intended? Quite all right for him to commit a criminal act to further his plan of vengeance? If the Philippe d'Icère he knew was such a bad lot, and a cold-blooded murderer to boot, and he believes he is still alive, then he should tell the police what he knows and let them get on with it. He has them in his pocket, they'd do what he asked and bring the man to justice. Only they'd do it legally.'

'You know Monsieur Ribérac is an old friend of Jean-Luc's? Jean-Luc is a big cheese in these parts. Heroic war record . . .'

'As we've just heard.'

'. . . landowner, now turned businessman, taking over ailing concerns and getting them going, boosting jobs and the local economy . . .'

'Father Christmas in person. No wonder everyone in St Aphrodise knew about Olivia, and no surprise that the police are reluctant to press charges. Where's our Dutch friend?'

'He thought he'd slip away before Jean-Luc got too nosy.'

'Very wise. We only have his word for his niceness during the Occupation. He may actually have been Gestapo and evil through and through. No one else is what they seem, why should he be?'

'One has to believe someone.'

'So I would have said a little while ago.'

They stood together in awkward silence, broken by Vicky. 'This Jamie Wright,' she began. 'He isn't my Philippe?'

'No. Yours was the real one. I'm certain of that now. Jamie took on his identity when he died. The real question is: who was the man that appeared on Jean-Luc's doorstep claiming to be d'Icère? It can't have been Jamie Wright. Which leaves us where we were, with too many Philippe d'Icères.'

'You don't think my Philippe betrayed all those people?'

'No, I don't.'

Chapter Fourteen

The next day they went to Nîmes.

This time they made no secret of their destination. They were going by train, so no one could tinker with the wheels of their vehicle. Julius couldn't face the prospect of another journey in the black Peugeot with Olivia in the back; the bodywork on his own car had been sorted out, but the garage was still awaiting the delivery of a new wheel.

'If you had a French car, M'sieur, it would be simple, and quick. Hire the Peugeot again, a very good car, and nothing conspicuous about it.' He himself would check it over, to make sure . . .

'To make sure what?'

Marcel had shrugged and sloped away.

Olivia was in a difficult mood, wrapped up in herself for most of the time, coming out of her shell to have a good grumble and then lapsing back into introverted silence. She didn't want to go to Nîmes. She'd stay in St Aphrodise, thank you. She didn't want to go off on some wild goose chase. However did Vicky think she'd be able to trace a woman when she had nothing more to go on than Susan, or Suzanne, and an English passport? And if by some miracle she did track her down, what was there to say? Excuse me, are you the mother of an illegitimate son called Philippe, fathered by Gaston d'Icère? She thought not.

'You're coming,' Vicky said. 'Either that or I phone Scotland.'

'I had no idea you were so horrible,' Olivia complained. 'Why can't I stay?'

'Vicky wants you where she can see you,' said Julius, who was losing patience with adolescent moodiness.

'Am I horrible?' Vicky asked Julius, as they waited in the taxi outside the Auberge Chameau for Olivia to join them.

'She's better coming with us than sitting about mooning over her handsome Frenchman.'

'You noticed, then.'

'Cupid may be blind, I'm not.' He said a few words to the taxi driver, a man of portly build who rejoiced in a most splendid moustache. The driver sounded a brisk fanfare on his horn, and Olivia came slowly out of the inn. 'Beasts,' she said, as she got into the back beside her aunt.

During the two-hour train journey to Nîmes, none of them had much to say to each other. Julius was engrossed in the copy of *Le Monde* he had bought at the station. He found the complex tangle of French politics under the Fourth Republic soothing after days spent unravelling the riddle of Philippe d'Icère's identity.

Olivia sulked.

Vicky looked out of the window, lulled by the steady rhythm of the train. Telegraph poles flashed past the window, and she drowsily remembered Sherlock Holmes calculating the speed of a train by timing the distance between poles. How come he'd been so alert and able to do sums in his head while the game was afoot, whereas she felt as though a bulldozer had her in its sights?

Some twenty minutes before they reached Nîmes, Julius folded up his newspaper, and asked Vicky what she intended to do when they arrived. 'I assume not stroll up and down the boulevards hoping for sight of a familiar face. I have heard there are splendid gardens in the city. Are we going to see if any resident members of the d'Icère family make a habit of taking a constitutional there?'

Vicky ignored his sarcasm. 'Cornelius van der Meulen knows Nîmes. He told me that there's a bookshop in the centre where they sell a lot of English and American books. It may be that if she's English, as the mad aunt declares her to be, this Susan woman will be known at the shop. A regular customer, possibly. If not, the proprietor may know the places where the English in Nîmes gather. English people abroad tend to cluster, have you noticed?'

'I have, indeed. It's worth a try. We have to hope that Susan is a clusterer, and not the kind of aloof English exile with a great but unspoken sadness in her past, who revels in solitude and never goes out into company.'

'We aren't living in the nineteenth century.'

'Might as well be,' said Olivia peevishly. 'For all the freedom anyone has. Might just as well be living in Victorian times. I mean to say, Grandfather's straight out of Dickens. One of the nastier characters, that is.'

'I didn't think you were talking about Mr Pickwick, and do stop being so dreary. Here you are, in the South of France, on your way to what is supposed to be a very pleasant and historic city. When you ought to be in a classroom doing maths or domestic science or whatever you do these days, and all you can do is moan.'

At the station, Olivia was no less tiresome, protesting at Vicky's suggestion that they walk into the centre.

'Along this boulevard, look how pretty, lots of shade. Don't you want to stretch your legs after the journey?'

'If I hadn't been forced into coming with you, then I wouldn't have been on a train, and my legs wouldn't need stretching, thank you very much. Let's take a taxi and get this over with, then we can go back to St Aphrodise as soon as possible.'

'We'll walk,' said Julius. 'Vicky, we'll need a map.'

'Got one,' said Vicky, delving into her bag and producing an ancient guidebook to the area, which Monsieur Ribérac had lent her. 'Street maps for all the principal cities in here. The maps mark places you should see, as well.'

'Spare me,' said Olivia. 'We aren't going sight-seeing, are we? I can't imagine anything more yawn-making.'

Vicky was regretting her insistence on Olivia's accompanying them. But what could she have done? She couldn't leave Olivia alone, and Monsieur Ribérac couldn't be expected to keep an eye on her for every minute of the day.

But even Olivia was impressed when they came to the huge Roman amphitheatre, still used for bullfights.

'Terribly cruel,' said Vicky.

'I expect the bulls enjoy it. Jean-Luc often comes to the bullfight, he told me so,' Olivia said, visibly brightening at the thought of Jean-Luc.

They came to the Maison Carrée, the famous Roman temple dedicated to Diana, which stood at an intersection, its stone pillars and walls blackened with soot.

'I'm not interested in the stupid old Romans,' was Olivia's defensive comment when they asked what she thought of it.

Vicky wanted to shake her; Julius raised his eyebrows, and walked on.

'Down this street here,' said Vicky, in as bright a voice as she could manage through gritted teeth.

'You've got the map upside down,' pointed out Olivia.

'I find it easier to orientate myself if the map and I are facing the same way,' said Vicky.

'It's clear you weren't much good at geography at school.'

'I know where London is, and Scotland also. I dare say with the help of this upside down map I can find the nearest *poste*, and put a call through.'

'Young people today don't respond to threats, you know.'

'It isn't a threat, it's a promise, if you're intending to carry on like this all day.'

'The Rue du Chat something,' said Julius, looking up at the street sign that was streaked with dust and barely legible.

Vicky consulted her map once more. 'Rue du Chat Gris. This is the street we want.'

'I wonder why it's called that.'

'Perhaps there was once an inn called the Chat Gris here,' Vicky said. She had spotted the shop, further along on the left. A sign in the shape of a book hung above it, and a small flagpole attached to the shutter of an upper window sported a faded Stars and Stripes.

Closer to, the shop had a small window full of dull-looking books, not a paper jacket to be seen. Macaulay, thought Julius, and old copies of Baedeker and thrillers from the twenties and a copy of *Jane Eyre*. He'd never been into a secondhand bookshop that didn't have at least one copy of *Jane Eyre*, not a book he particularly liked, but perhaps in Nîmes classics would be less in evidence.

He and Vicky went into the shop, leaving a fuming Olivia propped against the wall, glowering, her arms folded.

'I wish someone would come along and grab her right now, this very minute,' Vicky said in savage tones.

Inside, an angular woman of about forty sat behind a rickety table. Her hair was swathed in a purple turban, and she had bright red lipstick which glowed as though wet. A pair of half-glasses was perched on the bridge of her aquiline nose. She greeted them without enthusiasm, speaking French with a strong American accent. Vicky asked her if she had a copy of *Jane Eyre*.

'I did, but I sold it last week.'

'You didn't, Sonia,' came a deep voice, speaking in English, from the depths of the shop. Julius peered into the darkness, and stepped back as a tall, lean figure emerged to fix him with a penetrating stare, made more unnerving by a monocle on a chain. He was confused, was this a man or a woman? The shirt and tie and tailored jacket was masculine, but the short, very fair hair, although mannish, was too long for a man except perhaps a philosopher or poet. Only he thought absurdly, poets didn't wear shirts and ties.

'Don't interfere,' Sonia replied, rather rudely in Vicky's opinion.

'Rubbish, Sonia, I have it here, it was in the window. Don't you want to make a sale?' She held out a book with a dark blue cover.

'It's in French,' said Sonia. 'This girl's English, can't you tell?'

'It's in English. I was reading it in here last week. I nearly bought it. The Germans took my copy.'

'Lucky you to have had cultured Germans occupying your apartment,' said Sonia with an undercurrent of bitterness.

'I expect they used it to light the fire.'

'Well, do you want it or not?' Sonia demanded of Vicky. 'It's very small type, I suppose your eyes, being young, can cope with it.'

'Thank you, I'll take it,' said Vicky hastily.

'Good,' said Sonia, taking an old black cash box out of the drawer of the table. 'That'll stop customers reading it for nothing.' She raised her voice. 'I'm not a lending library, you know.'

'Perhaps you should be. A few francs per book per week, with business so bad it would be worth it.'

'Business wouldn't be so bad if my shop weren't always cluttered up with people browsing but never buying.' She shot an angry glance in their direction, shut the lid of her cash box with a defiant clang, turned the key and put it back in the drawer.

'Loyal customers are worth cultivating,' the monocled customer said.

Julius was looking at Sonia, and he was startled by the effect the words had on her; a nerve touched there, he thought. Sonia's incarnadined lips tightened, and her face grew paler under its layer of powder.

'There you go again. All of you are the same, you won't ever forget it, will you? Loyalty isn't everything,' muttered Sonia, burying her attention in a pile of catalogues which she spread out over the surface of the table with hands that shook. 'Go,' she said. 'None of you is buying anything else, and there isn't room, you'll put off customers who have money to spend.'

I wonder what all that was about, thought Julius, as he held the door open.

Vicky lingered in the shop.

Outside the shop, Olivia eased herself away from the wall and stared.

'Is she with you?' the monocled stranger asked, rather as one might speak of a dog.

'Yes,' said Julius, without enthusiasm.

'Stand up straight, girl, for heaven's sake. What do you look like? If you slouch around like that at your age, you'll end up with curvature of the spine.

To Julius's unholy amusement, and Olivia's own fury, she straightened herself up. Then she glared, to show her contempt.

'How old is she? Fifteen?'

That earned her another black look.

'Yes.'

'She's too old to be your daughter. Why is she with you?'

'Her aunt is the one inside the shop,' said Julius, not very coherently; he had an uneasy feeling he was about to be accused of cradle-snatching.

'Why isn't the girl at school?'

'Illness,' said Olivia promptly. 'Scarlet fever. I'm in quarantine.'

'Nonsense, if you were in quarantine for scarlet fever, you'd be locked away somewhere, not lounging about back streets in Nîmes. Been expelled, has she?'

'I have not,' said Olivia, flushing deeply.

'Run away, then. Deplorable habit. I had a friend who did it all the time. She ran away from school and from home, and finally, she ran away with a jump jockey.'

Before Olivia could come back with a suitable retort, Vicky burst out of the shop. Her eyes targeted the androgynous person. 'The woman inside, Sonia, says your name is Phil d'Icère.'

Julius stiffened, looked at Vicky, then at the monocled woman. 'It is.'

'Philippe d'Icère?' Vicky sounded confused. 'Gaston d'Icère's son?'

'No. I'm nobody's son. My name is Philippa. I go by the name of Phil. For reasons that should be obvious.'

They adjourned to a nearby café.

Olivia was so entranced at meeting a real live lesbian, dressed in men's clothes and altogether dashing, that she snapped out of her gloomy fit. She couldn't take her eyes off Phil, admiring the chic and the boldness of her. Mind you, there was something about her that was alarmingly reminiscent of one or two of her teachers at school. She meekly ordered a lemonade, and settled down to watch.

Phil had ordered black coffee. She pulled out a mother-of-pearl cigarette case that opened to reveal American cigarettes. Now she sat, one leg thrown over the other, a cigarette held negligently between her fingers, her monocle screwed into her left eye. 'I have a cousin called Philippe. Perhaps he's the one you're looking for.'

'Does he have a mole?' Vicky wanted to know.

'High on his leg? Yes.'

'I didn't know Philippe well,' Phil went on. 'I don't count as a member of the d'Icères, although I use the name. My mother never talks about my father's family, so all I know is gossip and hearsay. I did hear that Philippe got into terrible trouble during the war, so if he's the one, I'm not surprised he doesn't dare to show his face.'

How pale Vicky had gone. Olivia didn't blame her, it must be frightful for her, to have come to France to find out what had happened to the love of your life, and then to hear all these awful things about him.

'Thick as thieves with the Germans, apparently, and that doesn't make you Mr Popular. Take the American woman in the bookshop, Sonia. A German moved into her flat, but she made the mistake of staying there with him. She was lucky not to be hounded down as a collabo after the war. She only escaped because the concierge and the people in the other apartments didn't exactly have clear consciences where dealings with the occupiers was concerned and they all clammed up when questions were being asked after liberation.'

'What happened to her?' asked Vicky.

'He beat her up before he left,' said Phil matter-of-factly, 'and did her flat over.'

'How awful.'

'Nothing to what the Maquis or the police will do to people like my cousin if they ever lay hands on them,' said Phil.

'The war's been over for nearly four years.'

'There are still a lot of scores waiting to be settled.'

'Were you here in France during the war?' Julius asked.

'Yes. I and my friend were in Paris until the end of nineteen-forty, then we slithered across the demarcation line and settled here. After liberation, we stayed. We like it here, and we still have a flat in Paris for when we hanker after the bright lights.'

'And no doubt you spent the remaining years of the war sitting here with your tatting?' said Julius.

Phil threw back her head and laughed in a very unfeminine way.

Julius likes Phil, thought Olivia. She herself had thought Julius stuffy at first, but it turned out he wasn't at all stuffy. If only Aunt Vicky would listen to what Olivia could tell her about Julius, all the juicy items she had learned from Annabel. Julius was sophisticated, would count as a man of the world. Did Vicky's having been married for about five minutes make her a woman of the world? She hadn't been surprised when Vicky told her about marrying her Frenchman, and wasn't that sucks to Grandfather; it made her want to laugh every time she thought about it.

But even if a brief and clandestine wartime marriage didn't enrol you among the worldly-wise, her aunt still had a big advantage over a fifteen-year-old schoolgirl. Ex-schoolgirl, Olivia reminded herself firmly, and she forgot the cares of her elders and settled down to dream the dreams of youth.

Vicky was asking Phil about Philippe's parents.

'They died in nineteen forty-three, in a stupid motor accident. Tilly was killed outright, Guy lingered on for two days. They weren't old, it was a shocking business. Although Tilly was Jewish, so . . .' She drew deeply on her cigarette, leaving the sentence unfinished.

'And so when Bertrand claimed that Philippe was dead, he inherited?'

Phil's laugh held no humour. 'He did, at least, he had to do some sharing round, but he did very well. My word, he was pleased. He tried to show some sorrow at his brother's death, but no one was convinced. And he'd always loathed Tilly.'

'Philippe called Bertrand a Moscow man.'

'He would have done. It's true, Bertrand is a communist. Strange, when you consider how he loves money and possessions, and how rich he is. Guy hated it, he said it was as bad as being a fascist. Bertrand was very pro-German at first. Like all the Russian worshipers he had to be when Hitler and Stalin were on the same side. I think it hurt him to have to change sides. I don't think any of it really mattered to him, all he cared about was what would happen after the war. He longs for France to become a communist country. It's not an uncommon view.'

'I met Philippe in London in nineteen forty-three,' said Vicky. 'I last saw him in May nineteen forty-three, and in June I was told that he was dead. Bertrand claims he died in January nineteen forty-three.'

'Bertrand is probably lying. If not about Philippe being dead, then about when he died. Bertrand would pay a lot of taxes if he had inherited from Philippe and not from Guy.'

'Philippe gave me a butterfly.'

At that Phil lost her laconic air and sat up. 'Not the gothic butterfly?'

'Yes.'

'He gave *that* to you?'

'It was sent to me with the news that he was dead. And a letter. He wanted me to have it if anything happened to him.'

'Then he's dead. Philippe wouldn't give that away if he were alive. He took it from the church, you know, in nineteen forty-two. His mother told me. She didn't trust the man who'd hidden it in the cross, and she wanted Philippe to have it. But why did he give it to you?'

'I was his wife. And now, I suppose I'm his widow.'

Phil threw back her head and laughed, a spontaneous peal that amused Julius and wrenched at Vicky's heart; Philippe had sometimes laughed in just that way.

Phil calmed down, became serious. 'In which case, Bertrand is going to be very, very unhappy. Does he know?'

'I don't think so.'

'Take my advice, wait until you're back in England before the news is broken to him.'

'What can he do about it? Why should he care? Just because he wants the butterfly?'

Phil looked at Julius. 'Is she always this naive, or is it just shock?' Then she addressed Vicky. 'If you married Philippe, and Philippe was alive in May nineteen forty-three, then you're the one who should inherit, and Bertrand, and Isabeau, if it comes to that, wouldn't be entitled to a penny. Oh, my word. However is he going to account for those paintings and so on? Good heavens, he'd go to any lengths to hide his shady dealings in the art world.'

In the train on the way back to St Aphrodise it was hot and airless. Olivia leaned her head against the window and drifted off to sleep.

'Life's getting to her,' remarked Julius.

'Lucky girl,' said Vicky, who hadn't been sleeping very well these last few nights.

'What are you going to do now?'

'Go back to Paris, I suppose.'

'Aren't you going to make sure?'

'Make sure of what?'

'Whether your Philippe is hero or villain.'

'How can I ever be sure?'

'As Philippe's widow, you're his heir. Phil is right.'

'I've got the butterfly. I could sell that.'

Julius was shocked by the bitterness in her voice. 'Your most treasured possession? Your one memento of him?'

'The butterfly he nearly killed a man for.'

'I doubt if he did that. I think an angry German did that when he discovered the butterfly was gone.'

'I don't know what to believe.'

'I told you I ran into an old friend of mine, Adrian. He told me that after Philippe died, his papers were used to send another man into France.'

Vicky frowned. 'The one who betrayed Jean-Luc?'

'I don't think so. The timing's wrong.'

'I don't understand any of it,' said Vicky, turning away and looking bleakly out of the window. 'And I don't want to talk about it any more. Philippe's gone, and we're never going to get to the truth of it all.'

'Damned if we aren't,' said Julius cheerfully.

The train stopped everywhere, at stations and in between stations. Julius was heartily relieved when it finally pulled into St Aphrodise.

Odd, he thought, as he jumped down on to the platform and helped a yawning Olivia down. What was Monsieur Ribérac doing on the platform? Off on a toot?

From behind the innkeeper's rotund figure stepped two men, one in the uniform of a gendarme, the other in a rumpled suit. They walked towards Julius and his two companions.

'Monsiur Drummond?' said the man in the suit.

'Yes.' Julius was alert, suspicious. What was going on?

The gendarme moved behind him.

'Inspecteur Lestrange,' the other man said in a weary voice. 'Sureté. You are to come with me. We wish to ask you some questions.'

Vicky uttered a protest. Olivia stood still, the back of her hand pressed against her mouth, looking frightened.

Julius tried to move away, but the gendarme stepped forward and held his arms. 'Wait a minute,' said Julius. 'Questions about what? Are you charging me? Are you arresting me?'

'In this country, Monsieur, we ask the questions.'

Chapter Fifteen

———⟞◦◦◦⟝———

Vicky had to placate the alarmed and distraught innkeeper.

Abductions, arrests; never had such mishaps happened to his guests. His guests were happy, contented visitors to St Aphrodise. They came to walk, to look at birds, to observe the flowers, to admire the beauties of the landscape, to drink wine and savour the exquisite cuisine of the region.

They did not, he added glumly, come to find dead men, harbour runaway schoolgirls, who were then kidnapped, or be accused of nameless crimes.

'There is some mistake,' Vicky said firmly. 'Mr Drummond is a highly respectable lawyer, from a London firm that has been going for more than a hundred years. He has only been in France for a short while, on matters connected with his work, how can he have committed a crime?'

And the birds take my tongue, she thought; how much of what Julius had been doing could really count as lawyerly duties?

Monsieur Ribérac was off again. 'It is worse, then. He is arrested for some crime committed in England, he has come to France to escape from Scotland Yard's pursuit, Interpol will be involved, it will be an international scandal, the whole world will know that crooks stay in my inn.'

'That should be good for trade,' said Vicky, who had had enough of the innkeeper. 'If you want me and Miss Rowder to leave, we shall; I'm sure the Hôtel Donjon on the square will have spare rooms.'

That brought Monsieur Ribérac down to earth. Crooks were one

213

thing, francs walking out of the door and into someone else's pocket were another. 'The beds are hard there. Besides,' he went on, his face brightening, 'Georges has his troubles too. There is this Dutchman, whom Georges is sure is a Frenchman but who is no doubt in reality a Nazi in disguise, who has a room there. He has stayed there several times, he makes many visits to the chateau. What is he doing there? Suspicious, huh?'

'If you're talking about Mr van der Meulen, he isn't a Nazi, and he's an art historian.'

'So he says. What else should he say? You think he is going to shout to the world that he is a Nazi?'

Vicky gave up. 'I'm going to bed.'

That brought a fresh outburst from the innkeeper. 'How can you think of sleeping at such a time? Are you not going to rescue M. Drummond, rush to his assistance?'

'I can't rush anywhere at this time of night. Besides, from what I know of Julius, he'll do okay without assistance. You can be of assistance, though. Ask your gendarme friend where they've taken Mr Drummond, and if he knows why they've arrested him. The policeman in a mac, is he local?'

'No, no, no! The Inspecteur has come today from Carcassonne. He is a Parisian, a fine detective. A legend!'

Vicky found Olivia in her room, white with fatigue and panic.

'Don't you start,' Vicky said. 'Old Ribérac having hysterics is quite enough for one night.'

'What are you going to *do*?' wailed Olivia.

'About Julius? Nothing tonight. In the morning, first thing, I'll go round and see Monsieur Lamboley, the lawyer. Now go to bed, for heaven's sake.'

'You're unnatural,' Olivia said, her face crumpling. 'Don't you care at all about Julius?'

'There's nothing we can do until the morning.'

'I'd like to have him for an uncle. He'd be much better than Fergus or Edith's dull American husband.'

'There's no question of that.'

214

'Why not? You aren't going to eat your heart out over your dead Frenchman all your life, are you?'

Vicky cast her eyes up to heaven and set about calming the hysterical girl down. Olivia eventually went off to bed, lachrymose and bewildered. What an introduction to the grown-up world, thought Vicky, as she creamed her face. It wouldn't be surprising if Olivia fled back to England and demanded to return to her safe and orderly school life. She could postpone real life for two or three years yet. Of course, it would catch up with her in the end; only Peter Pans were spared the jolting shocks of adulthood. She herself felt about forty. It was hard to remember that she'd celebrated her twenty-fifth birthday only weeks ago.

Was celebrate the right word? she mused as she slid down between the linen sheets. She pushed the bolster off the bed and beat the single pillow into submission. There had been no cocktail party, no dance, no family gathering. Presents from her sisters and friends were still at her parents' house. Unopened. Unless Daddy had thrown them on the fire in a fit of rage. She had rung her mother on the morning of her birthday and could tell from the tone of her voice that Mummy knew she was about to go away. Which was presumably why her mother had given her her present a week before her birthday. A jewel that had belonged to her mother, Vicky's grandmother. A garnet cross, the square cross of the Templars and the Cathars, she thought irrelevantly. Set in gold. She had brought it with her, it was tucked away in her suitcase.

Her father hadn't given her a present.

She turned on to her side, trying to relax, convinced the bed was twice as hard as it had been the night before, noticed the moonlight creeping in through cracks in the shutters, considered getting up to pull the curtain across, decided not to.

Why wasn't she more concerned about Julius? Foreign prisons were hell, everyone knew that. She just couldn't imagine Julius sitting crumpled and bruised in a small cell, or sharing with some garlic-breathed ruffian sleeping off the booze. Julius, she felt sure, would be raising his own hell, arguing, outwitting and infuriating the authorities. They'd probably thought they'd arrested a tabby cat, too

English to make a fuss, only to find a lithe leopard swishing its tail at them instead.

She fell asleep, to dream of Nazis in clogs, leopards stalking their prey through the streets of Toulouse and Olivia, in pyjamas, climbing out of a window. This last dream was so vivid that she got out of bed, padded to her door and across the landing to Olivia's room to turn the handle and look in, to find Olivia fast asleep in a pool of moonlight.

She went back to bed.

'Mademoiselle. Mademoiselle Hampden! Please rouse yourself, it is urgent.' The words were accompanied by raps on the door.

Vicky opened sleepy eyes, saw the sunlight flickering through the room and realised that it was morning. 'What is it?' she called out.

'Mademoiselle, the telephone never stops ringing, and now there are two reporters downstairs, waiting for you.'

Reporters? 'Why? What do they want?'

'To speak to you, to anyone. It is in all the British papers, they say, that Mr Drummond is arrested, is an international art thief, that you are with him, his accomplice in crime, the reporters say.'

'What a heap of nonsense,' called Vicky, shooting out of bed. 'Tell them to go away.'

'Mademoiselle, they will not. They say this is an inn, that I am obliged to give them breakfast. This is an inn, yes, but a respectable one, I do not want notoriety and crooks at my inn! And besides, how do I know if they will pay for what they have? Reporters are cunning types, everyone knows that.'

'Coming, coming,' shouted Vicky. 'And tell Mademoiselle Olivia that she is to stay in her room, she can have breakfast upstairs.'

That brought a howl from Monsieur Ribérac. 'Who is to bring her breakfast when we are besieged, by reporters and by the phone, brr, brr, all the time!'

'Besieged, indeed,' said Vicky, flinging open her door, and causing the innkeeper to jump backwards. 'I'll deal with the phone. Who's ringing anyhow?'

'More newspapers! *The Times* of London, itself!'

'Oh, calm down, or you'll have a heart attack,' said Vicky brutally.

Downstairs, the phone was indeed ringing. Vicky plucked the receiver from its stand and listened. Then she cut off the caller and laid the receiver down. 'Leave it there,' she commanded. 'Now, I'm going to slip out at the back. You distract the reporters' attention for a few minutes, all right?'

'Mademoiselle, my guests do not slip out at the back, this is not that kind of an inn!'

'It is now,' said Vicky. 'Get moving.'

Early as it was, Monsieur Lamboley was at his desk. Before the clerk could announce Vicky, she swept into the lawyer's office and shut the door behind her.

'He was magnificent,' Vicky told Julius later. 'It took him about thirty seconds to find out what had happened, thirty seconds more to phone the gendarme and get the lowdown from him, and no time at all to agree to act for you. He was in the outer office, rattling off orders to his clerk, while I put through a call to London.'

'Why London?' asked Julius.

'To find out what the papers were really saying. It was amazing, you arrested in the wilds of France in the evening, headline news in London the next morning. Fishy.'

As Vicky waited for the call to come through, Monsieur Lamboley, gathering papers and packing them away into a briefcase, agreed with her. 'This is a fix,' he announced. 'Prearranged. A put up job. It is to cause embarrassment and inconvenience to Monsieur Drummond and to you, and the intention is certainly to make you leave St Aphrodise, and go back to England. I have no doubt it is all to do with this d'Icère business. Perhaps, now that our opponent has shown his hand, we shall be able to solve the mystery.'

'Opponent?' said Vicky.

'There is a single mind behind this, I am sure of it. Now, I feel, we shall discover the truth! We shall find how Monsieur d'Icère died. I go now to Carcassonne, to arrange for the release of Monsieur Drummond. Please, stay here as long as you wish. The reporters will not come looking for you here. Use the telephone, my clerk will bring you coffee.'

217

'Thank you. I'll wait for my call to London, then I'm going to find Mr van der Meulen, who seems to know all about arty crimes, and see what he thinks about this.'

'I was very glad to see Monsieur Lamboley,' said Julius, later.

'I bet you were,' said Vicky. 'Handcuffed and shackled, were you?'

'Not at all.'

Monsieur Lamboley arrived at the police headquarters in Carcassonne to be given, to his considerable surprise, a warm welcome. He was at once suspicious; long experience of the French police had taught him that an accused man's legal representatives were considered a troublesome element in the smooth workings of law. If they had detained a suspect, it was because the suspect was guilty. Why else would they bother? Therefore it followed that any tiresome details like the suspect's wanting to see a lawyer only served to delay matters and generate extra paperwork. Thus putting off the time when the criminal could be duly shut away to repent his sins and not sully society with further heinous crimes.

Members of the police force had more than once commented to Monsieur Lamboley how fortunate it was that they didn't have that ridiculous *habeas corpus* law that they clung to in England. Imagine having to charge a suspect within a set number of hours of his being detained. In England, if no charge could be made at that time, the suspect, although clearly guilty, could walk free! Only think how much better was the French system, where a person could be held as long as they liked. Months, sometimes, with no charge and no trial. They kept all kinds of villains out of circulation that way.

The police in Carcassonne had picked the wrong man in Julius, as they quickly realised. Acting on a tip-off, they had been full of glee at the prospect of having an Englishman to accuse of what, according to the experts, was a huge international art fraud.

They were less happy when Julius turned out to know much more about French law than was good for him. Or them.

The devil, exclaimed the Inspecteur in charge of the case, a big shot down from Paris. Everyone knew how insular the English were, why did the one man they arrested have to be the exception? Then he cheered up. Doubtless Monsieur Drummond's knowledge of law, acquired during a year spent at a French college – whoever heard of a respectable Englishman doing any such thing? – was what had enabled him to operate across borders in the matter of these paintings and other works of art.

Only to be cast down again when he discovered just how well-regarded Julius's firm was. 'They handle the affairs of many eminent men,' he was told. 'And politicians.'

That left a sour taste in his mouth, as did the discovery that the current British Ambassador in Paris was the suspect's godfather, and Madame l'Ambassatrice was a cousin.

The Inspecteur ground his teeth, a mistake, as many of them were false.

Yes, Monsieur Lamboley could take his client away. Monsieur Lamboley could have him with their compliments. No, the case was still open, and they must have all necessary assurances about Monsieur Drummond's continued sojourn in France. No, they could not give details of what lay behind the charge. Yes, they finally admitted after much pressing on the part of Monsieur Lamboley, they were not at present able to contact a vital witness, although once they had done, Monsieur Drummond could kiss goodbye to the open air, and think about a life behind bars.

'That means the information laid against you came from a dubious source,' said Monsieur Lamboley as he drove away with Julius beside him.

'An anonymous tip-off, I should guess.'

'I take it you are not involved in this art ring?'

'Certainly not. But I've got a damned good idea who is. Can you go any faster?'

Monsieur Lamboley obliged. 'Although I must take care not to exceed the speed limit. There will be a police car on our tail, and they would love to haul me in for a traffic infringement.'

'Muttonheads,' said Julius with feeling. 'Will Miss Hampden be in your office still?'

'Perhaps not. She mentioned that she was going to find your Dutch friend, Mr van der Meulen, is it?'

'The hell she did,' said Julius, startled.

Monsieur Lamboley shot him a shrewd sideways glance. 'This Dutchman is not what he seems, I think.'

'I fear not,' said Julius.

Vicky had waited for her phone call to London. She had decided against speaking to any of her sisters, who would want to harangue and criticise her. She wasn't sure whether to risk telephoning home, hoping to get her mother. Better not. Better keep her head down. So she rang her teacher from the Slade, whom she knew to be an avid newspaper reader. She felt quite certain that he'd be bound to read about anything concerning the art world, and knew that if he saw her name mentioned in one newspaper, he would send out for all the other dailies, heavyweight and scurrilous, in hope of finding out more.

She was right. His voice came down the line warm with concern. 'Vicky! What are you doing, what's this trouble you're in?'

'I'm not in any trouble, Ben, truly not. It's all made up by the newspapermen. You know what they're like. No, no, I haven't run away with Mr Drummond. Secret love nest? Oh, how absurd. No, I'm staying in the same inn, that's all, totally respectable. My niece is here as well, so you see how there's nothing improper. Mr Drummond is in trouble? Yes, well, that's why I'm telephoning. The English newspapers don't get to France for at least two days, and I do want to know what they're saying. Apart from the love nest bit. Smuggling? Art fraud? Forgeries and fakes and copies? No, no, it's all nonsense. He'll be able to sue them all and live in comfort on the proceeds. You can recommend a first-class libel lawyer? That's very kind, and I'll pass it on. Yes, Mr Drummond is a lawyer himself, but the trusts and old lady kind, I think. Is he married? No, he's not, and no, he's not the man I came to France to find. Have I found him? At least four times, only it's never him. No, I can't explain now, but thank you very much.'

She put the phone down, put on her hat and picked up her handbag and went to the door. The clerk was sitting there, together with the mousy woman who zipped off letters and documents on her huge and venerable typewriter. They watched her go, and then exchanged looks and disapproving noises before returning to their duties.

Olivia leant out of her window. The warm scents of the south, the brilliance of the geraniums, the intensity of the blue in the sky meant nothing to her. Imprisoned again, she said crossly to herself. Vicky goes running off, and she was left to fret the morning, or even the day, away in this room with nothing but an old copy of *Vogue* and a novel she didn't want to read to occupy her.

Then she heard a voice, and her world came alive. 'Jean-Luc,' she called down into the street. 'I'm here. I can't come downstairs, the inn is crawling with reporters.'

'Why?' His voice was warm and mocking and sent shivers up and down her spine. 'Have you committed yet another scandal? Has your terrifying grandfather arrived with detectives from Scotland Yard?'

Her clear young laughter floated down to him. 'Nothing like that. Julius, Julius Drummond has been arrested, and apparently, it's in all the London papers. And about Aunt Vicky being here with him.'

'That is scandalous.'

'Not with me as chaperone. Besides, Aunt Vicky hankers after her lost lover, she isn't interested in Julius.'

More laughter. 'She's looking for love, your aunt.'

Olivia was startled. 'Do you know, I think she is? Wouldn't you, if you had a tyrannical father and a browbeaten mother and a pompous brother and six older sisters? Wouldn't you be simply longing to have one person to love and be loved by? Only it's so sad that her husband was either a crook or dead.'

'If it's the man I knew, then he's a bastard. Perhaps he isn't, and she will have happy memories of him, and meanwhile find her true love and live happily ever after.'

'People never do,' said Olivia in tragic tones.

'Don't sound so miserable. Where is your Aunt Vicky? I want to talk to her.'

'Not if you're going to try to kidnap her and let that woman loose on her.'

'I've done my kidnapping for this week.'

'I can't come down, I told you.'

'Hold on, I find a ladder.'

He was back two minutes later. He whipped the ladder into place, and called up to Olivia.

'Quick, be quick.'

'Are there reporters about?' Olivia eased herself out of the window with considerable athleticism, and swung on to the ladder.

'Not reporters, but I have seen a man I very much want to see again,' said Jean-Luc as he jumped Olivia down on to the ground. He heaved the ladder out of sight behind some bushes growing round the side of the inn, took Olivia by the hand and broke into a run.

Vicky, enquiring at the Hôtel Donjon, was told that Monsieur van der Meulen was out. No, he had not told them his intentions. However, he often went to the chateau, the Château d'Icère. How far from here? A short walk, fifteen, twenty minutes.

Had Monsieur van der Meulen driven there?

Normally he used his bicycle. Like all Dutchmen, he cycled. Today, he had gone by car, not by bicycle. He had left the hotel in haste. Whether he was planning to drive to the chateau or had indeed gone somewhere else, in St Aphrodise or . . .

Before he could run through a list of places where the Dutchman might have chosen to go, Vicky interrupted. 'Bicycle? He has a bicycle here?'

'But yes, indeed.'

Then she would borrow it. No, no need to protest, she was a good friend of Monsieur van der Meulen's, and he would be happy to lend his bike. Stored in the old stable at the back? No, it wasn't necessary for anyone to help her.

Cries of it being impossible for her to ride a man's bicycle followed her as she ran out of the front entrance and headed for the stables.

Vicky found the bicycle propped against a wooden post in the second stable. It was a sturdy black model, with the seat high, but not too high, thank goodness Cornelius van der Meulen wasn't one of those giant Dutchmen. She wheeled the bicycle to the rear gates, gave it a push, hitched up the skirt of her dress and was away. She could just about reach the pedals while sitting on the saddle. Stopping might be difficult, but she'd cope with that when she got there; she had no intention of stopping en route. Praying she wouldn't meet a car, she pedalled through the market square, sending a cloud of pigeons into the air, bumped along several uneven streets and debouched thankfully on to the slightly better road that led to the chateau.

She didn't spare a moment to admire the ruined beauty of the chateau. Its twin, turreted towers, mellow stone and perfect position in an undulating landscape made no impression on her. She rattled over the cobbles and into the central courtyard. It was empty, and had the feel of a place long deserted. Weeds grew at the base of the stone walls and in clumps by the well in the centre. A once-espaliered tree had been left to grow unevenly and unrestrained. She had disturbed a pair of doves, pecking idly in the hot sun, who flapped indignantly up to shuttered window ledges.

The sound of their wings and her own footsteps were the only noises to break the silence. She propped the bicycle against the wall round the well and went to investigate the closed doors on each side of the courtyard. They were locked, with rusty chains and padlocks hanging from them.

She called out. 'Hello! Is anyone here?'

Her voice came echoing back to her. Now what? She noticed that the big double doors in the arch opposite the main entrance had a man-size door cut into one of them. She went over to investigate and found it wasn't locked. There wouldn't be any point, so much of it was missing. She pushed the door open carefully and stepped through it into another courtyard with a tree growing in the middle. It was overlooked by smaller windows, and Vicky guessed that these would have been the domestic quarters of the chateau, where servants and children would have lived. Some windows were unshuttered, their glass broken. A door in the corner was propped open.

She went across to the door, put her head round it and called again. 'Hello? Mr van der Meulen?'

This time, she got a reaction. To her left, she heard a door creak open, and a bent old woman shuffled through, muttering impreca-

223

tions. From behind her, she heard quick footsteps, and turned round to find herself face to face with Cornelius van der Meulen.

He spoke first to the crone. 'Leave us, Geneviève.' As she stood her ground, he waved the woman away, and ushered Vicky back through the door and into the small courtyard.

'Have you come alone?' he asked.

'Yes. I wanted to find you. Have you heard about Julius Drummond?'

'No. He isn't with you?'

'He's been arrested.'

His face took on a concerned look. 'What for?'

'Art theft. Or fraud, something to do with fakes or copies. What you've been talking about, I think.'

'Nothing is what it seems to be. Yes, this is true. But why arrest Mr Drummond, a harmless Englishman?'

'You tell me.'

'So how can I help, Miss Hampden? The police may at some point call me as an expert witness. I can say that in my opinion this painting is genuine, this is not. This can't help Mr Drummond.'

'I wanted to see what was at the chateau that was so interesting. And to see the place where Philippe came as a child. Who is that old woman?'

'Geneviève, the concierge, she wouldn't move from her rooms here. She remembers nothing. She is nearly blind and has fuddled wits. There's actually nothing to see here, except a ruin, so you have had a wasted journey. How did you come?'

'I came on a bicycle,' she said. 'Your bicycle, actually.'

His eyebrows rose. 'A bicycle thief,' he said with not very convincing joviality.

'Borrowed, not stolen.'

He was all the time guiding her towards the archway. Just as though she were a sheep, thought Vicky, but she resisted any temptation to demur. She found the Dutchman less amiable than hitherto. Domineering. Then he spoke.

'You are wrong to come here. You have made a mistake.'

The words froze in her mind, as other words tumbled into her head. 'Vicky, he intends to kill you. Run.'

Vicky stumbled on a patch of weed, was caught up by a strong arm. Too strong, too tight. A grasp that was no longer helpful, but menacing. She wanted to get through the door in the arch, to seize the bicycle, to ride away from this place, and away from this man.

'I think not,' he said. Still polite, still gripping her arm. 'We shall go this way.' He was at another door. He pushed it opened, drove her inside.

She had expected darkness, spiders and possibly bats. What she got was the base of a round stone tower, open at the top. A stone staircase curved up the wall to an arched opening some twenty feet above the ground.

'Up,' he said.

He had asked her to do something that she couldn't. All her other fears dissolved at the thought of ascending those stairs, to that height, with no rail to hold, nothing at all on the outside of the steps.

'Sorry,' she said. 'I don't like heights.'

'Then perhaps you'll fall. Easy enough. Rough stone steps, a stupid Englishwoman exploring on her own. Trespassing, in fact, on private property. She falls. How sad. She breaks her neck? That is quick. Just broken bones? Then it takes longer. No one ever comes here, you see.'

Famous last words, she thought, choking back an hysterical laugh as the door behind them opened and the old woman came in.

Vicky, wishing she had had Olivia's training, kicked the Dutchman in the groin, ducked, and twisted out of his grasp. She made a dash for the door, but van der Meulen, red with pain and anger, was there before her. 'Not so fast, bitch.'

Jean-Luc slammed his car into gear, reversed, and left the square in a squeal of tyres.

'What are you going to do?' shouted Olivia, as the postmistress's son, telegram in hand, flattened himself against the wall. A woman on the other side of the road shut her eyes and crossed herself.

'Kill him!'

'Who?'

'The man in the green hat with a feather.'

'Mr van der Meulen?' Olivia was astonished. 'Whatever for? He's a Dutchman, and an absolute sweetie.'

'He's a German. He was the man d'Icère betrayed us to. He was a Gestapo officer, they called him the Wolf.'

'You're mad!'

'His face has changed. I passed him in the street, thought nothing about him. His nose is different, and his jaw. But I saw him walking away, and I thought, surely I know that man. And now, just this minute it has come back to me. I have walked behind that man before, not here in St Aphrodise, but in Gestapo headquarters. It's imprinted on my mind. Nobody can change the way they walk.'

Monsieur Lamboley, confident on his own territory, and knowing that the local gendarme would never dare to book him for speeding, accelerated through the streets of St Aphrodise and screeched to a halt in front of his office. He leapt out of his car, paused for a moment to compose himself, and went in through the door.

The clerk stood up as the lawyer came in. 'M'sieur,' he began.

'Is Mademoiselle Hampden still here?'

'No, no indeed. She left a little while ago. We saw her going to the Hôtel Donjon. Then, just a few minutes later, she came past here on a bicycle, going very fast, and not at all steady. We fear she will have met with an accident!'

'Which direction did she take?'

'From here, she was going towards the road that leads south.'

A muttered word of thanks, and Monsieur Lamboley was gone.

'Well!' said the typist.

'He *ran*,' said the clerk in awed tones. 'Monsieur Lamboley actually ran to his car. I saw him.'

'I, too. It is an emergency,' said the typist firmly.

It took no time at all for Monsieur Lamboley to shake the information out of the receptionist at the Hôtel Donjon. 'Miss Hampden has gone to the Château d'Icère. She went in pursuit of Monsieur van der Meulen.'

'As fast as you can,' said Julius, holding on to the strap beside his seat as the car rocketed across the square.

'This man is dangerous,' said Monsieur Lamboley, gripping the wheel hard and not taking his eyes from the road.

'Very.'

The doves were startled yet again as a car swooped into the first courtyard. Jean-Luc leapt out. 'Now I get the bastard,' he yelled. 'Now I have his balls for ping-pong.'

Olivia ran towards the door to the tower. 'I can hear Aunt Vicky swearing.'

Jean-Luc overtook her, and hurtled through the door, sending Vicky reeling to one side. The Dutchman didn't wait, but took off up the stone stairway, three steps at a time. Before Jean-Luc had reached the bottom of the flight, van der Meulen had ducked through the arch and vanished.

Jean-Luc tore up the steps.

Olivia ran to help Vicky up. 'You know some choice words,' she told her aunt admiringly.

'Just let me get at him,' snarled Vicky, looking round for her prey.

'Jean-Luc's gone after him.'

'Too late,' said a calm voice. 'Vicky, are you all right?'

Vicky pushed back the hair from her face with a scratched and dirty hand, leaving a smudge across her forehead. 'Julius, Cornelius van der Meulen isn't Dutch. He's German, I'm sure he is. He was swearing and shouting at me in German. This woman, Geneviève, I don't know her other name, says he was here in the war, he keeps paintings here. He threatened her, told her if she said anything, he'd have her turned out of the chateau and put in a home.'

Monsieur Lamboley joined them. 'He got away. Driving like Lucifer with an archangel on his tail.' He raised his voice and addressed the crone. 'You are Madame Amboise?'

'I am, and my eyesight may not be so good, but there's no need to shout.'

'Is there a telephone here?'

'No. He cut the line.' Her voice rose to a wail.

'Calm yourself, Madame,' said Monsieur Lamboley.

Geneviève gave a few dismal sniffs, and continued, her voice rising again to a thin wail. 'He hurt me, he twisted my arm. He came with Bertrand d'Icère. I thought it was all right, that Madame knew they were coming, but this was not so. They made me show where the pictures were hidden, and Bertrand said he was going to hang them up again to look after them for the family. And all the other lovely things! He took them all, and then he brought them back, a few at a time, and then he took them again, and again returned them.'

She gave a little sigh and dabbed at her nose with a tiny shred of a lace handkerchief. 'I'm too old to look after a place like this. I wish Philippe would come back, he'd know what to do. My lovely Philippe, he was always kind to me.'

She broke into a series of dry sobs. Monsieur Lamboley put a kindly arm round her. 'Come with me. Your sister lives in the Rue Giverny, doesn't she? We'll go there.'

Moaning that she couldn't leave the chateau, that she wanted Philippe, Madame Amboise allowed herself to be led away. At the door, Monsieur Lamboley paused and turned round. 'Monsieur Drummond, are you coming? And Miss Hampden?'

'You take Granny,' Jean-Luc said. He was, Vicky noticed, holding Olivia's hand. 'I'll drive back to the inn with the others. You'll telephone the police?'

'Yes.'

They approached the inn cautiously, but Monsieur Ribérac came out to tell them with pride that he had managed to get rid of the reporters. 'They were getting bored with the lack of action at the inn, so I sent them to Béziers, which is where I said you were.'

'Well done,' said Julius.

'There are two telegrams,' the innkeeper told them, producing the flimsy pages with a flourish.

One was for Vicky, one for Julius. Vicky, longing for a bath, opened hers with strangely unsteady fingers. She read it, uncomprehending, and then, as the words finally registered, she let out a cry of dismay.

Julius, who had been reading his own telegram, looked up quickly. 'Bad news?'

'The worst,' said Vicky tragically. 'My father says he's coming to France!'

'Good God,' said Julius blankly.

Olivia, sitting happily until then with Jean-Luc in a corner, gave a squawk of protest. 'I won't go back with him, I won't.'

'Sssh,' said Jean-Luc. 'Nobody shall make you do what you don't want to do.'

'You don't quite understand,' said Vicky gloomily. 'I can kick up a fuss, but Olivia's only fifteen. He's probably had her made a Ward of Court already.'

Olivia was aghast. 'Oh, he couldn't have! Not so quickly.'

'What is this Ward of Court, please?' asked Jean-Luc.

'The court takes over responsibility for her. She can't do anything without their permission.'

'What, anything?'

'Oh, move or leave school or leave the country or get married. All kinds of things,' said Vicky impatiently.

'This court has no rights in France.'

'Tricky one, that,' said Julius. 'It will have, to some extent, but it could be a devilish slow business.'

'So if Olivia stands up to her grandfather. . . ?'

'No one stands up to my father,' said Vicky flatly. 'Not for long.'

'I see,' said Jean-Luc.

Olivia opened her mouth to say what she thought, but she shut it at a look from Jean-Luc.

How astonishing, thought Vicky with the part of her mind that wasn't filled with dread at the prospect of her father arriving. She saw Julius leaning against the desk in his usual insouciant way, holding his telegram loosely in his left hand. 'Is yours anything important?' she asked.

He smiled, looking far too cheerful to be the recipient of bad news. 'Merely the family firm dispensing with my services. One scandal too many, my uncle says, so will I get in touch to discuss alternative arrangements.'

'Julius, no! They can't do that, you haven't done anything wrong.'

'The name of Drummond has appeared in every paper of the land. People remember the accusations, not the denials or the fact that charges have been dropped. No smoke without fire and all that, you know.'

'Julius, you don't mind!'

'Not at all. We would have to part, sooner or later. Believe me, you don't know the half of it. Now, I suggest you go and have a bath, you look a perfect fright. I'm going to freshen up, as the Americans say, and then dive into a stiff drink. Meet you outside in half an hour? You'll need Dutch courage to face your father.'

Vicky shuddered. 'I never want to hear the word Dutch again. And I'm not too keen on the word father, if it comes to that.'

'Where's Olivia?' she asked some forty minutes later, as she joined Julius under the vine. 'She isn't in her room, and I can't find Jean-Luc. Has he gone?'

'But yes,' cried Monsieur Ribérac, putting down their drinks with a flourish. 'It is a romance, huh?'

'Romance?' said Vicky. 'They haven't?'

'Run away together. I believe so.'

'Why didn't you stop them . . . her? Julius, she's only fifteen.'

'Younger than she are mothers made,' he offered.

Vicky stared at him, then caught the allusion. 'This isn't *Romeo and Juliet*, however, and . . .'

Julius put out a hand and grasped her by the wrist. 'Sit down. Olivia is a born runner-away. What are her family going to do with her? Send her to that finishing school in Paris? She'll simply run off with the fencing master. Leave her with a chaperone somewhere in the country? God help the chaperone.'

'She's too young to get married. And she can't, not without her parents' permission. And what if Jean-Luc doesn't marry her?'

'He will. Didn't you notice how possessive he is about her?'

'He's French. He'll have a string of mistresses, she'll be desperately unhappy.'

'That's where her judo will come in handy.'

'Julius, you aren't taking this seriously.' Genuine fear had crept into her voice. 'How am I ever going to be able to tell Daddy what she's done? I think he'll go after Jean-Luc with a gun.'

Julius sat back and prodded the lemon in his glass with a cocktail stick. 'Vicky, I don't think we need to stay here any longer. I think for all kinds of reasons, it will be better for you not to meet your father.'

'It's cowardly to run away.'

'I don't think cowardice comes into this.'

'You're better off standing up to bullies,' said Vicky. 'I know this, and yet when my father raises his voice, all I want to do is be somewhere else.'

'Let's leave, then.'

Vicky felt light-headed, empty of emotion. It was all too much. She couldn't run away. Why not? She'd done it before. 'Where shall we go?'

'Paris. Your father won't find us in Paris.'

'You don't know my father.' The alcohol must have gone to her head, she felt most peculiar. Paris, she thought. Yes, Paris; they would go to Paris. 'I'll go and pack.'

'Vicky.' Julius put out a hand. 'Don't take more than ten minutes. If you can't pack in that time, leave things behind. Ribérac will send them on.'

'Daddy can't get here that quickly.'

'He might. There are ways and means. He may fly. We have to scram.'

'He won't do anything to me in public.'

'Trust me on this.'

In less than ten minutes, Vicky was down. Julius was at the desk, brown leather suitcases on the floor beside him. The innkeeper had a pile of notes, and was signing his name with a flourish across the bill.

'There, Monsieur. Everything in order.'

'You haven't paid my bill, have you?' said Vicky. 'I must pay for myself, and for Olivia.'

'Never mind that now. We can settle up later. The garage has rung, my car is ready. Can you manage your suitcase?'

'Yes, of course.'

'Quickly, then.'

They came out into the sun. There was a crack, and something whistled past Vicky's cheek. She jumped back; what was it, a wasp? a hornet?

Then there was another crack, and Julius gave a surprised gasp, then, very slowly, fell to his knees. After a moment, he toppled forward. He lay on the ground, unmoving.

It was imprinted on Vicky's mind, like a film playing in slow motion. People were running towards them. From the inn, from the shops, from the *place*. They jostled and cried out, gathering in a circle around the inert figure on the ground. Blood seeped from beneath him, dribbling over the cobbles and collecting in a puddle where a cobblestone was missing.

She had knelt down beside Julius and was attempting to raise his head. There was a smear of blood down the front of her dress.

A man standing to one side cried out that this wasn't an accident. It was deliberate. No car had come past, no thunderbolt had landed from heaven. A cry went up: He's been shot. The words were picked up and passed round. Men peeled off, darted about. The fat innkeeper bent and stood up, holding a bullet in his hand, consternation, horror, shock on his face. He told her that was the bullet that had missed her. Julius hadn't been so lucky. The other bullet was probably lodged in his flesh. Or in some more vital area.

'Listen,' said the innkeeper, 'they are discovering what happened. They have found where the marksman had stood. People say they had noticed a blond stranger in the town, drifting. He had called in at the Pâtisserie Dione.'

The assistant from the patisserie was exclaiming, wringing her hands. The blond man had described Vicky, had said that she was English, and she, might the Holy Virgin forgive her, had told him that the Englishwoman was staying at the Auberge Chameau. 'I thought he was an acquaintance of the young lady's.'

He must have taken up his position just before Vicky, with Julius behind her, had come out of the inn.

The innkeeper's thoughts had now turned to himself, and he was bewailing the misfortune that had befallen Monsieur Drummond, and also him and his inn. 'A respectable house, but ever since the English arrived, terrible things have been happening.'

The gendarme came puffing up on his bike, only to be roughly shouldered aside by the doctor who had been called from his surgery. He sank down beside Julius, ignoring Vicky, turned his head, flipped up his eyelids, felt his pulse.

Then he issued a stream of commands as a Citroën bounced over the cobbles towards them, and two ambulance men jumped out.

The hunt was on for the man who'd shot the English visitors. In broad daylight, outside the inn, just like the Germans.

They didn't catch him.

Chapter Sixteen

There was a tap on the door of Julius's room in the clinic, and Adrian's face looked anxiously in. 'Julius, old chap. How are you?'

Julius, his arm strapped to his chest, waved with his other hand. 'Come in. Pull up a chair.'

'I'd have come sooner, but I've been away. I read about the shooting, but in the first reports they didn't mention your name, and when they did, they implied you were at death's door. Were you?

'No. Unconscious and bloody, but breathing. The bullet went through my arm and ploughed a ridge in my chest, but no lasting harm was done.'

'You always did have the luck of the devil. Do you remember the time when Matron . . .'

Julius winced. 'Spare me. Now listen, Adrian, I asked Vicky to get in touch with you because I need your help.'

'Charming girl,' said Adrian appreciatively. 'A stunner, too. She's very fond of you, you know. I can tell.'

'I want to ask you about Duggie Fitzgerald. No, don't look like that. What is it about him that makes you look so wary?'

'I'm dashed if I know, but there's something about him that isn't quite right. Great hero and so on, but I've never felt entirely easy in his company.'

'I want to know about his politics.'

Adrian's face took on the give-nothing-away expression that Julius knew so well. 'Straight down the line Tory. Well, he would be, wouldn't he? Winchester man, army, merchant bank, old family, well-to-do. Bound to be.'

'Did he ever say anything that made you wonder if he really was the Conservative supporter he seemed?'

'Like what?'

'Oh, I don't know.' Julius shifted restlessly on his bank of pillows. 'Criticising some party policy, slanging Churchill. That kind of thing.'

There was a long silence.

'Come on, spit it out.'

'It's all nonsense of course. Just something he said when he was in his cups. He'd just got back from a tricky mission, nerves all shot to pieces, I dare say. Sorry, I could have put that better.'

'Go on.'

'I ignored it, of course. The next day he had a foul hangover. Came to find me, apologised for being so tight, hoped he hadn't said or done anything stupid. I felt embarrassed for him, you know how it is. I said he'd been so bloody pissed he was completely incoherent. That seemed to cheer him up, and he clapped me on the shoulder and went off quite cheerful.'

'Adrian, get to the point. What did he say?'

Adrian looked more and more unhappy. He stirred uneasily in his chair, uncrossed his legs, crossed them again. Then the words came out in a rush. 'He told me he was a communist. Had been since Cambridge.'

'Ah.' Julius gave a long sigh.

'There was more. He said he was working for Moscow. Under-cover stuff, buried deep, no one knew. He told me it had got bloody complicated when Stalin and Hitler were in bed together. There he was, English agent working in France – he was doing great stuff in Paris then, late forty, early forty-one – and at the same time passing stuff to the Germans and to the Soviets. He said it got easier when Hitler moved against the Russkies. Less complicated. Less danger of getting found out.'

'And you didn't believe this?'

'I told you, the man was drunk. Pie-eyed. And to be honest, it all sounded a bit like a *Boy's Own* story. As if he got some kick out of fancying himself a traitor. "I'm betraying King and country," he said. Over and over again.'

'Thank you,' said Julius. 'Thank you very much. You don't know how lucky you are, Adrian. Instead of me lying here, you could have ended up any time these last nine years stretched out on a slab with a bullet or two in you. Did you keep quiet about where you were living in France?'

Adrian was looking appalled. 'I suppose I did. Not intentionally, it just turned out like that. You didn't know where I was, did you, and we're old chums. You see, my parents are dead, I've got one brother, he lives in Canada. Peggy's Australian, her family know where we are, but I don't expect they go shouting it out to all and sundry; why should they?'

'No reason. But in time, Adrian, I think that some people might have started asking questions and found out where you were. Tell me, do you think Duggie plans to try for a seat in Parliament?'

'I know it for a fact. Got a safe seat in the Shires all lined up for him.' His face lifted. 'As a Conservative, of course. There you are, I told you he was true blue.'

'You did, Adrian, you did.'

'Have I tired you, old boy?'

'Not at all. You've made my day.'

Vicky tried to keep him in bed, or at least in his room. 'I don't want the mysterious marksman to get another pot-shot at you.'

'Nor do I, believe me.'

'This time, his aim might be better, and you're going to be a slow-moving target; how convenient for him.'

'He won't be expecting me to be up yet. And once I've spoken to a few people, I won't be in any more danger. Nor will you.'

Vicky wasn't too sure about that. Her father might be somewhere in France, and although she was hiding out with some American friends of Martha's, she lived in daily expectation of his turning up on the doorstep, demanding to see her.

'Will you come to Paris? When you're properly on your feet again, and the doctor says it's okay?'

'To Paris?' Julius sounded surprised. 'Of course I will. I can't go

237

back to London. It'll be rather too hot for me after I've spilt the beans.'

'Do you think you'll make it up with Drummond et cetera?'

'I doubt if my uncle will want me around.'

'Will any other firm want you?'

'There are a few who might. Most will be part of the cosy fraternity who are going to curse me for rocking the boat. Soiling the nest, not playing the game, letting the side down and all that.'

Vicky looked out of the window. The room had a balcony overlooking the pretty courtyard below. Very secure. 'I told Martha's friends about Bertrand. The people I'm staying with. He's at the American Embassy. I thought it might be a good thing if a few more people knew about what's happened.'

'Was he interested?'

'Oh, extraordinarily.' She leaned over the bed and gave him a kiss on his cheek. 'Please take care of yourself, Julius.'

'Don't worry. I'm not the stuff heroes are made of.'

'Thank God,' she said cryptically, and closed the door quietly behind her.

So much for keeping the gory details from her, thought Julius ruefully. Presumably you learned to face facts when you had Christopher Hampden for a father.

Five days later, pale and interesting, and needing to walk with care, Julius was escorted on to the Paris express by Monsieur Lamboley, Monsieur Ribérac and Marcel, with the gendarme, face pink with alarm, bringing up the rear. He was handed over to the care of the *conducteur*, installed in a first-class compartment, and bid a fulsome farewell by his friends from St Aphrodise.

'Don't linger in Paris. Come back to us to convalesce, the air in St Aphrodise is the best in France.'

'Please remember,' said Monsieur Lamboley, 'that there are many, many legal questions arising with reference to the d'Icère estate. It seems that Bertrand d'Icère has disappeared, and if so, there will be endless legal complexities to be dealt with. And the tax affairs! Only imagine!'

'Your car, M'sieur, will be looked after as though it belonged to the Président himself. Or to your King,' Marcel added in a flush of cross-Channel solidarity. 'Then when you are restored to health, you will come to St Aphrodise and drive it away, better than before.'

'And bring Mademoiselle Vicky with you.'

As the train drew out, Julius could see the little group on the platform, waving as the train rounded the curve and they were lost from sight.

There was a reception committee on line at the Gare de Lyon: Vicky, Martha, a large American with a crew cut and a smart Parisian police officer with a bored expression on his face. The American provided the transport in the shape of a large Pontiac, and Julius was whisked through the streets to an apartment on the Ile de la Cité, in the Place Dauphine.

'We're going to eat at the Lion d'Or,' said Vicky in a voice that brooked no argument. 'It's where this all started, in a way.'

'Is the food good?' asked Julius.

'If it's the place I've heard about, the cuisine's great,' said Martha.

The Lion d'Or was half way up the Rue des Saints Pères. A dim globe of light proclaimed its presence, just illuminating the swinging sign above the door. The windows were shuttered with old wooden panels, and the door, too, was old and worn.

A stout little man bustled forward and looked up at Julius. 'M'sieur has booked? No? In that case . . . ?' He spread his hands in a gesture of desolation. They were full, they had already turned away several customers, another night, next week perhaps . . .

The door leading from the kitchen opened and a woman came through. Vicky recognised her at once, she was the one from the café in Candle Street. 'Madame,' she called. She was frowning at an order in her hand, but at that she turned towards Vicky, looking at her without interest. Then, miraculously, her face broke into a smile. 'My customer from London, from Candle Street, the Mademoiselle who is a coffee connoisseur. How many are you?'

'Five,' said Vicky. 'Us three, and two more to come.'

Madame Lafarge hurled some rapid sentences at the little man, whose face was now similarly spread with smiles, and two minutes later, they found themselves installed at a table in a corner.

'Shoot,' said Martha, hands round the stem of her drink, her eyes on Vicky.

'No, we must wait for Olivia and Jean-Luc.'

'Here they are,' said Julius, starting to rise.

'Sit down,' said Vicky.

'Forget your manners,' agreed Martha. 'You're still not a hundred per cent, conserve your energies.'

A radiant Olivia led Jean-Luc by the hand to the table. She kissed Vicky and Julian and Martha.

Jean-Luc, smiling, handsome and charming, made his own round of greetings, although his eyes always strayed back to Olivia.

'Don't you think she looks beautiful?' he said with pride. 'Now she is dressed properly? My family adore her already, they greatly admire the English style of beauty. And while we are in Paris, I shall take her to all the houses, for the couture. She will look marvellous.'

'Sit down, everyone,' commanded Vicky, 'and then we can order.'

'You look like a truffle hound, what are you doing?' said Julius.

'Savouring the wonderful smells,' said Vicky.

They ordered, wine was brought and opened, glasses filled.

Jean-Luc was enthusing about the Lagonda. 'Julius, truly an astounding motor car, I want to have one just like it.'

'It's pre-war.'

'It's superb. Such performance.'

'Come on,' said Martha. 'Cars, indeed. Now, I want to hear all the latest, and then I want everything explained to me, just what happened. Vicky just dashes from one thing to another, and I can't make head nor tail out of it.'

Julius twirled his glass. 'Let's start with the hot news.'

'What news?' asked Vicky. 'Something I don't know about?'

'Yes. They've caught van der Meulen.'

Vicky put down her glass with a thump. 'When?'

'Last night, at the border. And he's squealing, as we call it in the trade. I don't think the police have been very nice to him. Not once they'd got hold of his war record,' he explained for Martha's benefit.

'Apart from various activities not covered by the Geneva Convention, he betrayed the Maquis.'

'The big no.'

'The story he spun us?' asked Vicky. 'No truth in it?'

'Not much. He was a one hundred per cent Nazi officer. He was an art historian, before the war, that much was true. He first came to Carcassonne before the German occupation of the south, as he said he had, but he wasn't the innocent abroad he made out. He was storing away useful information, ready for when the Germans were openly in control. At that time, he was pretending to. be a Dutchman – it's clearly a line of his. One of the things he discovered was that Bertrand d'Icère had sold the choicest items of the d'Icère's collection of paintings and works of art to Goering. He knew where Tilly had hidden them, and simply took them away, a few at a time.'

'So he and Bertrand went back a long way. That's how Bertrand knew I had the gothic butterfly; van der Meulen, or whatever his real name is, had told him.'

'When he saw the fortunes that were being made in the art market, he decided that, with Bertrand's help, he'd muscle in. An enormous amount of art was sold in Paris during the war. Black marketeers, all the people who were making fortunes and who had their wits about them wanted to convert cash into goods. Even the Germans were buying. Bertrand knew about the father and son team that had made the copies for Tilly d'Icère, and he and Bertrand got them going on lots more.'

'More copies? Surely it would come out in the end that two other people had the same picture as you, all of them supposed to be the original.'

'Copies and then fakes. The chaos of war and its aftermath provided just the right conditions for that kind of deception. However, things were beginning to get straight, and some of their chickens were coming home to roost. So up jumps a remodelled Cornelius, working – apparently – on the side of the gamekeepers. Of course he wasn't. He and Bertrand were just switching to new markets.'

'Don't tell me,' said Martha. 'Let me guess, might it have to do with all these rich Americans visiting Paris?'

'I think so.'

'Have the police arrested Bertrand?' Vicky wanted to know.

'No, not yet.'

'Bertrand is on the run, I think,' said Jean-Luc. 'I went to pay him a visit, with a few friends, you understand. There was no one there, and his housekeeper says she hasn't seen him for several days.'

'I'd bet he's dead in a ditch,' said Vicky. 'The Dutchman will have wanted to shut him up. Nothing silences a man so well as being dead.'

'Then I hope so,' said Jean-Luc. 'There would be satisfaction in dealing with him, but there is an irony if his associate killed him.'

'Was it the Dutchman who shot you, Julius?' asked Olivia, whose eyes were round at such a catalogue of wickedness. Not all Miss Calthrop's tough training had prepared her young ladies for a world where people betrayed and murdered family and friends.

'No. Too risky. I think Jean-Luc was right. He'll have headed for Corbières, taken Bertrand out, and then aimed to put as many kilometres as possible between him and St Aphrodise.'

'So who did it?' asked Martha.

'Oh, Duggie, don't you think?' said Julius, sounded suddenly very weary.

'Duggie!' said Vicky. 'Julius, I never heard anything so preposterous. Why should Duggie be in France, and even if he were, why would he want to shoot at us?'

'Jealousy!' declared Olivia, her eyes bright with romance. 'He'd heard about you and Julius being together, and he couldn't bear it. Maddened with passion, he leapt into the nearest plane, and . . .'

'That doesn't sound at all like Duggie,' said Vicky. 'He's the coolest person I know.'

'I tell you what,' said Olivia, fishing in her large envelope handbag. 'I forgot all about it. There's a picture of him in the papers, I bought a *Daily Mail* yesterday, out of date, of course, but never mind. Duggie's gone missing.'

Vicky was looking at Julius. 'You aren't surprised, are you?'

'No,' he said, reaching out to take the paper from Olivia. Vicky leaned over to look. There, on the front page was a picture of Duggie under the headline, MASSIVE MANHUNT FOR MISSING HERO.

Vicky ran her eye down the text. 'Douglas Fitzgerald, much

decorated hero of the war, whose book on his exploits as a secret agent . . . Not seen since last Friday . . . dinner with senior judge Sir Christopher Hampden . . . called a taxi, dropped at Victoria Station, vanished into thin air.'

'There's a whole lot about you, Vicky,' chirped Olivia. 'And a pic of you on page two, an awful one. It goes on about a long-standing romance, friends since childhood, expected to announce engagement, and then some snide stuff about you gallivanting round France with your good friend Julius Drummond.'

'Whose uncle,' Vicky read out, 'Edgar Drummond, of the well-known firm of solicitors was also a guest at the dinner party. Given by my father, etc etc.'

'And there's a bit more about Edgar Drummond further on in the paper,' said Olivia, who had clearly read the newspaper from end to end. 'It says he's retiring from the firm because of ill-health.'

'Did you know about that?' Vicky asked Julius.

'Let's say I expected it.'

Jean-Luc had picked up the newspaper. 'You know, I have never met this Douglas, and yet his face is familiar somehow.'

'Oh, he's been in lots of papers,' said Olivia. 'Going to the palace to get a medal from the King, and then his book coming out.'

'Has anyone got a pen?' Vicky asked.

Julius automatically reached for his inside pocket, and winced as a stab of pain reminded him of his injured arm and chest. He eased the pen out and handed it to Vicky.

She took off the cap, and holding it upside down, used the flat part of the nib to black in Duggie's fair hair. Then she added a moustache.

Martha frowned. 'Isn't that a bit tasteless . . .' she began.

Then Jean-Luc was on his feet, with a cry of rage that made every head in the place swivel towards their table. A torrent of angry French poured out.

'Hey, slow down a bit, will you,' said Martha.

'Julius, what's he saying?' asked Vicky urgently. She had caught the name d'Icère among the flood of furious words.

Jean-Luc, spent, sat down abruptly. He banged the photo of Duggie with the back of his hand. 'This filth, this piece of vermin, this so-called hero, this is the man who came to my house that night, calling himself Philippe d'Icère, claiming that his companion, the man Raoul, had been shot. This is the man we trusted, and the man who betrayed us.'

'Duggie!' said Vicky, in a whisper. 'Bloody Duggie.' She rounded on Julius. 'You knew.'

'I thought it had to be him,' said Julius. 'But it would be hard to prove.'

'No, it will not,' said Jean-Luc. 'I will stand up in court, I will point a finger at this Duggie, and say, you are the scum we sheltered and fed and gave false papers to. You are the man that had our girls raped and mutilated and killed on the hillside, and sent the others to death in the camps. I spit on you!'

Olivia tugged at his sleeve. 'He won't be in court, darling. I expect he's done a runner because he thought all this might come out.'

'Why did he betray them?' asked Vicky. 'How?'

'That's simple,' said Julius. 'He told Bertrand, the fellow traveller, about Jean-Luc's group, which just happened to have some anti-communists among their number. Apart from any private business in hand, both Bertrand and Duggie were answering to Moscow. Bertrand took instructions, and passed the word to his friendly Gestapo officer. That was the end of the network.'

'Are you saying Duggie's a commie?' said Martha with amazement. 'Douglas Fitzgerald? Oh, come on! Nobody's going to believe that.'

'I do,' said Vicky. 'Duggie's hidden side. Such a golden boy had to have one. He was brave and charming – very, very charming, people who'd only met him five minutes before felt that he understood everything about them, that they'd known him for years. Yet he didn't care a button about them. He always loved anything to do with secret societies when he was a little boy. A whole life of intrigue and danger, and laughing up his sleeve at everyone. That's Duggie all right. And, my God, I so nearly married him.'

'Philippe is dead, I suppose?' said Martha.

'Oh, definitely.' Julius said. 'You didn't doubt it, did you Vicky? Not really. The man you loved wouldn't have vanished out of your life if he'd been alive.'

'No. Philippe was all the things that Duggie isn't. Courageous and clever and funny. And he was loyal and honourable; no, he wouldn't have left me. It was only people saying they'd seen him, and the way I kept on hearing his voice.'

'Voices?' Olivia was interested. 'Hearing voices is bad news, Vicky. Perhaps you ought to have a course of psychoanalysis, I expect my friend's pa would do you a deal.'

'No, thank you, Olivia. I'm perfectly sane, and if I hear Philippe's voice, then I find it comforting in a strange way. As though something of him is still about.'

Olivia tore her roll apart. 'Duggie has absolutely no sense of humour, didn't you ever notice that?'

'You don't have to put me off Duggie, Olivia, whatever feelings I had for him died quite a while ago, even before these startling revelations. Julius, why did Duggie kill Philippe?'

'Duggie wanted Philippe dead for reasons of his own. His senior officer, who happened to be my Uncle Edgar, sanctioned it. The implication, in case anyone got nosy, was probably that d'Icère was a double agent.'

'Did his Russian masters get him to do it? So he wouldn't get even with Bertrand?' Martha suggested.

'That wouldn't explain Edgar Drummond's involvement.'

'My uncle was being blackmailed,' said Julius.

Jean-Luc, veteran of many daring raids, a man who had seen in his twenty-eight years more than most men did in a lifetime, was reproving. 'But this is shocking. This is terrible. I know we joke about the perfidious English, but this shooting friends and blackmailing uncles, it is unbelievable.'

'Honey, you don't know these Britishers. They're capable of anything. They all study Greek tragedies at school, and after that, anything seems kind of normal.'

'What had your uncle done, Julius?' Olivia was curious. 'Something scandalous or something really wicked?'

'God knows.'

'Is that why he's retiring?' asked Martha. 'Has news gotten around that all's not what it seems in the darker reaches of the Establishment?'

'I fear so,' said Julius. 'I think a good few reputations are looking tarnished. Chiefly mine, of course, for letting the cat out of the bag. A few phone calls: to my uncle, and then to people I know on the security side, and I'm afraid it didn't look too hopeful for Duggie.'

'Do you think he's killed himself?' Olivia asked in hopeful tones. 'Overcome with remorse, threatened with disclosure?'

'Not Duggie,' said Vicky.

'I think we'll hear nothing more of him for several months, maybe a year, and then he'll surface in Moscow.'

'Moscow!' said Vicky with relish. 'How he'll hate it.'

Jean-Luc was frowning. 'I still do not know why your uncle's blackmailer should want d'Icère dead.'

'I don't think we'll ever know. They won't get much out of Edgar, he's too frightened.'

Vicky sighed. 'I've got a pretty good idea who the blackmailer was. And it wasn't anything to do with politics and the war. I reckon it was my father, and he wanted Philippe dead because he hated him for loving me. And because I loved him, and wanted to marry him.'

Julius stretched out his good hand, and laid it on hers.

'It's all so horrible,' she burst out. 'How can such things happen?'

Madame flew to their tables, plates in hand.

Vicky looked down at the food placed in front of her. 'I don't think I'm hungry any more.'

'Of course you are,' said Madame. 'Because there are tragedies in life, you think no one eats any more? The past is the past, look at this man you have here, this is the kind of man who will make you a good husband, take it from me. Now eat.'

Vicky, dazed, ate.

LOSING LARRY

Elizabeth Pewsey

Larry Dunne divides his time between writing bad avant-garde poetry, working in a Bloomsbury bookshop, arguing with his girlfriend Pamela and putting the world to rights in a dive off the Strand named Joe's Club in honour of Stalin. Envious of Pamela and her upper-class friends, envious of the comrades' intellectual certainties and especially envious of friend Peter's book, Larry takes off to Hungary where he will at last breathe the purer air of an ideal state and bask in universal fellowship and equality.

Reality in late fifties Budapest is rather different. He soon finds out that the state runs on envy, paranoia and two-stroke, and wants nothing more than to get back to his cosy world of Bohemian London as quickly as possible. Then a woman is murdered in a neighbouring apartment, and he finds himself under suspicion with his passport confiscated. Larry realises that if the murderer isn't caught, he could be in Budapest for a very long time.

Praise for Elizabeth Pewsey:

'Delectable . . . she writes with tremendous vigour and wit . . . splendidly entertaining'

Sunday Express

'Wickedly amusing, sometimes outrageous and enchantingly amoral . . . Like good wine, very addictive. Strongly recommended'

Good Book Guide

HODDER AND STOUGHTON BOOKS

CHILDREN OF CHANCE

Elizabeth Pewsey

Prue Pagan knows nothing of family life, nor indeed of any life beyond the confines of her convent school and her aunt's suburban villa. Then a chance meeting with an old school friend leads to a journey north to work at Mountjoy Castle, where there's more than enough life and at least one member of the family who appears to have loved well but not wisely.

As the uncommonly sultry summer days pass, Prue tastes the pleasures – and dangers – offered by her new situation with innocent abandon, watched over by her worldly friend Cleo who is working at nearby Midwinter Hall for Sylvester Tate, a famous cellist. And while Lord Mountjoy's irascible heir, Valdemar, stalks his prey, Cleo pursues her own quarry in typically uninhibited fashion.

Nothing is quite what it seems, however, and only Sylvester's witchy housekeeper knows just how many secrets lie between castle, hall, vicarage and village. By the time the summer is out so are most of the secrets, and Prue is not the only one wiser in the ways of the world.

Praise for *Children of Chance*:

'A deliciously wicked tale of the shedding of innocence'
Company

HODDER AND STOUGHTON BOOKS

DIVINE COMEDY

Elizabeth Pewsey

One dark night, an exhausted young girl tumbles impulsively off a coach in the cathedral city of Eyot. Fleeing from family, friends and her much older lover, Quinta has nobody to turn to and nowhere to go, until she is rescued by a kindly stranger.

Now, eight years on, she has achieved an orderly life, balancing the demands of her daughter, her work as a violin maker, and the composer she lives with. What's past is past, and Quinta is determined it will stay that way – until an unruly element in the shape of Lydia, a friend from Quinta's schooldays, arrives in Eyot. Smarting from a sudden break-up with her Oxford boyfriend, Lydia hurls herself into a new affair with a most unsuitable man and draws Quinta out of her safe, careful ways.

Around them, the cathedral world ferments with a heady brew of scandal, threatening its ancient and cloistered tranquility. A new Bishop is due, complete with a wife one member of the choir knows remarkably well, and by the time Quinta comes face to face with her past, no one's life is left unchanged.

Praise for *Divine Comedy*:

'Sharp, invigorating and enormous fun'

Elizabeth Buchan

HODDER AND STOUGHTON BOOKS

A selection of bestsellers from Hodder & Stoughton

Losing Larry	Elizabeth Pewsey	0 340 71863 3	£6.99	☐
Children of Chance	Elizabeth Pewsey	0 340 61820 5	£6.99	☐
Divine Comedy	Elizabeth Pewsey	0 450 65420 1	£6.99	☐
Unholy Harmonies	Elizabeth Pewsey	0 340 64911 9	£6.99	☐
Volcanic Airs	Elizabeth Pewsey	0 340 65393 0	£6.99	☐

All Hodder & Stoughton books are available at your local bookshop or newsagent, or can be ordered direct from the publisher. Just tick the titles you want and fill in the form below. Prices and availability subject to change without notice.

Hodder & Stoughton Books, Cash Sales Department, Bookpoint, 39 Milton Park, Abingdon, OXON, OX14 4TD, UK. E-mail address: orders@book-point.co.uk. If you have a credit card you may order by telephone – (01235) 400414.

Please enclose a cheque or postal order made payable to Bookpoint Ltd to the value of the cover price and allow the following for postage and packing:
UK & BFPO: £1.00 for the first book, 50p for the second book and 30p for each additional book ordered up to a maximum charge of £3.00.
OVERSEAS & EIRE: £2.00 for the first book, £1.00 for the second book and 50p for each additional book.

Name ....

Address ....

....

....

If you would prefer to pay by credit card, please complete:
Please debit my Visa / Access / Diner's Club / American Express (delete as applicable) card no:

Signature ....

Expiry Date ....

If you would NOT like to receive further information on our products please tick the box. ☐